THE ANSWERS

'Not your typical romance, *The Answers* verges on the dystopian'
Radio Times

'A slyly subversive and funny take on the modern dating game'
Psychologies

'A multi-pronged satire which takes shots at misogyny, the "gig economy" and our obsession with data' *Sunday Telegraph*

'An ingenious sci-fi scenario that tweaks at the edges of what we believe about that part of us we call a self . . . Lacey has sly things to say about equality too . . . Why things should be this way, and whether they can be better, are great questions'
Guardian

'Delight at *The Answers'* suggestiveness, its lovely clean prose and its lack of answers' *Literary Review*

Also by Catherine Lacey

Nobody Is Ever Missing

THE ANSWERS

Catherine Lacey

GRANTA

Granta Publications, 12 Addison Avenue, London W11 4QR

First published in Great Britain by Granta Books, 2017
This paperback edition published by Granta Books, 2018
First published in the United States by Farrar, Straus and Giroux, New York, in 2017
Copyright © 2017 by Catherine Lacey

The right of Catherine Lacey to be identified as the author of this work has been asserted by her in accordance with the Copyright, Designs and Patents Act, 1988.

A CIP catalogue record for this book is available from the British Library.

1 3 5 7 9 10 8 6 4 2

ISBN 978 1 78378 218 5
eISBN 978 1 78378 219 2

Designed by Abby Kagan

Offset by Avon DataSet Limited, Bidford on Avon

Printed and bound by CPI Group (UK) Ltd, Croydon, CR0 4YY

www.granta.com

THE
ANSWERS

There was at least one morning I was certain, though only for a few hours, that everything that could ever really happen to me had already happened to me. I woke diagonal in bed, no place to go, no immediate needs to meet, no company expected or calls to make. I watched red tea steep in hot water. The mug warmed my hands. I believed it was over.

When I opened the blinds, she was standing in the middle of the street, staring hard at my second-floor window as if she'd known exactly where I was, had been waiting for this moment. We locked eyes—Ashley.

The tea slipped, shattered, and scalded my feet.

I try not to be so certain anymore.

PART ONE

One

I'd run out of options. That's how these things usually happen, how a person ends up placing all her last hopes on a stranger, hoping that whatever that stranger might do to her would be the thing she needed done to her.

For so long I had been a person who needed other people to do things to me, and for so long no one had done the right thing to me, but already I'm getting ahead of myself. That's one of my problems, I'm told, getting ahead of myself, so I've been trying to find a way to get behind myself, to be slow and quiet with myself like Ed used to be. But of course I can't quite make it work, can't be exactly who Ed was to me.

There are some things that only other people can do to you.

Pneuma Adaptive Kinesthesia, PAKing—what Ed does to people—requires one person to *know* and another person (me, in this case) to lie there, not-knowing. In fact, I still do not know what Pneuma Adaptive Kinesthesia really is, just that it made me (or seemed to have made me) well again. During our sessions Ed sometimes hovered his hands over my body, chanting or humming or silent while he supposedly moved or rearranged or healed invisible parts of me. He put stones and crystals on my face, my legs, sometimes pressing or twisting some part of my body in painfully pleasurable ways, and though I didn't understand how any of this could remove the various sicknesses from my body, I couldn't argue with relief.

I'd spent a year suffering undiagnosable illnesses in almost every part of me, but after only *one* session with Ed, just ninety minutes during which he barely touched me, I could almost forget I was a body. Such a luxury it was, to not be overwhelmed by decay.

Chandra had suggested PAKing, called it *feng shui for the energetic body*, *guerrilla warfare against negative vibes*, and though I was sometimes skeptical of Chandra's talk of *vibes*, this time I had to believe her. I'd been ill so long that I'd almost lost the belief I could be well again and I was afraid of what might replace that belief if it disappeared completely.

Technically, Chandra explained, *PAKing is a form of neuro-physio-chi bodywork, a relatively obscure technique either on the outskirts of the forefront or the outskirts of the outskirts, depending on who you ask.*

The problem was, as always, an invisible one. The problem was money.

I needed a minimum of thirty-five PAKing sessions, at $225 each, to complete a PAK series, which meant a complete treatment would cost me the same as a half-year's rent on that poorly lit and irregularly shaped one-bedroom I'd had for many years (not because it suited me—I detested it—but because everyone said it was a steal, too good to let go). And even though my paycheck from the travel agency was decent, the monthly credit card minimums, student loan payments, and last year's onslaught of medical bills were all reducing my bank account to cents or negatives each month, while the debt always seemed to grow.

One dire morning, starving and cashless, I ate the last of my pantry for breakfast (slightly expired anchovies mixed into a tiny can of tomato paste) and I often Hare-Krishna'd for dinner, leaving my shoes and dignity at the door to praise Krishna (the god, as far as I could tell, of cafeteria-grade vegetarian fare and manic chanting). By the fourth or fifth Love Feast, white tilaka greased on my brow, pasta wiggling around the metal plate as if independently animate, I knew that the boundless love of Krishna would never be enough for me—no matter how hungry or broke or confused I became. It was a few days later that answering that ad for an *income-generating experience* tacked to a bulletin board at a health food store seemed like my only real option, that somehow giving away the dregs of my life might be the best way to get a real one back.

For a year I'd had no life, just symptoms. Mundane ones at first—tenacious headaches, back pain, a constantly upset stomach—but over months they became increasingly strange. Persistent dry mouth and a numb tongue. A full-body rash. My legs kept falling asleep, stranding me at the office or in a bath or at a bus stop as the M5 came and went, came and went. At some point I somehow cracked a rib in my sleep. These strange lumps began to rise and fall on my skin, like turtle heads surfacing and sinking in a pond. I could only sleep three or four hours a night, so I tried to nap through my lunch hour, forehead to desk, on the days I didn't have a doctor's appointment. I avoided mirrors and eye contact. I stopped making plans more than a week away.

There were blood tests and more blood tests, CAT scans and biopsies. There were seven specialists, three gynos, five GPs, a psychiatrist, and one grope-y chiropractor. Chandra took me to a celebrity acupuncturist, a spiritual surgeon, and a guy who sold stinking powders in the back room of a Chinatown fishmonger. There were checkups and follow-ups and throw-ups and so on.

It's just stress, someone said, but they couldn't rule out cancer or a rare autoimmune disorder or a psychic attack or pure neurosis, all in my head—*just don't worry so much*—*try not to think about it.*

One doctor said, *That's just bodies for you*, sighed, and clapped my shoulder, as if we were all in on the joke.

But I didn't want a punch line. I wanted an explanation. I hesitated at storefronts for palm readers and psychics. I let Chandra do my tarot a few times but the news was always bad—swords and daggers and demons and grim reapers. *I'm new at this*, she said, though I knew she wasn't. I held my spasming legs to my chest, chin to knees, and felt like a child, dwarfed by everything I didn't know.

I came close to praying a few times, but everything felt unanswered enough and I didn't want another frame for the silence.

Something in the genes or a consequence of ill choices, one might rationalize, but it could have just been a hefty stroke of bad luck—senseless, or a karmic bitch slap—somehow earned. My parents would have said it was just a part of *His plan*, but to them, of course, everything was. How someone wants to explain catastrophe isn't important—that's what I know now. When shit happens, it doesn't really matter what asshole is responsible.

Two

For five years, I had a life.

My childhood wasn't my life—maybe it had been Merle's life, but not mine. And the time I lived with Aunt Clara hadn't really been a life, more like rehabilitation. And college wasn't life at all, just a gestational period, four years of warning and training for this life that was coming, that future thing.

My life began on an airplane, the moment we left the ground. We ascended and I wept against Chandra's shoulder as silently as I could, and when the flight attendant came around, Chandra asked for a cup of hot water, adding her own tea bag and holding it still in the turbulence until it was the right temperature to drink, giving it to me then. She knew so much, knew all the best ways to do things. She unfurled her massive scarf, wrapped us together, and I fell asleep against her shoulder. We woke up as we were landing in London, holding hands in our sleep, and minutes later she guided us through Heathrow, a place she already knew. It wasn't that she felt like a mother to me, but I was still somehow her child.

It must have been her hundredth trip, though it was my first, a graduation present from her parents, Vivian and Oliver. Viv and Olly, she called them. I'd spent most holidays and long weekends at their place in Montauk all through college since I had nowhere to go. The house was full of expensive things that didn't really matter to them—chipped antiques, forgotten gadgets, scratched CDs in stacks—and it wasn't uncommon to find random twenties between sofa cushions or strewn around the kitchen amid magazines and candies from foreign countries. At the dinner table her family spoke loudly with their mouths full and Chandra lovingly argued with her parents about books and art. Everyone made and laughed at jokes I didn't understand, though I learned to laugh anyway. We all drank wine, even when I was nineteen and a tablespoon of it made me blithe and sleepy.

It was the two-month round-the-world ticket from Viv and Olly that began my years of compulsive travel. I saw the Galápagos birds, cherry blossoms in Japan, Egyptian pyramids, the Catacombs, Burmese snake pagodas, and that eerie neon-teal lake in New Zealand. I loved the leaving, even the 5:00 a.m. flights, silent subway cars rattling through desolate purple mornings, predawn airports filled with limp people. I read somewhere that the first thing you learn when traveling is that you don't exist— I didn't want to stop not existing.

At home the debts were always growing. Strangers called at all hours, spoke hatefully about what I owed them. I received serious letters with large bold numbers, each higher than the last. Other envelopes came with new credit cards, new ways out, new trips. I stopped wondering where I might go next but what would happen if I never returned. But I always returned. And each time

I hit the tarmac I had this terrible feeling that the trip I'd just taken had never even happened, that I'd spent hundreds for a memory I could barely recall.

The back pain started first, which seemed innocuous enough (didn't everyone get back pain?), though I was only twenty-five or twenty-six at the time. I blamed the knotty hostel beds and kept traveling beyond my means, though in less adventurous ways after a bout of muscle spasms were so strong they left me stranded on a trail in Abel Tasman for an hour until a group of hikers from Japan carried me out.

A few months later, while fighting off the first in a plague of stomach bugs, the headaches began and with the headaches came the full-body pains, pulsing and huge, pain seeming to stretch me from the inside. I was pregnant with it, labor that never ended, just ebbed. I had to stop traveling, to spend all my time and money trying to feel alive again—referrals, appointments, inconclusive results, more referrals, bills. Stern calls came from receptionists who had once seemed so kind—when would I pay, how would I pay, did I realize that missing payments came with fines? And even more calls came from debt collectors, three or four of them. They asked if I knew what I owed or they told me what I owed, more, often much more, than I thought. They told me that contrary to what some believe, it was possible to be jailed for one's debts. I said I found that surprising and they told me not to be so surprised. *It's theft, a form of theft*, one of them said, to which I said nothing. And didn't I worry about my credit score, planning for the future, home ownership, retirement, providing for my family, and I said, quickly and not kindly, *No, I didn't think of that, I never thought of that.*

Well, maybe you should, he said.

I sometimes wondered why I even answered the phone, but I guess I always had the hope that it would be someone else, some other way of life calling for me. One of the collectors spoke so fast that when I listened to him, the back of my head seemed to emanate heat through my hair, and another spoke so slow and softly I felt I was sinking or drowning, that the air had become thicker around me and would take me down if I kept breathing.

It felt possible—though I know this is absurd—that the use of my own body, the only thing I really owned, had somehow been repossessed.

For a while Chandra's constant care may have been all that stood between me and the total loss of my mind or life, and looking back at that year—when I'd wake up most nights hardly able to breathe, lying there for hours, mouth hanging open like a gargoyle—well, I don't want to think about what I would have become if she hadn't been there for me, stopping me from falling out of myself. (I don't mean I wanted to kill myself—I've never had that kind of nerve—but sometimes the pain was so unfathomable and large that I wondered if I might, unintentionally, be killed by myself.)

When Chandra suggested PAKing for all the pain, and when PAKing necessitated getting a second job, I was desperate—ready to do anything for relief, no matter how expensive or ridiculous it seemed. She'd become an expert on illness and wellness, on traveling the distance between these places. Two years earlier, standing on a street corner, she'd been violently clipped by a city bus and had since been living on the settlement, devoting her time to healing herself, completely, of everything: the broken leg, twisted wrist, busted face, fear of street curbs—and the preexisting stuff—anxiety, caffeine dependence, pollen allergies, self-diagnosed chronic candida, disillusionment, thwarted intuition, commitment issues, trust issues, all her traumas and the habits they'd left. She had an herbalist, a Reiki master, a Rolfer, a speech therapist, a movement therapist, an art therapist, and a therapist.

Retreats and pilgrimages took her in and out of the city for a while, but she always sent postcards. I kept them in my purse and stared at the images of oceans and temples, hoping to get some residual calm while I sat in another waiting room, clutching the part of my body that was currently killing me. First she swore by ayahuasca, then it was all about sensory deprivation chambers or MDMA, wheatgrass, body alkalinization, or a certain guru. Every day, she said, a new layer of something was removed between herself and her *self*. She was fulfilled, she said, for the first time in her life, and though I envied her, a more cynical part of me couldn't help but wonder, *Filled with what?*

When she was in town, she came over weekly with an arsenal of cures—herbs, powders, oils, bitter tinctures so powerful I had to take them by the drop. She burned sage, chanted, meditated, and sometimes—though this always embarrassed me—she'd hit a small gong or play this wooden flute. I never knew where to look or whether to suppress or release the impulse to laugh—even my embarrassment was embarrassing to me—and why couldn't I just chant with her, be at peace with her stupid flute or that little gong? I was lucky she was there at all, that I knew at least one person who wanted to help me not because it was her job, but because she just wanted to see me healed.

The day she came back from Bali, she appeared at my door unannounced, all sleek and tan, draped in white linen.

I can tell you're suffering, she said.

Out of anyone else's mouth I'd be bothered by a statement standing in for a question, but she was always right about me. She walked through my apartment with an alluring, eerie calm, as if she were no longer interested in anything other than the slow purification of her body, other bodies, the whole world. She draped scarves over my toaster oven, alarm clock, and telephone, whispered mantras in each cardinal direction, spread a circular tapestry across the cracked hardwood in my living room, then settled into an elegant meditation posture. I tried to copy her, but my knees were too stiff and the twitching foot made it hard to keep still so I gave up and went full starfish on the floor.

I'd sold most of my furniture in a stoop sale to make rent, so lying on my floor doing nothing in particular was a habit I was all too familiar with. When she was here, I called it meditation, but I always fell half-asleep, my body exhausted by itself. I woke this time to Chandra standing over me. When she met my eyes, I noticed her face change a little, in ways I couldn't exactly explain, but could feel. Our twelve years of friendship made silence soft and easy between us, though it wasn't just the passage of time that had created this intimacy. It had somehow been there immediately, this mysterious closeness, as innate as an organ. While lying on the floor just then, the real weight of our love became palpable, pushed tears out of my head. She was all I had.

Are you still taking those medicinal fish oils?

I nodded. She crouched and wiped the tears out of my face, smoothed my hair.

And the geranium–hemp powder?

In porridge, like you told me.

Well, let's try to get your weight up. She looked away from the little shred I was. My appetite had departed long ago; all soft parts of me followed.

First all my coworkers assumed I'd taken up yoga and commended me for it. They said I looked good, that I'd gotten into shape, asked for tips on motivation, healthy recipes. But soon they were saying I shouldn't lose any more weight, that I was *just right*, that I must be working out too much, that I needed to build muscle, put on some weight, start eating more red meat or peanut butter or full-fat grass-fed dairy. Someone gravely recommended their thyroid specialist and Meg suggested I see a hypnotist to fix my eating disorder, but when I said I didn't have an eating disorder, that I was just sick, she just said, *I know*.

When word got around of all my midday doctor appointments, everyone began speaking to me as if I had no body at all, everyone except Joe Nevins, who once interrupted our discussion about a missing invoice to say my face looked different, and when I asked what he meant by that, he wouldn't or didn't say.

Just different, he said, and went back to talking about the invoice.

I got used to it, in a way, being this sack of skin full of problems, because having a body doesn't give you the right to have one that works correctly. Having a body doesn't seem to give you any rights at all.

You'll get over this, Chandra said while unpacking the new herbs and roots she'd brought for me. *This pain is just a teacher for you.*

This was how she saw the world, that everything went according to plan, that we subconsciously made our own problems, that every cancer had been invited, every injury earned. I wasn't sure if I had the nerve to believe this, and if I did, if I really accepted I had asked for everything that had happened to me, I wasn't sure I could ever forgive myself. But thinking this way seemed to calm her. If she deserved her pain, then she deserved all the good in her life, too.

I could have used a sense of acceptance like that. I hated the pains in my body, struggled against them and cursed them so much I'd even grown to fear good feelings—a settled stomach, a relaxed back, a full night's sleep, or a whole day without crying. Even Chandra's care grew to terrify me. What if it vanished? What if she just gave up and stopped coming by?

Her kindness, as if we shared blood or history, had always

been hard to accept. I was just a person who appeared in her life at random, her assigned college roommate, a homeschooled semi-orphan from a barely literate state, but she still spent hours going over financial-aid and student-loan paperwork I didn't understand. She lost sleep listening to me debate the merits and demerits of what I should major in—religion, philosophy, history, or English—though she'd made up her mind from the start: theater major, marketing minor. And most crucially, she decoded the world for me, explained all the pop culture I'd never heard of, and let me evade the answer to how I'd made it to eighteen without ever hearing of Michael Jackson. I'd blame the home-schooling or say, *We were poor.* (She seemed terrified by that word: *poor.*) Once I mentioned that I'd been raised, for a time, by my aunt, a detail that stopped her questions. People like her didn't get raised by aunts.

After Chandra and I meditated, or, rather, after she meditated and I did whatever I did there on the floor, she served me maté in gourds and crudités with homemade allergen-free, vegan, sprouted pepita paste she had made, she said, while sending nourishing vibes to my astral body. It tasted grassy, felt thick in my throat.

Pepitas absorb toxins, she said, watching me eat as if watching someone parallel park. I sat there filling myself with pepitas, as the pepitas, I imagined, filled with my toxins. Chandra took the pulse from each of my wrists and examined my tongue. She closed her eyes for a little while, then told me her spirit guides had just advised her to advise me to complete a full PAK series, as soon as possible, with Ed, her PAKer. It had something to do with past lives or future ones, or perhaps even current lives that Ed and I were somehow living in another dimension. She spoke unflinchingly, as if her spirit guides were a real group of people, a flesh-and-blood committee.

PAKing changed my life, she said. *Not just a door opening . . . but . . . a whole house of doors opening? It's going to do that for you, too. My spirit guides have never been so clear. This is your future. You just have to take it.*

I'd always been skeptical of Chandra's reports from her spirit guides, as they always seemed to have these plans for her that she couldn't explain to me yet. She'd once told me they were preparing her for incalculable fame and financial wealth, that her accident was part of a strengthening regimen for this future greatness, that she was going to eventually have her own talk show.

I didn't know you wanted a talk show, I told her, but she just smiled.

It's not about what I want. The fates are beyond desire.

I wanted to believe that she might actually have some understanding of fate or any kind of intel on the future, because she seemed to believe in it and she also believed in me. But I also didn't want to lose her to the belief that life had a code that could be cracked, that there was some ideal way to live.

Regardless, I trusted her. Perhaps someone would say I had no choice but to trust her and perhaps that is true, but also, and I understand this now, I loved her and I loved her in that rare way, that non-possessive and accepting way that it seems people are always trying and failing to love someone, so I sipped the last of my maté through the metal straw, looked into Chandra's profoundly healed and spiritually realized eyes, and asked for Ed's number.

Three

I woke as if I'd been slapped. My neck brace had been removed.
I was lying on my back. Ed stood beside the massage table, staring down at me.

How long have I been asleep?

He pushed a frizzy chunk of hair from his eyes that immediately fell back in.

Only a few days.

For a long moment I wondered if sleeping for a few days was
some PAKing fine print I hadn't read. I could barely remember
coming into the office or signing anything or even starting the
session—just the empty all-white waiting room, no music, no
receptionist, two white chairs pushed close in one corner, like
twin children cowering in fear.

I'm kidding, he said, *you were asleep for a few minutes. It happens a lot during this first assessment. I hope Chandra warned you
that my readings are very powerful.*

I said she had though I still knew almost nothing about PAKing or what it was or how it worked. Maybe, I worried, PAKing was just an excuse for this guy to have a woman strip to her underwear and fall asleep in his office. Since I'd become so absurdly thin, I had noticed a certain kind of look I'd get from a certain kind of man, a mix of pedophile and vampire. (I would be so easy to conquer, to feel large above.) Ed didn't seem to be that sort of man, though when I considered the legions of semiconscious and desperate women who had likely come before me, it wasn't hard to imagine he might fondle their feet while pretending to read their auras, or maybe he would just stare at their undressed bodies, uselessly thinking good thoughts in their direction, or, worse, jerking off into a bare hand, or, even worse—all sorts of things—but I needed to be well again more than I needed protection from someone's possible perversion. And what if my skepticism of Ed was already working against me, preventing me from getting whatever he might legitimately be doing or healing on some dimension I couldn't yet see?

How is she, by the way?

Who?

Chandra—how's she doing?

Oh. She's good, I guess.

Of course she is, he said, nodding and smiling in a way that suggested he knew much more about Chandra than I did.

I touched my neck, noticed the throbbing pain had been replaced by a warm fizzle.

You won't be needing the brace anymore. That much was easy, but the assessment uncovered several blockages that will take much longer to resolve, so . . . I need to ask you, Mary—are you really ready for this work?

I think s—

You need not verbalize, he interrupted. *I'm speaking to your aura . . . Okay?*

We were silent but open-eyed for a long while. I was still just lying there. He was still just standing over me. If he was going to talk to my aura, I thought he might seem to be concentrating, not just staring off in that waiting-on-a-bus way.

Okay? he asked again. *Is that okay?*

He was staring at my knees. He raised one hand as if he had a question and moved the other in circles above my head.

Okay?

I wondered if I should answer, thought I shouldn't, but couldn't, for some reason, help myself.

Is what—

Shhhh . . .

The hand over my face was shaking slightly.

I'll wait, he said, so we did for a while, a minute or five, until he finally lowered both his hands.

This is going to take some additional effort, I see.

He pinched the bridge of his nose in a functional way, as if turning something on or off in him. My foot had stopped twitching for the first time in a week, and the cluster of painful lumps that had risen up on my right arm that morning had dissolved back into my body. Ed sat on something across the room that almost looked like a hammock. I didn't know if I was allowed to move yet or not, didn't know if I should even look at him or speak. I shut my eyes.

So, Mary . . . This is serious work. Chandra certainly told you about the seriousness of this work, didn't she? The equal amount of concentration and mindfulness I'll need you to bring to this in order for us to make progress?

I didn't say anything for a while, not sure if he was still talking to my aura.

You can verbalize now, Mary—do you understand this work is deeply serious?

I understand, I said, but I know now that I didn't understand then, or maybe ever. (Serious as opposed to what?) What I did understand was that whatever Ed had done to me so far had already relieved pain that had been stubborn against thousands of dollars of treatments, though I couldn't be sure if Ed was responsible the way penicillin is or the way a sugar pill could be. There was no explanation for what he had done to me—I felt almost normal. I braced for a new symptom or an old one to return, but nothing came.

Listen—and I don't say this to scare you—but PAKing will deeply alter the way that you live—your relationships with others, the way you conceptualize yourself—everything. If you choose to complete a full series, your life and body will never be the same.

We listened to the white-noise machines for a moment. I thought about how much I wanted everything in my life to change.

Are you familiar with the concept of the pneuma?

Not really.

Not really what?

Ed never seemed to try to earn my trust, which made me trust him more. His voice was simultaneously gruff and ditzy. Every day he wore the same baggy hemp pants and tunics. Sometimes he had ashy smudges on his face that seemed only half-accidental.

I just mean I'm not that familiar with pneuma. Something about the soul, I think . . .

The literal translation from Greek is "breath," but as a concept in my healing practice it has to do with the creative life force within each of us. Kinesthesia is also of Greek origin, meaning, roughly, "an awareness of movement"—so, a question, Mary. Are you moving right now?

I was still lying on the padded table, motionless, so I said, *No*, though I knew he'd only asked in order to correct me.

Wrong. Your body is actually moving a tremendous amount right now, far more than it needs to be. This is what has happened to you: your pneuma is in a state of chaos and stress, which has set it into constant motion, but your awareness of that chaos has been suppressed out of fear. This pneumatic agitation has gone unchecked for so long that it has been translated into the physical language of your body, hence all your symptoms. Your pneuma is both trying to be ignored and trying to be treated. It's simultaneously asking for help and trying to avoid receiving that help.

It was a relief for someone to explain what was wrong, what had happened. No one else, none of those doctors in their white jackets or their scrubs—or their comically patterned scrubs if they were trying to bring a sense of humor into a place of smashed bones and dead hearts—none of those people had even tried to explain anything to me. All they could say was that they couldn't say anything for sure, that bodies were a mystery, that even blood tests, ultrasounds, X-rays, MRIs, were only little guesses. Whole hospitals shrugged.

But now Ed was giving me an answer: the pneuma. It didn't matter if I believed in the pneuma or not. It didn't even matter if he was right. It was an explanation. A story.

The root of your symptoms is deeply embedded and intertwined with your nonphysical self, so it makes sense that Western medicine hasn't been helpful for you.

Ed's hair frizz swayed in a draft. I had the odd sense that time had somehow bent, that it was coming at me on a diagonal. My scalp covered itself in sweat.

Your energetic body is telling me that you want to be healed so desperately you are actually stopping yourself from being healed. Are you aware of that?

Isn't it funny that a person could want something so much she might do everything she could to stop herself from getting it? So funny.

That sounds about right, I said.

He nodded slow and deep, the moral to his own story. *All your problems and all the answers to those problems exist in the boundaries of your body.*

I thought I might start crying though I didn't know why. There was a humming behind my eyes but nothing came. Ed picked up a pale gray stone and came back to the table, held it a few inches above the bridge of my nose.

I've created a deionized field around your body, a temporary splint for your aura, and that is giving your pneuma some relief, but in order to create a lasting solution we'll need to go through a complete PAKing cycle over the next few months, maybe longer. I realize it's expensive, but you should know I have to prepare for a full day before a PAKing session and it takes at least two days to recover. My waiting list has a dozen people on it, but because of Chandra's recommendation and your condition, I could start seeing you as soon as next week.

He was moving the stone in an arc above my face, lightly touching each temple. Somehow it was clear I didn't have to say or do anything.

But for now I'll administer some more dramatic energetic maneuvers to open those blockages, so if you could just totally relax, remain attentive to your energetic body, and trust my guidance, that would help us out tremendously.

He put the stone down on my sternum and closed his eyes, then extended his hands to hover over my chest. I tried to clear my mind and maybe I did or maybe he did because the rest of the session was a blur and all I remember now was the slow walk home, my foot not twitching, my neck brace half-stuffed in my purse. I wasn't in pain but I wasn't completely out of pain either. I felt as if several strong hands were gripping my legs, my back, pressing the muscles closer to the bones.

No fighting. No flying, Ed said as I left. *Just float.*

Four

My first PAKing session had taken me out of the office for almost three hours, so I was staying late—*to catch up on some invoices*, I explained to Meg as she left, but I actually meant to use my work computer to apply for a second job to raise the cash to pay for a complete PAKing series. There weren't really any invoices to catch up on, I just needed to put in some hours at the office, pretending what I did was useful. Travel agencies, we knew, were dying, and Universal Travel had been downsizing almost constantly since I'd started working there. I didn't have any of the skills they were looking for in an accounts manager, but the pay was too low for anyone qualified for the job. I'd only applied because I thought free travel might be a perk, but even the agents only got slight discounts and I never became an agent—*You're not the type*, I was told. I remained in the fluorescent-lit, low-ceilinged back part of the office, sending e-mails to people who owed us money and excuses to people whom we owed money. Checks. Invoices. Checking invoices. E-mails. That's all I ever did.

But that night all I sent were cover letters and résumés to random night gigs culled off Craigslist—restaurant hosting, temp stuff, various forms of assisting. Somewhat reluctantly, I also responded to an ad I found on a health food store's bulletin board.

The ad listed several qualifications (*Ivy degree, CPR training, spotless mental health record, knowledge of foreign affairs, strong communication skills, and—above all: discretion*), though the details of the job, the ad noted, could not be specifically described in the ad, *NOT because of the legality of the job*, but because describing the *specific duties* of this job would likely attract candidates poorly suited for this (*high-paying, low-time-commitment, weekends and occasional weeknights*) job, which, the ad said, wasn't even really *a job*, but a sort of *income-generating experience*.

An auto-reply came a few minutes later—

> We are moving very quickly to fill the positions. Please complete and respond as quickly and as thoroughly as you can.
> Best Wishes,
> Matheson.

—with a full application attached—several forms; a personality test; a handwriting-analysis worksheet I had to print, complete, and scan; a natal-chart questionnaire; a clearance for a background check; and ten short essay questions on disparate topics.

I immediately went to work, completing it two hours later. What would a background check even uncover about me? My debts? That I was a medical mystery? The places my passport had been? (If anyone could run a truly accurate background check on me, I knew all they'd find would be Merle and Mother in that dusty brown cabin. The name Junia. The navy Bible I'd left behind. But no one would ever find that.)

Walking through the inert office that night, the dark broken only by the flicker of a screen saver dancing alone, I thought that if I could ever do a background check on myself, I knew exactly what I'd do with it. I wouldn't even read it, just take it somewhere sacred and set it on fire.

The next night I was belly down on the living room floor trying to read a book when the phone rang. It was a quarter till eleven. No one called anymore except for Chandra and I knew she was religious about not using any technology after dusk.

May I speak to Mary Parsons?

This is she.

Hiii, Mary. Forgive me for calling so late. How are you this evening?

I'm—fine . . . But really I felt odd and alive, my body still throbbing from whatever Ed had done to me.

Good, good. Well, my name is Melissa and I read your application—you responded to one of our flyers? Anyway, we'd like to invite you in for an interview tomorrow.

She told me to arrive at suite 704 in a building near Union Square at 1:23, exactly, and it was 1:23, exactly, when the door to suite 704 swung open before I even had a chance to buzz. A pale blond girl exited, hunched and glanceless, as if she had just endured something unspeakable. Melissa and Matheson offered soft handshakes—*Hi, hello, Mary, nice to meet you, how are you, thanks for being prompt*—their voices overlapping so that I didn't know how to respond.

Of course, I said, afraid my nervousness seemed condescending.

I am so *sorry about the lighting*, Matheson said, flicking an overgroomed bang from his forehead, *but we'll just have to deal, I suppose.*

Suite 704 was an anonymous conference room, an overpolished faux-wood table nearly filling the space. I took a seat as Matheson wrote something on his clipboard, inhaling and exhaling like a yoga teacher in preparation. The asymmetrical cut of Melissa's neckline below the extreme symmetry of her face created a deep sense of inferiority in me. She stared at me as if she was unable to conceal her contempt for anyone who was not as groomed and sleek as she was. I couldn't tell if she was a very young woman disguised as someone older or the other way around. Matheson was dressed like an executive of some fashionable company, but still had the face of a teenage model—suspiciously clear skin, high cheekbones, square jaw, attractive in a surreal, alarming way.

Do you have any favorite celebrities? he asked.

No, I said.

Well, do you know about the personal lives of any celebrities?

That they have personal lives?

Ah—no. Do you follow the lives of any celebrities, in particular? Through websites or magazines? Melissa chimed in.

No. I don't actually, um, read any magazines.

Melissa blinked hard and looked at her notes. *What kinds of movies or television shows do you watch? Are there any actors or directors you enjoy in particular?*

I was beginning to sense that I'd been duped, that there was no job, no income-generating experience, that this was some poorly funded marketing firm's attempt at research.

The truth was, I had this not-so-fun party trick called Guess What Movie I Haven't Seen? *The Wizard of Oz? Star Wars? The Godfather?* The answer was always no. A film studies major at

Columbia—a beady-eyed Christopher who wouldn't answer to Chris (*That's not my name*, he would say, producing his driver's license)—had tried to force me to watch my first movie, *Citizen Kane*, when I was twenty. He wanted to curate my entire experience of film, spoon-feeding me black-and-white classics first, and telling me what to think of them, building in me his own empire of taste. It failed because I fell asleep after a few minutes of each movie or else just couldn't concentrate on the screen, had to get up and find something to read or do instead. I'd never gained the skill or desire to watch things like that, I suppose, in the same way that people who grow up without a religion rarely feel the lack of one as an adult. (*Adult-onset ADD*, Christopher told me. *I've seen it before. You know you can take something for that, right?*) After a few weeks of failure, I told Christopher I couldn't do his project, that I didn't have it in me, and he said I'd ruined his entire thesis and wasted his time. *I didn't know you were such a vapid pleaser*, he said. I asked him what that meant and he said, *You know, one of those women who want male approval so badly they go along with whatever a man asks them but ultimately end up failing because they never think about what* they *actually want*. It was a beautiful autumn day and we were standing in front of the old library, the concrete steps strewn with students. My veins dilated. I said, *I didn't know you could be one of those pretentious assholes who think they have a right to something just because they have one stupid idea, you skeezy fuck*. I had never felt so large and small at the same time. I didn't recognize my own voice and words. Shame and pride swirled together in a way that felt animal, so I darted away from him. I was still new to this kind of adrenaline, the immediate release of anger instead of gnawing on it like overdue gum.

I really don't know, I told Melissa. *I don't watch things.*

Do you mean, like, recently? Like a tech cleanse?

I've never had a TV.

So you watch things online?

I just use a computer at work.

What about your phone?

I have a landline.

She looked at me as if I were a hallucination, then lowered her gaze, bewildered, to her clipboard.

Wait, what about movies? What was the last movie you saw?

I've never been to one. I watched some of Citizen Kane *one time, but I fell asleep. I've seen the beginnings of a few others but I don't know which ones.*

I couldn't tell from their expressions if this was a deficiency or impressive.

Well, I guess—um, let's move on for now, Matheson said. *Is there anyone in your life that you tell everything to?*

Like a best friend, Melissa added.

Yes, or a relative. A parent? Sibling?

No siblings, no parents anymore.

What about friends or a boyfriend? Melissa asked, noticeably unslowed by the speed bump that mentioning my parents usually was.

I have one good friend, but I guess I keep a lot to myself.

Forgive me if I'm prying, Matheson said, *but are your parents still living?*

They weren't dead, or if they were, I didn't know how I'd ever find out. I assumed Aunt Clara would call me if anything happened, but we had spoken so rarely since I stopped visiting Tennessee and not at all in the last few months or year or so. I wondered if we were just trying to let enough time pass so we could forget what had happened.

They're off the grid, I explained, though that didn't really explain it.

Oh my God, were you like Amish or something? Melissa asked.

Just homeschooled, I said, but homeschooled didn't even begin to explain it. I always avoided talking about the way I'd been raised. *Are you going to ask me about my résumé or those essays?*

We read your application, Melissa said.

And it's fine, Matheson interrupted. *Admirable. Columbia. Steady job. CPR training. Scuba certification. Spanish, French . . .*

Yes, it's all very impressive, Melissa said, *isn't it?*

So, you don't have any questions about—

Matheson held his hand up to stop my voice. *Mary, we appreciate your cooperation as we go through this very rigorous selection process, and we can assure you that should you be selected for this work, you'd be pleased with both the compensation and the extremely interesting experience.*

We work for a very interesting and influential man, Melissa said.

Wise beyond his years.

And talented.

And wealthy, of course.

Of course.

And we are responsible for assessing candidates for a very innovative project, a state-of-the-art inquiry into some of life's most challenging questions.

That's all we can tell you.

For now.

Right.

Candidates who pass additional interviews will be given more information.

As needed.

A cell phone pinged and Matheson and Melissa rose in unison, extended their hands for shaking.

So, unfortunately our time is up today, Matheson said. *Thank you very much for your time. You're a very interesting candidate. We'll be in touch.*

A girl in a boxy beige outfit was at the door. I couldn't tell if she was poorly or well dressed, stylish or just a mess.

Hi, I'm Matheson, Melissa, yes, hello, Rhoda, nice to meet you, how are you, thanks for being so prompt.

Five

Ed had me by the wrists, pulling the left one up and slightly right, the right one up and slightly left. He was crouching on the table and I was kneeling, my ankles and knees held down by soft leather straps attached to the floor. We had scheduled the next seven sessions, and he agreed to let me pay at the end of the month, twenty-five days to come up with $1,575 in cash. My only backup to the income-generating experience was being a host seven nights a week at a pan-Asian restaurant, which seemed to be a front for something in the back room. I couldn't quite tell. It wasn't enough to cover my PAKing sessions, but they paid nightly, under the table, and the guy who'd interviewed me said there was the possibility of more money, though he didn't say how. He asked a lot of questions about my shoes and ankle strength—*There's a lot of standing involved in . . . you know, in hosting, being a hostess.* He asked me what size shoe I wore three times and seemed to be implying something I didn't understand, though this was a feeling I had often, the sense of a subtext. On the back of his card he wrote another number, said to call him whenever I liked. I hoped I'd never need to.

Since you're ovulating right now, I'll only be actively working above your heart and below your knees today, Ed told me. *We don't want . . . to interfere.*

Oh, I said, *okay*.

One doctor had told me to keep strict records of my cycle, basal body temperature, and cervical position, so I knew Ed was exactly right though I hadn't given him any of that information on the intake form. Could a person appear ovulatory? I was accustomed to being blind to what others found obvious, but this felt extreme. I tried to forget Ed's ovulation comment and focus on my breathing or something, but it was all just too weird, as if I'd caught him going through my purse.

I, um, didn't give you any cycle information, I said after a long silence.

Root your knees into the earth, he said, so I did (or attempted to, or something, and what did that even mean?). He started to chant.

Without contracting your lower back, he added, breaking and immediately restarting the chant.

I wanted to ask, more specifically, how he knew I was ovulating, but I was concentrating on uncontracting my lower back as he chanted above me. My shoulders shook as if generating a low-pitched sound.

A woman's aura noticeably shifts with her cycle, he said later. He attached sensors between my eyebrows and on the underside of each wrist. Cords ran to a small white machine about the size of a mini-refrigerator. He turned it on and it started whirring, a cool blue light flashing on and off in a senseless pattern.

At the count of seven please hold your breath and concentrate on the first color you feel.

I was belly down on the massage table, face cradled, staring at the floor. He pressed his elbow between a muscle and bone just below my neck and counted in a whisper. On seven I saw a pale yellow light and felt my arms go slack. When I woke up a few minutes later, Ed was sitting on the floor beside the table, cross-legged and quietly chanting. I felt as if a swath of molten wax had hardened down my spine, but when I reached for it, there was just my skin. It seemed I had been crying, that I was still crying. Tears rained straight out of my head, fell to the floor.

Tears are a flow of energy that can be channeled into more progressive pathways, Ed said. *Tears are a choice you make.*

I stopped immediately.

There, he said, *now isn't that better?*

Six

How was your day?

I was staring into a black lens embedded in a wall in a small white room in a building in SoHo, reading a list of phrases. Matheson and Melissa sat to each side of the lens, occasionally taking notes or exchanging glances.

How was your day? I asked the lens again. *How was your day?*

I had been instructed to say each phrase three times: *That must be hard for you* and *Whatever you want is fine* and *You're right* and *What are you thinking?*

It was my third, maybe fourth interview. Nothing, as usual, had been explained. I was only told to vary my inflections slightly, imagine I was speaking to someone I deeply cared about.

Excellent, Matheson said, *but moving forward, could you pause a little longer between repetitions?*

Does the job have something to do with acting? Is that part of it?

No, Melissa said, *we can assure you there is no acting involved.*

I missed you was next on the list I'd been given.

I missed you, I said, wondering who else had made it this far and who or what was on the other side of that lens. *I missed you*, I said, wondering what missing even is. *I missed you*.

Melissa uncrossed and recrossed her legs. The dozen small sensors that had been taped on various parts of my body felt sometimes fizzy or warm, but being measured by some technology or another had become such a normal part of my life in doctors' offices that these sensors hadn't surprised me at all.

I love you, I said to the lens. *I love you*. I let the pause linger. *I love you*.

Melissa stood and left abruptly, saying she needed to check on the results in another room.

Matheson smirked. *The other girls have been a parade of disappointment. So fake and weird. But you were almost totally unpretentious.*

To my left was a large mirror, and glancing at it, I realized it had been built into the wall, which made me wonder if it was a mirror on one side and a window on the other. It depressed me to think that I might have been looking at another person but seeing only myself.

Is this one of those mirror-window things? I asked, but Matheson didn't react, pressed his earpiece, looked up, and asked, *Mary, why do you think people pair up, so to speak? Why do human beings couple off?*

I thought of the year I'd been one-half of a pair, a little while before all the sickness began.

Paul. We met on a rooftop, at a party one of Chandra's rich friends was throwing, and we somehow said hello to each other at the same moment, both of us with the vague feeling that we'd met before, that we'd known each other for a long time, that this meeting had occurred before, would occur again, had always been. Looking at each other, something made sense that hadn't made sense before. We talked about whatever we talked about, smiling so much it was actually painful, then it was dusk and we left in the dim, forgetting goodbyes to the others, overcome. For hours we walked the streets of that neighborhood, found a park and walked around the outer edge of it, talking and talking, though I don't remember what about—there was just something in his voice, something deeper than just the sound or words or how he said them. (He said *together* with more *a* than *e*, so it came out sounding like *to-gather*, and this had a tremendous effect on me, *to-gather*.) It still makes no sense, even all these years later. I still don't know what it is or was about him, about us together (his pronunciation), that made us bind so decisively, two indecisive people so clear, for a time, about each other.

At some late hour we decided to take the subway back to our homes, but he missed his stop and stayed on to keep me company, then I missed mine and we kept right on along, not noticing it at first, then noticing and not caring. We went all the way up to Queens and had to wait on a platform for an hour with a swelling crowd, some annoyed, some tipsy, some commuting to early jobs, and I'm pretty sure I knew, even then, that I was doing what people in books did when they fell in love, romanticizing ugly things, the grungy station, the air weighted with the evaporating sweat of hundreds, that massive stink—but I didn't care that I was romanticizing it. I didn't care that I was in a hideous MTA station mid-renovation, with the jackhammers wailing and greenish dust in the air and all the tired, angry, sweating people gathering around us, complaining so loudly. I was in some other place. I wasn't waiting on anything. I knew that this sort of love, technically, was just a neurotransmitter cocktail designed to make you feel invincible and infinite—beyond language, beyond logic—but I also knew that love was as thrilling as it was temporary, a prelude to pain, though I only knew this through reading—which is just to say I had not really learned it yet and may never. That little shimmer in the chest. How simple it seems. It only seems that way.

This paradox of feelings and memories filled me in the instant Matheson asked this question, but I couldn't speak. It all sat impossibly just below my mouth.

Do you mean . . . why do people just get together . . . (to-gather) *for the long term?*

Yes—long-term relationships, marriage. What's the point of it?

Maybe because they think it will be easier that way? A division of labor?

(I didn't believe this. It seemed he could tell.)

Chores, creating income, raising children, he asked, *that sort of thing?*

Maybe?

And what are maybe some other reasons?

Maybe . . . people fall in love. And that makes them stay.

And what, exactly, is falling in love?

It makes sense of something that doesn't make sense.

He nodded at me and made a note. *Do you think of this a lot?*

Not in particular.

You seem to have some ideas about it.

I just think a lot. I don't have much else to do.

Right, I guess without TV or anything you have a lot of time . . .

That wasn't what I meant but I didn't correct him.

He made another note, put a finger to his earpiece. *Mary, we live in very strange times. Knowledge is always second to data—big data, data as a form of war, and meanwhile adults are taught to be anxious about not having enough sex while teenagers are shamed for wanting to have it all the time. Haute couture uses emaciated children to sell sex as art, while toddlers are wearing high heels and doing abdominal exercises. The ways in which our culture expresses value and collective sexuality has become, to put it lightly, demented.*

None of this exactly made sense to me, but I nodded as if I understood. Matheson pressed his earpiece and kept talking like a bad actor imitating a worse politician.

In the greater context of human history, wealth and power have been indications that a person has secured excess resources for survival. The wealthy and powerful of the world should therefore be nodes of philanthropy and evolution, the ones who move us, as a species, forward with thought and generosity. However, the American concept of celebrity has developed and become deformed in tandem with the rise of the information age. The paparazzi are now everywhere because anyone can be one with nothing more than a cell phone. What used to just be in Us Weekly *is now on every corner of the Internet, constantly dehumanizing many of our most emotionally intelligent and talented members of society.*

I didn't interrupt his rant to ask what *Us Weekly* was, but looked it up at work the next day. Will I ever stop being surprised by the ways people make hell?

The value we have placed on superficial knowledge of the personal lives of our celebrities is quickly creating a sort of emotional vacuum for many respected, talented, wealthy, and otherwise evolved individuals . . . And this paradox relates back to what I was saying about the wealthy and powerful needing to move the human race along. Celebrity obsession is often emotionally and logistically shackling to the country's most prominent and successful people, and this ultimately hinders those wealthy, powerful, and celebrated people from being the nodes of evolution and progress they should actually be for the culture at large.

(Matheson seemed to briefly notice I didn't understand what he was saying, but he continued just the same.)

For example, let's say the financial resources of an extremely successful actor-filmmaker who has lived the majority of his life in the public eye are rich, but his ability to connect deeply and intimately with another person has been compromised by the fact that anyone he meets feels as if they already know him from his film roles and media coverage. On top of this, there's also a pervasive and inescapable surveillance of his public activities that is shared continuously online. Strangers tweet his whereabouts and every movement. Discreetly and indiscreetly taken photos are posted of him standing on a sidewalk or driving a car or eating in a restaurant or walking a dog or vacationing or anything else he might do in view of another person. As you can imagine, this creates an overawareness of the self, even in the most resilient people. Then there's all the official appearances and interviews he must do for marketing his films: questions about his personal life, his creative life, what movies he likes, what he does in his free time, who he's dating, who he used to date, where he travels, what he's done, what he's doing next. All this privacy is sacrificed already, and anything he intentionally tries to keep private is hounded all the more for it. Can you imagine what this might do to a person?

But he wasn't asking for an answer from me. Matheson put his hand, again, to his earpiece, and it occurred to me this might all have been scripted and I couldn't decide how to feel about what he was saying, whether it was all nonsense or just more evidence that I would never understand this world.

Because of his films and his perpetually compromised sense of privacy, anyone who meets this hypothetical actor-filmmaker tends to have complex opinions about him and the false sense of already knowing him long before they exchange any words. In this way, he has lost all control over his ability to make a first impression or genuinely meet and interact with another person. Instead he is subject to whatever knowledge a person happens to have about him, regardless of its integrity. But what else can that hypothetical actor-filmmaker do? How does he find meaningful human connection in a world of people who falsely believe they are already connected to him? How does he make friends who don't just want to ride his coattails toward their own fame or the afterglow of his celebrity? How can he ever really trust someone, and thus, how could he ever safely be in love?

(Safety seemed, to me, to be the opposite of being in love, though my experience was limited to, maybe, one tangible experience and some secondhand understanding.) I wasn't sure if this was still part of the interview or if I was now being trained for the income-generating experience. (Chandra had always said accepting uncertainty was the key to happiness so I accepted all this uncertainty, but I still felt as if I were looking over my own shoulder, watching the quiet moment before everything fell apart—this white room, this man speaking in such a strange, written way.)

Look at TMZ *or any celebrity magazine online or at the grocery store and all you'll see is substance abuse and divorce and meltdowns. And why do you think that is? Could it be the constant pressure of being observed and scrutinized? Could it be the way our culture constantly looks for a way to cannibalize its most interesting, talented, and powerful citizens? It's just further evidence that this country is always stopping itself from progressing in any way—whether culturally or politically or emotionally—*

I wanted to ask him whether I'd been hired or not or remind him I was the one who didn't know about celebrity things, but he never seemed to notice my pre-speech inhalations.

And we all have needs. Don't we? To be heard and understood, to feel less alone. Those needs don't go away, no matter how famous or wealthy or celebrated you might become, no matter how many movies or television shows you're in, no matter how many awards you win . . .

His attention fell inside himself for a moment, making his face soft and childlike until he flicked at his bangs and began again.

Now, let me ask you something—are you familiar with the procedures used in ovum donation?

Um, egg donation?

Correct.

Ah, a little, I guess? (I had once seen a girl self-administer a subcutaneous injection of hormones in our dorm bathroom while explaining to me how she was furthering her bloodline without the risk of pregnancy—*like men have forever*, she said bitterly. I remembered the bead of fresh blood rolling down her leg.)

Well, here's the funny thing about egg donation—let's say you want to make a person. That used to mean you needed to have sex, get pregnant, survive childbirth, and raise the kid, right? Even like twenty years ago that was almost the only option.

Sure?

But now, of course, technology is expanding the routes you can take to create a new person. If a woman can't get pregnant easily, she might take some drugs. Or if you're single or gay or your partner is infertile, you can go to a sperm bank. If you can't carry a baby, you can hire a surrogate. And if your eggs don't work, you can actually buy eggs harvested from another woman. So, theoretically you could buy eggs, buy sperm, hire a surrogate, hire a wet nurse and an army of nannies, and theoretically you would be the legal *mother of that child, but the egg donor would be the genetic mother and the sperm donor would be the genetic father and the surrogate would be the birth mother and the wet nurse would have the milk bond or whatever and the nannies would do the actual parenting—*

I can't donate my eggs, I blurted.

Oh, dear—we totally don't want your eggs. No offense. What I'm saying is that technology now enables us to divide up the relationships and roles that were previously wrapped into one person. The question of who is that theoretical child's mother has many true answers.

I don't see how this connects to what you were talking about—

Well, it's in the fact that our project is also concerned with evolution—emotional evolution—*specifically the development of a more honest, nuanced view of human pair-bond selection, behavior, and maintenance. We know marriage started as a way to control land and wealth, but that's not how we ideally think of it today—we want our spouses and partners to be everything to us: a lover, a best friend, a confidant, a nurturer, an intellectual equal, sometimes a coparent, sometimes even an oblique replacement for a lost or failed parent. Furthermore, it's more accepted now than it ever has been that love and attachment don't always fall along heterosexual gender lines. We have reached a point, as a culture, where the predominant view of romantic partnership is no longer about survival or wealth or creating progeny. Ideally a marriage or long-term relationship should be built upon a profound feeling of love between two people; however, the presence or intensity of this feeling is extremely difficult to accurately measure or explain. What we are trying to research here is the physiology of that sort of emotional equilibrium. What is happening within the brains of a truly happy couple and how can we know if a couple is actually happy? Are there habits and practices that could actually create this contentment from the inside? And when people say that when they met their partner "they just knew," what is it that they knew? And what does it mean if a person is continually trying and failing to reach this sort of emotional steadiness with one person? Might it be impossible for some people to only rely on one person for all of one's emotional, social, sexual, and daily support? Might there be a kind of technological, therapeutic, and/or medical solution for those who continually try and fail to find contentment in a romantic pair bond?*

I stared at him, utterly lost.

Basically, he continued, *our bodies evolved from animal to human. We evolved from nomadic tribes into structured civilizations and now we are continuing to evolve, to make the human experience a more harmonious thing.*

I guess that I'm still just wondering what this has to do with this . . . job?

What I can tell you at this stage is that I work for a very prominent film artist—he's a director and actor, but he's truly so much more than that. A real artist. And based on the last couple interviews, it seems you've never heard of him and that's great. What I can say is that you're in the final running for a very exciting opportunity. He's quite the idea man, brilliant but very humble about his success. But this is why we had to be so obtuse in the ad—if we mentioned the fact that this involved a high-profile personality, we would have had a billion applications from fangirls—which is exactly what we are not looking for. But, Mary, we really do appreciate how patient you've been with all these interviews—he slid an envelope of what felt like cash into my hand—*so here's a token of our appreciation.* I tried to accept it with nonchalance, suppressing the feeling that a bag of snakes had just been shaken up and set loose in me. The tendons in my neck and behind my ears tensed. I thought of the money I already owed Ed.

The same silent man in the white lab coat who had applied a dozen sensors to my body came back in, removed all the sensors, put them in a special case, and left. I had to wonder how much he might know or whether he might be the actor Matheson was talking about, happy to look at someone who didn't know who he was.

We'll be calling you very soon, Matheson said, escorting me to the door, then to a waiting elevator. He pressed a button and waved as the doors shut.

Seven

I felt well and wealthy enough (the envelope held ten new fifties) to buy real food—roast chicken, mashed potatoes, and creamed spinach—at the deli for rich people near my office. I even got a bottle of wine, though the corkscrew, I realized later, had gone in the stoop sale. Sitting against a wall in my living room, I ate straight from the paper box while staring at the un-opened wine—a nonessential, a luxury item. It was a victory to buy (with *cash*) even the cheapest bottle at the nicer store (be-spoke wood shelving instead of bulletproof glass), and they carded me, too, the first time I could remember (though it had been a long time since I'd bought anything or been anywhere to warrant it).

As the clerk handed back my ID, hard-won at a midtown DMV, I thought back to my first driver's license in Tennessee, long expired, though I still kept it in the small box of objects I'll always keep. In the photo I am seventeen, my skin wan from years of long-sleeved dresses, forest shadow, and wide-brim hats. I used to think, *Junia*, when I looked at the photo, as if Junia were someone else, not me, not the name I'd first been given. It seemed that my identity had necessarily split, that I'd turned into a different person. I could look at her now and see all that stoic ferocity in her eyes, how she wanted to do something that could never be undone. Something permanent. Some little forever. But I'm not interested in forever. Not anymore.

What kind of name is Junia anyway? Aunt Clara asked as she drove me away from the cabin for the last time. *That's just Merle for you, a name like that. I mean, what's wrong with Julia or Julie? Too normal for him, I guess.*

She laughed, trying to get me to laugh, it seemed, but I couldn't. In the car she renamed me Mary, and when I later saw my reflection in the glass door of the courthouse in Knoxville, I didn't know whom I was looking at, didn't know where I was in all of this.

Good Christian name, Clara said. *You could be anyone you want with a name like Mary.*

Aunt Clara's house was listed as my home address even though it was never quite my home, just a house I slept in for a few months. I took her last name, Parsons, instead of my parents' name, Stone (though I still don't know which name is more mine than the other). Parsons had been her husband's last name, dead then for longer than he'd been alive. All she ever said to me about him was *You can only love a person that much once in your life*, and I didn't know enough to agree or disagree with her. What a terrible and beautiful delusion, and how sad if it's true. I wouldn't know, might never.

That afternoon I went to the DMV, drove around a block with a man riding shotgun, and a half hour later I had the very first picture I'd ever seen of myself in my hands, still warm from the machine. I kept my ID displayed on my desk at all times, and as my other documents came in—my Social Security card and birth certificate and SAT scores and GED—I added them to the spread. Here was this person. Mary Parsons. Here was proof that she existed.

But it was everything Merle had taught me to fear. I'd been at the center of his life's work, though not his life, as he had and would always have a love for the Lord greater than any he could have for me or my mother. This was not a secret, and I'd been told to do the same, to love the Lord above all others, been taught that love belonged only to the divine, not here on this broken world. I've found it difficult, maybe impossible, to undo this way of thinking. Maybe I will always have to love the idea of love or a concept of God more than I can love a person. But then, these things are so difficult to measure—how could you even quantify or compare one love to another? By weight? By volume? And who is to say that loving a person isn't just loving the idea of that person and not the actual person, all these incomprehensible clots of flesh with all their years gone by and vanished, all their history stored in basements even they cannot reach?

So it makes sense that so many people decide to love God so much, as that's the only love that has a chance of never changing, never leaving (though even a person's love of God isn't guaranteed to last). When I think of Merle this way, I can almost forgive him, can almost understand how intensely his devotion to loving God directed everything in his life, fueled his hands to type and burn and retype all those pages—a purpose he was sure the Lord had given him. This one certain thing.

He was writing a manifesto, of sorts, a creed on the impossibility of living a truly Christian life at the behest of any government. He believed that all forms of government were spiritually bankrupt, that the only true way to follow Jesus was to be radically self-reliant—off every grid. The energy grid was wasteful and corrupt, and the food grid devalued and destroyed the planet, and the culture at large was full of pain and deceit, and money itself was truly evil, and even the church (or, as he would say, the corporation that calls itself the church) was the most corrupt—contaminated by money and political greed and widespread land ownership. Worst of all, they called themselves holy.

His plan was to raise me in a state of complete purity, to protect me from the terrible world, and my life would prove his point. I suppose he expected me to be a prophet, but I had nothing to say. Eventually, with Clara's help, I left and joined this broken country, began following its rules, breathing its air, began my debts, joined all these terrible grids.

My birth certificate came seventeen years late, so the official word on my beginning is murky—my time of birth, mother, father, and location are all *unknown*. But finally I was born.

When it was decided that Merle and Florence would come visit Clara and me for Thanksgiving, some months after I left, all my days sank toward that day like water toward a drain. Then the day arrived and they arrived and they came in through the same door that all my *Mary Parsons* documents had come through. Florence hugged me as if I were too delicate to really touch and Merle's eyes refused to meet mine, opposing magnets. He sat in the living room reading his Bible and I passed some time in the bathroom, dry heaving, throwing water on my face, practicing a calm smile into the mirror.

Over supper Florence spoke about the beet crop and how the string beans had gotten so tall she had to build new scaffolding. *Our vegetables just haven't been like this in years*, she said, and

Merle said almost nothing the whole afternoon, until just before they left, all of us refusing pie despite Clara's insistence, and in the moment Merle could have said goodbye to me, he just said, *You're a fool*, and left.

Later, as Aunt Clara and I dismembered the turkey into plastic containers, I couldn't stop wondering if he'd intentionally been referencing that scene in *King Lear* where Lear calls Cordelia a fool. He'd been so proud of the essay I'd written about Lear's materialism being intrinsic to his insanity, that the play dismantles the lie of acquisition, how the spirit is at odds with the accrual of wealth and power. He would bring up that essay out of nowhere sometimes, interrupting anything to compliment it again. While tutoring me in a subject I was having trouble with, he'd cite it as evidence that I was gifted, capable of creative thought and would therefore soon be able to understand whatever algebra or chemistry I was struggling with. We had staged *King Lear* several times, the three of us cast in every role, which sometimes meant we'd have to speak both parts of a dialogue. Florence would read one part in a high voice and the other in a low voice, but Merle would just shift his weight from leg to leg, never breaking pace or altering his diction, every line cascading directly into the next, rushing like fire across a field. His voice, for some reason, never let on that he'd been raised in the shadow of Lookout Mountain, the way that Florence's and Aunt Clara's long vowels gave them away. Clara once mentioned how she thought Merle moved out to California for a few years before he met Florence, but I never found out, for sure, what happened out there or why he'd gone or why he'd returned.

The Thanksgiving dinners never got easier, just, for a few years, quieter. After I'd gone away to college, returning each fall, it seemed we had reached an almost-comfortable stasis, that we could go on like this indefinitely. But then Merle said something about me living so far away, something about me forgetting about my roots and I snapped.

New York wouldn't seem so far away if y'all just got a phone already. Really, you're not making a statement about anything by not having a phone. It's not going to eat your soul or whatever it is you believe.

I thought I had the right to argue. I thought I knew more. No one answered me for a while and that sentence hung there— *It's not going to eat your soul or whatever it is you believe*—and I had to confront the caustic inanity of what I'd said. I mashed the stuffing into the asparagus casserole with the back of my fork, and when I looked up, Florence was pale and still and Clara had bowed her head. The only movement at the table was in my father's jaw, his face looking unnourished and hollow, his fork hovering over his plate. Sometimes I remember him with his eyes shut. Other times I see him staring through me.

I was twenty-two, had a degree, a job, had traveled the world with Chandra, had read all sorts of books they'd never read, knew all kinds of things they refused to know. I thought I'd *make* them understand, with rhetoric, with everything I had learned. I didn't realize I was ending it all, that it would really be that easy for me to vanish from the family.

It's astounding how ignorant and arrogant you've become, Merle said after a long silence.

Oh, Florence said, *let's not fight about this. We all know this fighting won't get us anywhere.*

Damn right it doesn't get us anywhere.

Damn was the only curse I'd ever heard him use, a total of four times: when his toolshed collapsed; when he chopped his fingertip; when an oak fell on our goat during an ice storm; when he found someone's escaped pet python had swallowed two hens from the coop—easy fixes, all of them; he rebuilt the shed, cauterized the wound, cooked the goat, and shot the python, but solving the problem of me was not so simple.

Aunt Clara dropped her fork hard on her plate and spoke gently: *Merle, darlin', I'm so sorry, but I can't put up with that kind of language at my dinner table and surely not on Thanksgiving.*

He regarded Clara as if she were just a house cat that had sauntered into the room, then went back to his food.

I'm sorry, I said to no one in particular.

I was already prepared to retreat, to sink back into my once-a-year role as the permanently prodigal daughter, our unspoken agreement that I show up at Aunt Clara's house, eat a meal, sleep a night, and leave the next day on the Greyhound. This was all that kept us a family.

I shouldn't bring it up, I said. *It's my fault.*

Though Florence had tried writing me letters for a while—telling me of the tomato, squash, and string bean harvest, the tally of animals Merle had killed, how many pounds of jerky one deer had turned into—those had stopped after a year or so. They'd always been signed *Love, Your Mother and Father*, always in her hand. There was never an ounce of anything personal, never a question about me, and though I half hated those letters, I loved them, too.

She can do whatever she wants, Merle said as he stood up, and walked calmly to the back door, slamming it shut.

He just needs some air, Florence said. *You know how he gets without a good lungful of air.*

It was well after dark when he walked out of the little patch of suburban woods behind Clara's house. He was gripping the shotgun he kept in the truck in one hand and two skinned squirrels dangling from a branch in the other.

Listen, he said as he stepped inside, not bothering to remove his muddy boots, and I thought he was going to go on one of his rants about my way of life creating income that became taxes that supported war, about war being inherently at odds with a life following Christ, that the only way to live was to refuse all forms of capitalism and subsist on God's gifts, tending land and animals, but he just paced around—almost speaking, then not—tracking mud across the beige carpet.

Clara loudly began the dishes.

The daughter shall not bear the iniquity of the father, he said eventually, a hacked quote from Ezekiel, *neither shall the father bear the iniquity of the daughter: the righteousness of the righteous shall be upon him, and the wickedness of the wicked shall be upon her.*

I tried to come up with a verse of my own, but all I could think of was Nietzsche, as if philosophy had fully displaced all the Bible verses I'd memorized in childhood. I wonder what he would have done if I had come up with something from the New Testament about kindness and tolerance.

Provoke not your children to wrath, I said, hesitant, dusting off my memory of Ephesians.

How can you quote from the Word you've rejected? He squinted as if I were so far away from him he could hardly recognize the face that echoed his. *There's no room in you for the sanctity of the Bible when you believe anything you read.*

I tried to remember another quote—one I had leaned heavily on in my early years away, when I was still trying to make room for Christianity among other philosophies and long discussions with atheist valedictorians—but nothing came. I looked at Merle for a moment, and now that moment stretches out long in my memory—his skin had thinned across his face and his beard was longer and grayer than I'd ever seen it. I remember noticing, perhaps for the first time, the thick creases just below his cheekbones.

He slammed the back door again, moved toward the carcasses with a knife, and from the window we watched him gut the little animals, their blood pouring onto the deck.

Florence was sipping black coffee from a teacup.

She didn't look at me. She may have never looked at me again.

She said, *Oh, he got some squirrels.*

Eight

It was hard for me to take this seriously. Ed was on his back on the floor, legs straight toward the ceiling, and I was draped over them, arching my back across his socked feet, arms overhead, body hanging in a C. This was the second time we'd done this particular move and I held a heavy metal ball in each hand, to which Ed had told me to send my breath, but I couldn't tell if I was doing it right. He flexed his toes against my back in a slow, deliberate pattern.

I'd been hanging there a while when he broke the silence.

So, do you have a boyfriend, girlfriend, partner, anything?

It was hard to talk, blood weighting my face, but I said, *No.*

Oh, well, that might be for the best. Lots of people get divorced or separated during a PAKing series.

Gravity contradicting my head—I could barely speak.

Because you're reorganizing the way your energetic body processes the external world. People you seemed close to suddenly become very

foreign, though it's always for the best. A whittling away of the ener-
gies that can't exist harmoniously with your pneuma.

His silence was expectant, but I had nothing to say and no
way to say anything I could say. I felt this spiraling sensation growing in my legs while a sharp, warm oval formed between my
shoulder blades.

Really, you're not even seeing anyone?

I said nothing.

Because it feels like someone is sending out psychic cords to you . . .
Are you familiar with psychic cords?

No.

Ah, well. They're fixations, attachments, psychic energy that one
person directs toward another, often in a nonconsensual manner.

He slowly pressed his toes into and out of my back. I became
incredibly dizzy.

Say, an overprotective parent or a needy partner or whatever the
case may be. Those sorts of psychic cords can interfere greatly with
my practice, so I do need to know about any situation you may be in
that would involve psychic cording. It presents a major hazard to my
work and safety. Did you recently end a relationship? Lose a family
member?

No one, I said, wishing he would just stop talking. I'd assumed
that PAKing would be serene, silent. Soothing music of an unde-
terminable spiritual origin. Sage, sandalwood, something. Not all
this small talk during the most awkward maneuvers. During our
second session, while I was secured in this medieval-looking
wooden apparatus, he'd asked if I had any recent dreams. *I hardly*
ever remember them, I said, so he asked if I had ever heard of the
band Yo La Tengo, to which I had no answer (of course I hadn't)
so I just pretended that I was concentrating on my breathing. Ed
began explaining this Yo La Tengo thing, how he was listening

to a record of theirs, *on vinyl*, he emphasized, and he'd been thinking about a genre of music called *shoegaze*, something about the body language of the shoegazer, the perpetual crumpling or downward slope of the gazer's neck, and then he changed the subject, abruptly, to nettle root—had I ever taken nettle root? Had anyone ever advised that I take nettle root? I was in a subdued, semi-meditative state, but he repeated himself, louder—*Mary, have you ever taken nettle root?*—and I said, *Um, no*, to which he immediately began chanting.

And where should I have looked when he chanted? Did he want an audience or was this supposed to be the sound track to my introspection? Also, what was nettle root?

I had to constantly fight the feeling that PAKing was just absurd—two adults in a room, contorted with each other, one of them occasionally chanting in what didn't even seem to be a language, occasionally making random small talk, an odd blend of exercise, therapy, first date, and ceremony. All his talk seemed like a distraction from our supposedly *serious* work, but it was Ed—the expert, the PAKer, the possible psychic—who always started the small talking. So maybe idle chatting *was* somehow necessary to my possible healing, and maybe my reluctance to respond to Ed was further evidence that my aura was uncooperative, unwilling to be healed. I understood nothing, felt child-dumb and strange.

There's likely someone in your future, he said. I was prone on the massage table, hooked up to a machine by these little metal clips on my earlobes and fingertips. My face felt cool, as if covered in aloe, and I had no memory of getting from the last position to where I was now.

That's probably what I'm sensing, he continued. *Some premonitions. Someone is just around the corner for you. Have you ever met*

someone and felt like you already knew them? Your spirits were prob-
ably preemptively sending psychic cords to each other, without even
realizing it. Our spirits know so much more than we can.

I remembered Paul, the thrilling and terrifying feeling that he
already knew me, but when I opened my eyes there was just Ed,
his clumpy blond hair and limp gaze. I closed my eyes again and
my lids pulsed with a bright blue light. What was I doing here,
spending all this money I didn't have for this man to talk and hum
and touch me? I couldn't deny that it was giving or correlating
with the only relief I'd felt in a year, but did I have to trust Ed or
just endure him for PAKing to work?

Perhaps I should leave and never come back. I didn't have a
solid opinion on the possibility of anyone's having psychic abilities or a fluency in reading auras, nor did I want to form an opinion about these things, to be one of those people with convictions
about things they can't prove or disprove.

And yet, I can't find a way to explain what began happening
at this session. He put a pink crystal in my right hand and was
pressing an oily wooden sphere into my biceps when he'd started
muttering something. At first I couldn't hear what it was or I
thought it was in another language, one of his chants, but he
spoke up—

E . . . Six . . . Four . . .

I thought of Ephesians 6:4—*provoke not your children to*
wrath—felt my heart spike and flutter. The thought of Ephesians
brought the memory of Merle and this immediately exhausted
me, or maybe it was something Ed was doing, or maybe it was
just my life, my strange and always stranger life, taking all the
life out of me. I closed my eyes, tried to get as far away from myself as I could.

E . . . Six . . . Four, he said again. *The E stands for something.*

Was he waiting for me to tell him what? Did he already know?

I didn't want to say it, didn't want to give him any clues. I think I fell asleep here or time compacted and passed quickly for some other reason, but later Ed asked me if I knew a man who wore a red hat.

A bit older, perhaps, like a grandfather, something like that. I said I didn't know anyone like this and he nodded and smiled. He said I would soon, that he was certain. The rest of the session went quietly, and after I'd gotten redressed he told me, his hand on my shoulder, that he knew I was undergoing a huge loss.

I realize that you're not able to talk about it yet, but just to let you know, you will need to find a way to open up in order for us to effectively continue our work, and the sooner you allow yourself to do that, the better off we'll be, okay?

I don't know what you're talking about.

And I didn't. I think back to this moment sometimes now, look back at that person I was, months before I couldn't unknow what had happened. He held his hands a few inches from my waist.

There's a large, dark cloud hovering on the lower right side of your rib cage. A woman, something like a mother figure, has passed on to the other side.

On a reflex, I looked down, but nothing was there. Nothing I could see.

Oh . . . well. I guess I'll just let you know.

When you're ready, Ed said, nodding, unashamed in his eye contact. *And, oh, one more thing. Do you know anyone named June?*

I said nothing.

I keep hearing it around you—June, June—almost like there's some spirit calling for someone. I don't always get such messages like this, but it was very clear with you today. Do you know anyone named June? Perhaps a relative, a pet?

No. I knew who I was and who I wasn't.

Anything significant ever happen to you in the month of June?
Nothing I can remember.
A birthday or anniversary of something? Anything?
No.
No clues. I would give him no clues at all.

We stared at each other, and though I wanted to look away, I found I somehow couldn't. What were we to each other, Ed and me? Was this a kind of love, a relationship? A willful manipulation—almost a kind of church, two people alone, doing things to each other. What more could anyone want than to try to change and be changed by someone?

I said, *See you next week*, and left.

Nine

My PAKing session had stretched my lunch break to almost three hours, but no one seemed to notice. When my tongue had gone numb a few weeks back, I sent out a memo about my lost voice, so no one even bothered to speak to me anymore, e-mailing everything. Though I could talk again, I hadn't told anyone, preferring the silence, but the moment I returned to my desk that afternoon, my phone rang.

Mary? Matheson asked, but he didn't wait for me to confirm myself. *Sorry to call you at work, but we're wondering if you can come in this afternoon to discuss the position.*

I slipped out the back, took the service elevator to the street, dashed to the subway as if being chased. The address he gave me was in a neighborhood full of French patisseries, chocolatiers, and the sort of high-fashion shops that seemed angry to be themselves. The doorman already knew my name, walked me to a specific elevator, pressed PH, turned a key, and waved goodbye as the doors shut.

Matheson was there when the elevator opened on the top floor. He smiled and led me down a gray hallway with high ceilings, then through three doors to an all-white office—white desk, white walls, white chairs, white rug on a white floor. Behind him, a sweeping view of the water and bridges.

I'll have to ask you to sign this nondisclosure agreement before I can give you any more information. Is that all right with you?

As I read the contract, not quite understanding it or perhaps not even really reading it, the three smallest toes on my right foot throbbed and a crick took root in my neck. I couldn't remember whether Ed had told me the neck had something to do with expression or abandonment or intuition, but I signed the contract, pushed it back across the desk to Matheson.

So everything I tell you from here on out is confidential.

I nodded.

And you won't relay any of the information or questions I or anyone else on the team will ask you, whether publicly or privately, regardless of circumstance, and you further realize that even accidentally revealing any classified information could put your standing with us in jeopardy and potentially could be the grounds for legal action taken against you.

I understand.

All right, great. So. I'm quickly going to show you a few photographs and I want you to tell me if any of these people look familiar to you, all right?

He held up a portrait of a man in a white shirt. The man—I didn't recognize him—seemed to really enjoy being himself. I nodded no.

Not even a little?

I looked at him harder, but he seemed to exist solely as a photograph, as if knowing him would have required being in that photograph, too.

No.

What about this one?

He held up a different photograph, a different man, same answer, then a woman, another woman, another man, a woman and a man together, another man, two more men after that, but none of them cued anything.

Okay, so. Mary, have you heard the name Kurt Sky?

I don't think so.

And just double-checking, you haven't heard of the movie Diamond Lives?

No.

Okay, and what about The Palace Island? That was with Allie Benson—have you heard of her?

No, neither.

But you're probably familiar with the TV series City of Men, right?

I'm not.

You haven't even heard of it? It was very respected. Even the public-radio crowd was into that one. You didn't see the billboards? Subways ads, nothing?

They all sort of blend together to me.

Wow. Okay, so that's actually great. That's what we suspected. Kurt Sky, my employer, is a very well-respected and recognizable actor and, I should add, a . . . phenomenal person—Matheson teared up quickly, as if he'd rehearsed it—*who has changed my life . . . in . . . tremendous . . . ways. Excuse me, I just—well.*

He took a shallow breath, fluttered his eyes.

With the help of a team of biotechnology researchers, as well as Kurt's meditation counselor and psychoanalyst, we have devised a plan, based on empirical evidence, that essentially assigns the roles fulfilled by a life partner to a team of specialized team members to enact Relational Experiments meant to illuminate the inner workings of love and companionship. This endeavor is both a scientific experiment we're conducting for the good of society at large and a healing exercise for Kurt in particular, a sort of recalibration of his understanding of himself in relationship to others. We're calling it the Girlfriend Experiment—GX for short—and we're considering you for the role of Emotional Girlfriend to Kurt.

I was briefly shocked, not that someone even had such an idea, but that it was feasible that *I* could be someone's girlfriend of any kind. I had forgotten, in a way, that I was a girl, that people had girlfriends, that girls like me were sometimes those friends. To be hired as a girlfriend, sure, this seemed abnormal, but then again so many things seemed abnormal to me that I'd long ago learned not to trust that instinct.

We believe you are capable of understanding this situation, Matheson added. *Kurt and his meditation counselor watched a livestream of your auditions and Kurt feels a strong energetic kinship with you. Of course, this feeling will need to be reciprocated, by you, but based on the personality test in your application and the astrological analysis, we believe this is likely.*

Matheson put a finger to his earpiece again, nodded, and continued, *We realize this might be a lot to take in at this moment, so what I'm going to do now is outline the responsibilities of the Emotional Girlfriend so you have some context to go on, but please hold your questions till the end.*

He flipped to another page on his clipboard, cleared his throat. *Responsibilities of the Emotional Girlfriend will include but may not be limited to:*

One: Coming to the loft or off-site locations for two to four Relational Experiments per week, which will be scheduled at least one week in advance.

Two: Being completely fluent in the various guidelines, expectations, and protocols outlined in the Emotional Girlfriend handbook and enacting these tasks with accuracy during your sessions.

Three: Listening to Kurt talk while remaining fully engaged by asking questions, maintaining eye contact, affirming his opinions, and offering limited amounts of advice or guidance that may or may not be entertained.

Four: After the first week you will begin sending texts to him each afternoon that you are not scheduled for a session. Texts should arrive after at least five hours have passed since you've seen him in person and none should exceed 120 characters. We will provide the phone and it should be used for GX purposes only. Text frequency and content will change as the weeks pass, and the Emotional Girlfriend will be required to adopt these changing assignments as they arise.

Five: After three weeks of successful employment you need to leave no fewer than three personal objects in Kurt's home, e.g., a toothbrush or book or sweater.

Six: After five weeks, you will be given keys to the penthouse and you will need to give him keys to your apartment, though you shouldn't expect that he will visit you.

Seven: At some point after two and four months we're going to need you to be able to cry in front of Kurt and to do so during one of the Vulnerability Relational Experiments. Also within that time frame you'll need to say I love you *after an emotionally intimate moment. You will also need to explain that you usually never say that sentence first, that you have fallen in love more quickly with Kurt than with anyone else in your life. Crying or telling Kurt that you love him before two months is not acceptable and may or may not result in termination.*

You should also note that we are requiring a three-month commitment, at which point there will be a reevaluation based primarily on whether the data the Research Division collects about the Emotional

Girlfriend Relational Experiments is consistent and valuable. At this point both parties will need to decide to continue the relationship, and a new job description will be written. This may or may not increase or change the Emotional Girlfriend's working hours.

Matheson removed his reading glasses, crossed an arm over the other, and leaned forward, posing in a way meant to convey his intellect.

It's important that you understand the GX is so much more than a relationship—it is part of a large-scale inquiry, a very serious research endeavor. In order to maintain the security of the project and the safety of all participants, we must take discretion very seriously and even the smallest security breach will likely result in serious legal action. This great compensation comes with great responsibility and we need to be absolutely certain that we can trust you.

Okay, I said, though he didn't seem to hear.

I know exactly what you're thinking, he said. *What about sex?*

I wasn't. I almost never did anymore. With all the illness and pain filling my body to the teeth, there was no room for desire, and even before I'd become sick, sex seemed like a thing that might only happen to me at random, outside my control, like weather.

At this point we have decided that sexual intimacy will not be expected of the Emotional Girlfriend. Any physical contact between the Emotional Girlfriend and Kurt should be restricted to the list of preapproved Signs of Affection that you'll find in Appendix F of your Emotional Girlfriend handbook. In the event that sexual desire arises in Kurt for the Emotional Girlfriend, the Research Division will need to first give written approval to alter the nature of the Relational Experiments between Kurt and the Emotional Girlfriend; however, the Emotional Girlfriend will not be required or expected to consent to any sexual intimacy. In fact, the selection criteria used for the Emotional Girlfriend required Kurt to score below a certain threshold of sexual interest toward her—which is to say, Kurt does not find you sexually attractive. However, in the event that this feeling changes in Kurt during a Relational Experiment with the Emotional Girlfriend and a consensual sexual act between Kurt and the Emotional Girlfriend occurs without prior contractual agreement and approval from the Research Division, this will be done so at the Emotional Girlfriend's own risk, and no additional payment or promotion should be expected. The Research Division has strongly advised against it, and for the time being the Emotional Girlfriend should realize and accept that all sexual responsibility has been assigned to another team of specially trained women—the Intimacy Team.

The Emotional Girlfriend should take care to ensure that she does not become jealous of the IT, and she should never, under any circumstance, mention the existence of the IT or any of the other girlfriends in Kurt's presence. The Emotional Girlfriend should also avoid maternal activities such as buying groceries, preparing meals, cleaning anything in his house, offering interior design suggestions, or even watering his plants—even if one of them seems like it may need to be watered. Those and other tasks have been assigned to the Maternal Girlfriend in order to keep the relationship between Kurt and the Emotional Girlfriend as pure as possible. We've also just signed on the Anger Girlfriend, who will be responsible for fighting, nagging, and manipulation, so all of Kurt's interactions with the Emotional Girlfriend should be entirely pleasant as he will conduct more volatile emotions with the AG. The Emotional Girlfriend should therefore never disagree, challenge, or complain to Kurt. The Emotional Girlfriend will need to take care never to criticize him for anything, no matter how honest or caring her tone might be.

At present the position pays $1,450 a week, cash, which, I should tell you, is the project's highest-paid team member, though also the most demanding position. Should any additional responsibilities be presented to the Emotional Girlfriend, her salary will be renegotiated. Any questions?

The whole thing seemed at once terrible and logical, my only option. I couldn't afford to go back to where I'd started—emptying my bank account each month on pills, treatments, lab fees, copays, and premiums. I could be redeemed, have a life worth living, maybe even a chair, socks without holes, maybe even a false tooth to put in the hole where that molar had been that I could only afford to get pulled. And if I could stand it long enough, I might even be able to get out of debt completely, to end the calls from the collectors, to go back to having the freedom to *do* things again, to live without constraint. The hope for that freedom steadied me, so I nodded no—no questions.

Depending on performance and Kurt's needs, we may collapse the roles of other girlfriends into the Emotional Girlfriend's duties or expand her position to include new Relational Experiments, but should any expansion of your position breach thirty hours per week, you'll be considered full-time and offered the same health and dental coverage that I have, which is excellent. For the time being, you should have enough hours off to keep your current employment, as your sessions will only occur in the evenings and on weekends.

I look back at this moment sometimes, the moment I accepted this job, and I have to wonder what kind of decision it really was—the right decision that is the wrong one, or the wrong one that's actually right. Someday I hope this is clear to me, that I can find the right end, the right moral to this story. Am I the sort of person who makes life harder than it has to be? Did I actively invite all this trouble into my life or was I just doing the best I could? But it's as terrible as it is true: everyone has something in them they cannot yet see.

Ten

Not realizing it was past seven, I went back to the office. Most of the lights were off but I could hear the rumble and click of a computer somewhere. A sticky note from Meg was on my screen: *Where are you?*

With so few hours in the office today, e-mail had piled up. There was never a ton of it and it was hardly ever urgent, but still, there it was, the hundred tiny responses to give, invoices to receive, to check and cross-check and send. As I started in on it, I remembered what Ed had told me, that I had experienced a loss. I was pretty sure he had to be talking about Clara—we'd fallen out of touch.

First I'd stopped calling because all my news was bad and I didn't want to hear myself tell it or lie by talking around it. Then I hadn't called because I was too embarrassed by how long it had been since I called. Then I didn't call because she hadn't called. Then I didn't call because I feared I'd created something I'd have to deal with, that I would have to explain to her what I'd been doing all these months, then a year, then longer. Somewhere along the line I must have begun avoiding her because I was afraid she'd be ill or just not there. But before it became fear, it was just selfishness. And I didn't want to face that selfishness, to atone or make sense of it.

I knew I owed my whole life to Clara, that letting myself drift from her was inexcusable. She had taught me everything— how to drive a car, how to talk to a stranger, use chopsticks, put on panty hose, put a quarter into a gumball machine. She explained basic etiquette, answered every question I had about the billboards we passed. (*What is Rock City? What are fireworks? What is a state line? Hampton Inn? What is a Dollar Menu? Powerball? 1-800-Marines? Hits 96?*) She guided me through the plastic madness of a grocery store, though for the first couple months I couldn't stand to go inside—all those smells, strange music overhead, the mounds of produce all so large and bright—it was grotesque and eerie, too strange of a dream.

Clara was always so gentle with me, soft knocks on my bedroom door, a hand just barely on my back as we walked, her voice always low with me, like speaking to someone ill who had just woken up. She once came to my room with a sack of clementines and asked me if I would like one. I didn't know what a clementine was but I said yes. I always said yes. We sat in the living room and she showed me how to puncture the skin, tear back the peel, divide the sections out like a strange bloom. I ate one after another just so I could peel them again and again. (Did anyone else notice how citrus skin released a wet blast of oil with each pull?)

As I was going sick on clementines, Clara told me that I needed to know something about Florence, that if I wanted to blame someone for how I'd been raised, I shouldn't blame her—

You know, there just wasn't much she could do, though she did try, she really did try to make things better for you. Since you were still little she'd been asking Merle about when they might move to town, since God didn't seem to be sending any more children and you needed to be around other kids. And he kept saying he needed to finish writing this manifesto, this book or whatever—but after a few years he said a move just wasn't going to happen, that she should listen to the Lord. Imagine saying that to a grown woman—to tell her No like that. And I'm not trying to judge—I do know there are certain compromises you have to make in marriage—you'll see someday, you'll see for yourself—but this just wasn't fair. All those years out there and you with no one to know . . .

I couldn't tell how it really felt to hear this. Mother had never said anything about wanting another life for us, had never contradicted a word that Merle said, aside from that one time I had overheard them argue late one night. Anytime I think of Florence, even now, all I can see is her just staring out a window, washing dishes, nodding to herself, nodding as if everything was just as it should be. And that afternoon as Clara told me this while I ate those clementines, it was all I could do—nod, stare off.

He's a violent man, your father.

I kept my mouth full of citrus, rubbed the oil from the peels against my palms and wrists, and still every time I see a clementine I think of this moment, think of Clara. I cannot eat any sort of citrus anymore, though I do remember how to peel them.

Somewhere else in the office I heard a door close and I caught myself staring into the spongy gray nothing of the cubicle wall, where a window would be if I had a window. All at once I was overwhelmed with the need to talk to Clara. I picked up the phone, dialed her number from memory. No answer.

I called her again. Again, no answer.

I thought of the worst, thought of her dead in her home for months, years even, decomposing—who would know? Who was there for her? Why had I never realized this before? Who would make the funeral arrangements? What if there had already been one? Or what if I got called down immediately, today, this evening, for a funeral? I'd have to delay training for the GX—would they just hire someone else? How else could I pay for PAKing? And where would I stay if I had to go down to Tennessee for a funeral? In the home where she'd died? In the backseat of a rental car? In a motel? One of those roadside motels? Would my parents come pick me up at a motel? Did Merle still drive the same truck? What would they say to me? Who were those people? What did they do to me? How much of me was still their daughter? Did they even still count as my parents since they no longer parented me? Or was parenthood inextricable, a matter of biology, of cells? A forever no one agrees to?

I called Clara again and it rang nine times before I gave up, hung up. I remembered that she'd been religious about having her hair set at a beauty parlor on Main Street, and if anything had happened to her, I knew they would know, so I hunted down the number. Mona's on Main. The Internet had given it four out of five stars and they were open for another half hour.

Now, let me get this straight—you're asking me *to tell* you *if a certain customer has been at the parlor lately?*

Clara Parsons. Yes. I called her house but she didn't pick up and I'm just worried. Has she kept her appointments recently?

Well, honey, I can't just tell you stuff like that, you know. Private citizens deserve their privacy. Security and everything, you know.

But I'm her niece.

And you sound like a nice young lady, but I don't know you and there's all this terrorism now and I'm just doing my part, okay, honey? I can't just give out classified information.

But you're a beauty parlor.

Yes ma'am, and we're proud of it. We're proud Americans.

For a long moment I didn't know what to say. She coughed—loud—into the phone.

If she comes in, will you just tell her that Mary is trying to get ahold of her?

I think I ought to just leave that up to you, hon. We're not an answering machine.

She had a point. She owed me nothing. Who was I, even? What right did I have?

Meg appeared, so I hung up in a rush.

Got your voice back?

Oh, yeah, I said, startled, forgetting where I was, *it got better.*

What was it, laryngitis or something?

Something else.

Hey, just wondering, but were you in the office today?

I had some appointments but I was here in between.

And did you get my note?

The staff meeting, yeah, it just didn't cross my mind that the second Thursday—

It's just weird because you never miss meetings.

Meg was known, I had been told, for being a snitch. She kept a log, Sheryl said, a detailed log about when you arrive and when you leave and how long your lunch breaks are. Someone else said that some form of blackmail was involved between the company owner and Meg, so she made the highest salary in the office for ordering supplies, signing checks, and reading magazines at her desk. Every time I spoke to her, I got the sense that I was somehow ruining her day.

I know, I said, *but it was a last-minute thing and I had to. I didn't have a chance to—*

No, it's fine, it's no big deal, I'm just checking, but you probably should have taken a personal day, seems like. Maybe you should just take one tomorrow—get your head straight? How does that sound?

Okay, sure.

K, she said, like a shrug, and left.

Just before I left for the night, my phone rang, but when I picked up, it was just the rustling of some papers, then a click and whoosh of dial tone.

When I got home, an elderly man wearing a bright red cap was sitting on my stoop. He looked at me and said, *It's a beautiful night to become a new person*, slowly and seriously with relaxed eye contact, as if he had been practicing the line all day. I said, *Sure*, a reflex, while wondering if Ed had really predicted or hired this guy, though I was pretty sure I'd never given Ed my home address.

As I turned to lock the front door behind me, the man in the red hat was standing at the edge of the sidewalk, looking at the sky, one arm raised, waving up at it. He was just crazy, I decided, and just happened to be wearing a red hat. No reason to read into anything.

Once inside I called Clara again. It rang twice, then I heard a click, a hanging up, and dial tone again. I willed my heart rate to lower. I did my breathing exercises, sat on the floor, and thought about what Ed had told me about awareness, slowness, these better ways to live.

I called again. It rang. I remained calm. Then again. Again.

Hello, Clara said, sounding irritated and quiet, as if someone were sleeping close to her and she didn't want to wake them.

Clara, I said, relief spiking my voice.

Who is this?

Your niece, Mary. I'm calling from—

Oh, Mary! Well. You just about startled me half to death. These . . . damn telemarketers keep calling. I've just about had it with them. I'm too old for that crap. And how are you?

It's just been a while since I've called—I just wanted to check in, make sure you were doing all right.

Oh, I'm fine, fine, you know. Same things here . . .

Have you seen my parents lately?

Now . . . who's that again?

Your sister, Florence. And Merle?

Oh, sure. Why, yes, yes. We had a nice meal the other day, didn't we?

My neck released—Ed had been wrong. Everyone was fine.

Oh, you did? You had dinner with them?

Well, yes. Merle and Florence were there. And Tom, of course, and you. Thanksgiving is my favorite.

My pulse returned. Her words came quickly, the story without hesitation.

Clara, it's been, um, a few months since Thanksgiving.

Well, I'm just getting so old, I reckon. Everything sort of mushes together. You said that just the other day, didn't you, Tom?

She spoke away from the phone.

Oh, now quit it, you just quit it, Mr. Parsons . . . you little devil. He is such a little devil, Mary. Did you just hear what he said?

. . . No.

Well, that's probably for the best. That little devil . . . Her voice carried a smile. *Well, sugar, you better run on now, Tom is getting antsy for his supper.*

And before I could decide what to do she'd said her little Southern *bye* and hung up. Clara—alone in her kitchen, talking to her dead husband.

Eleven

I woke on my personal day feeling impersonal. I'd slept long and late, so much I barely recognized the time of day in my bedroom, dust made obvious in the hard light, no job or appointment or interview to rush toward. I needed nothing and was needed nowhere. I almost doubted I was alive. In fists I fingernailed my palms, to make sure I was still in there. Hands above eyes, I watched the skin flush and release the dimples.

I walked to that restaurant in my neighborhood where a bare piece of toast cost seven dollars and came with a marble of hand-churned butter and salt from a far-off sea. It had been years since I'd been there, a place I went with Paul, back when I spent money as if we had everything I'd ever need, as if I were debtless and immortal. The walls were painted this frosty, pale green and the silverware and china felt like art in the mouth. They served omelets stingy with filling and magnificently complicated fruits—

soaked mulberries, candied lemon, papaya crescents, cubes of heirloom melon, a black grape sliced into a bloom. A little dish of it cost sixteen dollars to account for carbon offsets and living wages, which made it more than organic, they said—this fruit salad was ethical. People swore it was the only place in New York where the produce tasted as good as it did in California. Tourists would approach the windows, look in at this diorama of people in expensive clothes, then move on.

Before I lived here the only place I'd ever heard of in New York was the Metropolitan Museum because it was in so many captions in one of my history books. I went there every free day or afternoon I had my freshman year, until I'd been in each room, looked at every piece. I was methodical, reading all the cards, taking notes.

Once a security guard asked me if I was a student and I said I was and he said to study hard and I said I would and I turned a corner, sat down, and wept quietly for five minutes. I wasn't entirely sure why. I became accustomed to these unexplainable moments, emotional things. It was just a part of living in the world, I told myself, of not having an obvious god.

Maybe spending so much time at the Met had something to do with why the city also seemed like an exhibit, or maybe that's just what Manhattan is—a bunch of shrines and reenactments. I'd overhear conversations about what this building used to be or who used to live in that place or what it was before it was whatever it was. (It always used to be something better.) Restaurants listed the origin and history of every ingredient they served, archaeology of a salad, a stew. And the people, the characters in the streets, they were always so arranged, layered with clues about who they were and where they were in their history. Leather purses carried hieroglyphic messages about the carrier's taste and socioeconomic status. The young wore their tribes overtly, with messages on T-shirts, brands or bands. The rich looked out their cab windows the way painted eyes looked out of a frame.

I ordered forty-seven dollars of breakfast with a whole pot of tea because I was going to spend as much of my personal day right here, trying to reenact my history, pretend Paul was here, pretend I was younger and in less debt and in less trouble. Maybe I somehow knew it would be one of the last calm days before the GX began—that I needed to spend a little time looking back before I could go forward.

I thought of Ed hearing the word *June* and Ephesians 6:4 and seeing the man with the red hat standing so strangely in my future. I took a heavy sip of tea, tried to scald these thoughts out of my head. I watched the people eating or barely eating, eaves-dropping on them as Paul and I used to—that *her spring collection was horrendous, embarrassing,* and someone else was *just going to outsource the whole thing* or that he *didn't fucking believe this guy wasn't checking his phone*—but my attention kept drifting back to Ed's predictions, premonitions. How had he heard these things? Where had they come from? I had once been sure there was al-most no difference between hearing a voice and hearing your own desire to hear a voice, that we make what we want, but this didn't explain Ed, the window he seemed to have on me.

—*June, June, I keep hearing June like someone is calling that name—*

Ed was always looking at me with this expression of curiosity mixed with concern, an expression similar to the way that Paul had looked at me, as if I were a puzzle he was waiting to com-prehend. And how sad it is that the last face someone makes at you is always the face you remember the most. Some days I felt haunted by Paul's last face. I'd seen it after we had taken a couple weeks *off*—his term—which meant that during the time we would have been together, we stayed alone in our respective apartments, doing nothing in particular, because being alone had somehow become more compelling to us than being together. How sad our respective nothings had seemed at first, the cool absence in a bed, the dinners with a book. Then, even sadder, those nothings became preferable. The simplicity of being alone won out over the complexity of being together.

And that last day—a July afternoon, immovable heat—we sat on a park bench and watched a pack of kids shooting each other with water guns, fighting with cool relief. They screamed at and with each other, dizzied themselves with pleasurable aggression, but I felt no aggression and no pleasure. Paul asked me why I wouldn't open up to him, why I was always so cagey, said he couldn't help me if I wouldn't let him, and I said, *Why do I need the help?* And he said that wasn't what he meant but I said, *It's what you said, that I need help, and who are you to tell me what I need, to think you're so necessary?* I was spitting these words at him, but I did not recognize my own ferocity, so I stamped it out like embers. It seems to me that we can be the angriest with those we love most—what a curse, what a trick. We sat there in silence for a while until he said, so softly, *That's not what I meant.*

It seemed we were always saying things we didn't quite mean.

I said, *I used to miss you when you were out of town, but now I have that feeling when I look at you, when you're right here.*

This was true. I did mean this. He said something about how hard that was to hear or how it hurt or maybe he didn't say anything and I saw that hard hurt in his eyes, that it came out wordlessly.

What had started all this *time off* was the morning I'd woken in his apartment, got dressed, splashed cold water on my face, brushed my teeth, and hesitated before putting the toothbrush back in the cup beside his. I held still for a moment, then slipped the toothbrush into my pocket, then the cheap moisturizer I'd left in the medicine cabinet, the bobby pins that were collecting rust on a metal shelf, the black hair elastics circling nothing. I went to the living room, found the few books that I'd finished and abandoned months ago, put them in a paper grocery bag, put the bathroom things in there, too. I took the scarf that had lingered since the snowy spring and wrapped it around the good knife I'd brought over to make dinner with because all his were dull and cheap. I went back to his bedroom and noticed he'd rolled over but his eyes were still closed. I removed the few clothes I had in his closet, the underwear, the extra bra, the dress, the other dress. I was shaking. I was afraid I might cry or vomit, that I would wake him. Why did this feel so large? All I was doing was taking what was mine and getting away from him, but I felt somehow as if I were killing someone, myself or him or us. I didn't know.

I looked at his face in the pale dawn, sleeping or just still, and I let myself completely feel the pain of missing a person who no longer exists. Not missing a person who has died, not mourning (I had yet to feel actual grief), but the strain of trying to see the person I'd fallen in love with inside the person he had become. Now I know this just comes with love, that there's no way to avoid seeing a person gradually erased or warped by time, but the first time I realized this with Paul—it felt apocryphal.

But what had really happened? It was still unclear. Was it possible nothing of any significance had ever happened between us and our ending was just the sad process of realizing this? It was too sad to believe that we had just been two people staving off loneliness together. Perhaps I had just ruined it by reading Barthes at the wrong time. (*A Lover's Discourse*, Chandra said, was *relationship poison*.) But no—I had to trust my memory of those easy early days, when words passed between us like water, when we were always quick to laugh, when we had held each other as if we were part of the same body, built to be like this. It seemed, on nights like those, that a whole lifetime of such feelings could be right there, ready to be taken. Hadn't I woken up some mornings so sure that all my life must have been leading up to this for a reason? And what had happened to those easy days and what had happened to our laughter and what had happened to us? Suddenly, it seemed, they'd been replaced with copies of those people, then copies of those copies, blurry and blurrier still.

Losing Paul to time was far from the worst thing to happen to me, but the feeling doesn't always match the loss. Sometimes the bigger ones are easier to take, like ocean waves. Smaller, human losses, the ones that carry a sense of fault, a choice, a wrong turn—they haunt, fuse in you, become impossible to remove.

The night before I left Paul's apartment with all my things we'd gone to a party at his friend's house, and when he talked to other people, I noticed how his face seemed to go backward in time, how his eyes lit up when we spoke to anyone new and how he smiled in a way that he never smiled at me anymore. And how sad and stupid it was that I believed it would always be that way, that our love wouldn't dissolve into the ordinary. Believing in exemptions, maybe everyone has to make this mistake once.

I wished that seeing Paul talk to new people at the party that night hadn't hurt as much as it had. I barely managed to do the small talk—the *what-do-you-do*, the *where-are-you-from*, the *what-neighborhood*, the *what-college*, the despair of trying to explain oneself. I deflected questions about where I'd been raised. I answered the terrible, terrible question about how Paul and I had met—*at a party, at a party like this one*—but internally I was obstinate and childish and furious, so furious over not being back there at that time when I met Paul, the original Paul, when all my life had a happy, drugged feeling in it. I had nothing to say to these strangers, whoever or whatever they were.

You know, it was so stupid. Of course people become accustomed to each other. Of course you don't put on your first-impression face when impressing yourself on someone for the nine hundredth time. What a child I am.

I miss you to your face, I said to Paul, too quietly, as we were walking back to his apartment after that party, not looking at each other, just hand in hand, walking.

You missed what?

And I said, *No.*

And he said, *What?*

And I said, *Nothing, never mind.*

In the months and years since Paul, I began seeing his features in other people. Someone would walk by with a shoulder span like his or his eyes or his jaw.

There's Paul's jaw, I'd think.

Here it comes.

There it is.

There it went.

That was Paul's jaw.

Several months after I had last seen him it seemed that every third man in the city had Paul's haircut or glasses, and on a crowded subway car one morning I was surrounded by memory and suddenly incensed—*This is mine*, I thought senselessly, helplessly. *This is my men's haircut and my glasses on all these strangers' heads, all those people going places I didn't know.*

When my stop came, I faked lateness and ran.

So I killed an hour of my personal day in that café, with all this nostalgia, which I suppose is what I wanted, was the reason

I'd gone there, to borrow the past. Leafy tea dregs were cool in the pot. I paid my check, tipped extravagantly, not because I felt generous or wealthy, but because I wanted to pretend to be. Spending money was a luxury in itself. Having it. Giving it away.

As I was leaving, I saw a woman who, in profile, looked so much like my mother everything in my body told me to sprint, every organ jolting. She was long limbed and underfed, sixty or so, holding a spoon to smack the shell of a boiled egg cradled in a red cup. As I pulled open the glass door, we caught eyes through the frame, though she likely felt nothing, oblivious of how we, two women who were strangers to each other, echoed two women who were estranged from each other. She struck her eleven-dollar egg, scooped the white, and dipped toast points in the molten yellow, thinking nothing of it as I drifted into the city's ever-moving bodies. But the image of her face turned my stomach in on itself—or perhaps it was all the caffeine and cream, or perhaps I hadn't been healthy enough to stomach real food. I turned a corner and let out my expensive breakfast churned with acid against a building and sidewalk.

I leaned into the wall, held back my own hair, stared at the errant beads of vomit on my shoes. I tried to contain myself, to ignore and be ignored in the street. It was what we did here, one of the urban agreements I'd observed, learned, upheld. A hand offered me a tissue and disappeared before I could see where it had come from. How utterly isolated we were and still never alone. As a child I felt lonely but knew *He* was always up or out there. Then, as a woman in this city, I spent all my public time in a sacred privacy, though sometimes when my eyes briefly darted over a stranger's eyes I felt a silent flash, a visit from the god in other people.

I spat up the last bit of acrid vomit and felt a fresh push of sweat cool my head. Three decades had turned me into a woman, but girlhood memories still sat in me, steering—I could almost hear the pot rattling on the stove, so many years ago, steam illuminated in a diagonal of afternoon sun.

Mother asked, *How long do you let it boil?*

I must have been ten, if that, eight or nine or ten. I didn't know what she was talking about, only that it wasn't right for her to not know something like that, for her to ask me how to do something in the kitchen.

Do you let it sit for . . . How long is it?

I was silent for a moment, the most uncomfortable nothing I'd ever known, though it may have only been two seconds. The way children stretch time and the way adults forget that stretch could be one of the saddest differences in the world.

To boil an egg? I asked her.

I'm forgetting everything these days. Her eyes went red and glassy. *You're such a good help around the house. God blessed me with you as my daughter.*

She pulled me into her body so I couldn't see her face.

Thank God. Praise God, she said, soft and low.

She clenched me and it hurt but I was silent. Affection didn't come with this sort of intensity in the cabin, so I gave her the privacy of her feeling. A couple days before this I had woken in the middle of the night to the sound of the kitchen table skidding across the floor. Then the silence kept me awake—so still—not even crickets or the night wind or the grandfather clock ticking outside my bedroom. Where did the crickets go, that wind, that clock? I heard my parents' voices and mother weeping.

In the morning it was clear that something had happened that should not have happened. Too many things were wrong.

The stove was cold. She wasn't there. Wet chicory grounds were spilled in the sink. Even the light seemed strange, as if part of the sky had gone missing.

Merle was sitting at the kitchen table but he was elsewhere, praying or otherwise lost. He didn't open his eyes when I came into the room. An unconscious frown. Hair askew, shirt cuffs undone, flayed open like animal skin, and when he opened his eyes, I could see the dark fear in them. No child understands how well she knows her parents' faces, how much they tell her without speaking; that language is writ so deep she could never back away from herself far enough to see it, but she always feels it. It registers in there.

I didn't ask where Mother was and reacted not at all when she came back as if she'd just been in the garden. I can't remember if she was gone for a whole day or overnight—all I remember clearly was that afternoon she couldn't remember how to boil an egg and how hard she held me, as if I were about to float away. (I suppose I was. I suppose she knew.) When I saw those dark bruises on her arms, they explained it, though the bruises weren't the worst of it. It was that she'd been moved by an instinct deeper than deference that made her leaving and coming back terrible. She'd been moved by something embarrassingly deeper than the sanctity of marriage or her husband's authority or her fear of God.

Now years have gone and that old idea of God has gone and I've also left, left my family, my name, the whole simple way I could have let my life pass.

I keep wondering what, in me, might be constant. I catch myself looking for that remainder, retracing my steps as if in search of lost keys. I am always wondering if there's something holy between people, a formless thing, something that can't be bruised.

Your mother is forgetting everything, she said, watching the water roil and ripple. *I can't seem to keep my head straight.*

She was shaking. It wasn't cold. She held the side of my face to her chest and I watched the dust move in the sunlight the way tadpoles move in a creek and years later, in a biology class, a professor told us about a recent study on fetal cells, how some cells from a child in utero seep into the mother's body and remain decades after a birth—even from aborted children or stillborns or children who grow up and go away. But the study was inconclusive. The researchers weren't sure if those children cells helped or hurt the mother or if they had some effect that wasn't particularly helpful or hurtful. Some scientists discovered that these children cells collected around illnesses and tumors, but they couldn't quite tell what they were doing there, if they served any real function. It just wasn't clear.

Still, I wondered whether any of my cells were in that bruise and what they might have done in there. Was there anything left of me in my mother? What order, what rules, were there in the world, a body? And why did I still hope for answers that I knew weren't coming? It could have just been a craving for the kind of certainty I'd been born into—having a user's manual for life and an unmovable, divine love. But maybe I really did sense something vague and holy in others' eyes, something sacred in crowds, in a bus of people staring out their windows, watching life. There should be a middle ground between believing in a certain god and believing that some mysterious third substance was between people. Like churches, I thought, there should be a place for people who just weren't sure. There should be a place for people who see something but won't dare say what it is. Maybe there's something, something between people that is more than air and empty space, something holy in that nothing between one face and another.

Sometimes it seems all I have are questions, that I will ask the same ones all my life. I'm not sure if I even want any answers, don't think I'd have a use for them, but I do know I'd give anything to be another person—anyone else—for even just a day, an hour. There's something about that distance I'd do anything to cross.

PART TWO

1

A camera watched each woman as she arrived, as she exited the elevator, as she stood on the taped *X* and stared neutrally and square into a lens, said her name, turned left, right, and said her name again. Mary hesitated, caught *Junia* in her mouth, and the others remembered past mug shots or passport photos or auditions they'd given, past faces they'd had, people they'd been or tried to be. They filled out forms and waited, filled out forms and waited, waited and kept waiting.

A dozen dime-size sensors were applied to each woman's body, their chests and bellies, wrists, clavicles, armpits, necks, and faces, and as they were activated, the screens in the Research Division's office grew animate, blue and red lines worming and peaking across the graphs. The monitors showed how each woman's heart was flexing blood, lungs pumping, nerves shimmering with electricity, voices and inflections, pores pushing up

little smears of sweat, a twitch in the face, the vagus nerve pulsing between brain and chest—all of this was tracked, recorded,
and archived—a file for each test subject, the analytics already
running, looking for patterns, trying to find the logic of each of
them.

As Mary took a seat on a sleek white sofa in the living room,
she noticed how it exhaled instead of squeaking in that doctor's-
office way, and even the air felt exotic in the lungs, as if it had
been imported. Being in that room was like being inside a furniture catalog, everything so placed, all human evidence scrubbed
out, the real/unreal of a photograph. The blank white walls seemed
to blaze, as if covered in something more than paint, and an
abstract gold statue sat high on a white pedestal in one corner
while a Warhol hung high above it, watching.

More cameras (some obvious, others hidden) were trained
on each woman's face while she waited for on-boarding to begin,
facial-detection software already analyzing the quick, passing
expressions that let an honest feeling out, like heat exiting from
a briefly opened oven. Through the various data streams, the Research Division could track each woman's arc from one mood to
another, the steady decline they all made toward dehydration
over an hour, the way their attention became concentrated or scattered, the little sway of thoughts and feelings. One woman
showed signs of duplicity as she spoke to another. One was quite
significantly depressed and another oddly euphoric. Some daydreamed; some were amused; one was aroused. Ashley was angry or detached in turn; another woman was sleep deprived and
undernourished; one was lying in her small talk to another, who
was, in turn, heavily bored. And Mary, all gangly and graceless,
her activity patterns were the most erratic—breathing shallow,
heart rate inconsistent, attention always fluttering. It seemed she

might, at any moment, need to run away, but her background check explained this, at least partially, the way she'd come to be.

Mary had woken up that morning with a swollen throat, every swallow scorched and meaty. Her right ear and jaw throbbed. The pain fenced her from the room, separated her from the other women as their heels staccatoed across the hardwood, as they spoke to each other with ease, some even shaking hands as if this were really the beginning of something. They laughed, leaned toward each other. Some wore their sensors with the unbothered cool of a model in haute couture, though others didn't seem so calm, kept touching the tape. Did anyone know what these things were doing? No one did.

But *on-boarding*—as Matheson called it, as if this were the sort of job that would come with business cards, a stapler, a phone extension—was no stranger than all the interviews that they'd all been through. They had acclimated to the weird, curiosity and nerve and need carrying them through. They thought of their rents, their debts, their ailing parents, their families and their constant bills, tuitions, payment plans, groceries, all those end- less appetites. Some had expensive habits: motorcycles, children, drugs, obscure bodywork treatments, lingerie, high-end kitchen appliances, and a few still had that youthful habit of daring life, of running toward risk, of wanting to do something wild before (or because) something wild was done to her. Some of them were excited, hopeful, optimistic, though most held some skepticism beneath the optimism, and some had genuine fears beneath the skepticism and some had a good deal of rage beneath the fear. A few women carried Mace disguised as lipstick or hot-pink Tasers and Ashley had her fists and Mary thumbed a smoky quartz from Chandra. At least one of them believed rage was her most reliable bodyguard, and often that is true, and Ashley could dislocate a person's arm in three different ways and Vicky could torque a man's nut nearly off if she ever needed, and even Mary, who hardly even looked at men anymore, even she remembered the moves learned in those self-defense classes with Chandra, years ago. None of them knew how those defenses, here, would be useless.

2

Was Ashley really going to take a job as someone's *Anger Girl-friend*? And what the fuck was that? They'd been vague with her in the interviews except about the money and assuring her it had nothing to do with sex, but she knew better than to take them at their word. Still—she wasn't afraid.

She'd worked, for a while, as the desk girl (the boss literally called her *the desk girl*) at the massage parlor where she'd met Vicky, who took Ashley out for dim sum twice before realizing she was straight, which embarrassed Vicky enough for her to apologize four times before the end of the night, though Ashley hadn't been offended as she'd often wondered, like almost every other woman living in this late patriarchy, if that kind of life might be available to her. Not being gay felt like a failing, somehow, less evolved. But they still shared an undeniable comfort, an innate understanding. Both had immigrant mothers and New

York–born fathers, whom they'd both lost at the same age. Both had ambition—Ashley wanted to be a pro fighter and Vicky wanted to make films or maybe plays, she wasn't sure. Conspiring, they quit the massage place the same week, Vicky to go into domming full-time and Ashley because she got more shifts at that overpriced restaurant in NoHo where she hid behind thick-rimmed glasses that men who claimed to be *agents* (they never said what of) were always asking her to take off so they could get a look at her eyes. (*Nah, I'm good.*) Some nights after her shift she'd walk down to Vicky's dungeon to hang out in the dressing room to complain about work, and one night there Vicky had told her about this weird job she was taking, something called the GX, which wasn't really sex work and wasn't really not sex work. *They just want me to sit around this guy's apartment for a few hours, and the money is crazy.*

Two weeks later Ashley had, herself, made it to the final interviews, albeit for a different role.

I'm not stupid, she said to Matheson as he explained the responsibilities of the Anger Girlfriend.

—Sorry?

I said I'm not stupid. Anger Girlfriend? I know what a dominatrix is, so you don't have to call it something else.

Okay, Matheson said, *so, it's actually not, but I do like that tone. We really think you'd be great at this*, and he passed her an envelope of cash and began explaining the scheduling system and nondisclosure agreements, and though Ashley still had more questions than answers, she said yes. Anything was worth the chance to quit waitressing and start training full-time—all she'd ever wanted.

She'd started boxing as a teenager, her father's idea. *Self-defense*, he reasoned to her mother, who just said, *Be careful with your face*, to which Ashley said nothing, already exhausted of this lie, that the best thing a woman could become was a magazine page, motionless, silent, shreddable.

Even years after that winter morning her father didn't wake up, she could still hear him shouting angry encouragement at her in the gym, could feel him holding the strike bag still, counting the reps. Every hour in her day bent toward her training, muscles quivering and knuckles going raw under the wraps. She was twenty the year he died, but when she fought, she felt a thousand and zero and alive and nonexistent at once.

Eventually she switched from just boxing to MMA, planned to go pro next year, but next year was always next year as time and money and injuries kept thwarting her schedule. Every job she took—waitress, bartender, desk girl, maid, receptionist— was supposed to just be the thing she did to support her real work, but if she didn't get bored and quit, she got angry and was fired. Too often she injured herself from overtraining and sometimes she'd give up for months at a time, wonder if she might waitress her life away, but she always returned to her dream— training and protein shakes and ice packs. Nearly a decade passed this way and all that stopped her from giving up was the belief that only incredibly boring people have lives that go the way they expect.

She was the first to arrive to on-boarding, ten minutes early after a morning of training at the old boxing gym that had persisted through this neighborhood's gentrification, from back when these streets were a better place to get a gut shot than a single-origin espresso. A new girl in a hot-pink sports bra and volleyball shorts had come in, insisted on sparring with her.

You don't want to do that, she said, eyeing Hot Pink's yoga-toned and yogurt-fed arms, but the chick just asked if Ashley was *scared*, and seriously—who the fuck did this woman think she was? Just stupid or still coked up from the night before? She was used to men doubting her, but when another woman failed to recognize Ashley as a fighter clearly out of her league, the insult was sharper. Guys at the gym sometimes looked at Ashley as if she were someone's daughter, someone's little princess, and even when they saw how brutal she could be they still grunted at her hooks (half-astounded, half-aroused) and some of them still had the fucking nerve to call her *girl* after it was over. She ignored them usually, but after that one dude slapped her ass, she spun around and knocked one of his teeth loose. Word got around not to fuck with her. These men, these bitches of their boneless limbs—didn't they know being a woman meant being at war?

Hot Pink fought as if she'd once impressed herself in a kick-boxing class and thought that meant something, so the spar took less than a minute. Ashley returned to her drills with an easy strength, rhythmically pummeling a punching bag. *Serves her right. Everyone should know where they belong.*

But it was this—knowing where you belong—that made her suspicious of being someone's Anger Girlfriend. Ever since Jason she'd openly disdained actors, as it seemed to her that the more a man wanted fame, the weaker he became, that craving external approval atrophied inner strength. (Nothing was dumber than people en masse, she knew. Our worst impulses live there.) So as she walked from the gym to the loft for on-boarding—for this job that would either buy her the time she needed or cost it again—she steeled herself for what she couldn't see.

3

Before the women began showing up, Matheson had been enjoying the near silence in the loft, staring at his pint of seltzer, listening to the bubbles chime against the glass. Then the first elevator arrived. Ten minutes early. The nerve of some people. He moved to his office and closed the door.

Matheson was unaccustomed to so many people being around, and though he'd always been told he worked well with others, that he was a natural *leader*, blah blah blah, he didn't actually *like* having people answer to him. Sure, once or twice a year Kurt would host a party that required Matheson to manage the florists and waiters and bartenders and security and catering teams, and of course the maids came a few times a week, but they all knew the drill by now, and the in-house chefs would just as soon never talk to anyone, communicate entirely in notes taped on the fridge. Bless them. Otherwise it was just Matheson and Kurt in the penthouse (which sometimes felt, a little, like *their* home).

Years ago the loft had briefly become the headquarters for postproduction on *The Walk*, the film that Kurt had written, directed, produced, designed, and starred in. They had just finished an on-and-off shoot of many years and were beginning to edit, but Kurt had soon dismissed all the editors and sound people and everyone else for not sharing his vision, just as the original director, cinematographer, set designer, costume designer, lead actor, and others had been let go over the years. Though Matheson knew that all these firings just gave more work to Kurt and delayed the film's completion yet again, he was happy to share the space and Kurt's attention with fewer people.

But now, here they were again, the living room filling with all these women he'd have to manage and pay and schedule and call and send e-mails to and follow up with and on and on. The Research Division had already been around for a few weeks, preparing the loft for the GX to begin. Matheson didn't mind them, as they all kept to themselves, didn't ask many questions, were monomaniacally focused on whatever they were doing, skittering around in their white lab coats, eyes always averted, but all the equipment they'd brought in had taken over Matheson's office and forced him into a smaller room on a lower floor. And as if that weren't bad enough, they'd turned the place into a complete mess for three weeks before on-boarding, with loose wires and cords and cameras and microphones everywhere, random electricians stumbling around, ladders being constantly set up, then left unattended in a room for *hours*. It was exhausting.

Matheson believed in Kurt's vision and was sure the GX would hasten a new era of *emotional evolution*—as Kurt called it—but all these people in the loft were a disruption, complicating the space with various smells and outfits that messed up the aesthetics and voices that echoed, shrill and grating, against the high ceilings.

Spatial harmony had once been Kurt's highest priority, and he'd even commissioned a minimalist sound installation for the loft a few years ago, a nearly imperceptible drone calibrated to fluctuate with the weather and time of day so that it always vibrated at the exact pitch that allowed Kurt to be his most relaxed and creative. The installation was intended to hasten Kurt's editing of *The Walk* by stimulating gamma waves, but it had taken several months of trial and error to sync the correct tracks with patterns in cloud coverage and atmospheric pressure, a process that had *creatively derailed* Kurt to the point that his meditation counselor, Yuri, suggested Kurt spend some time doing something repetitive and therapeutic to allow the psychological impact of the installation to set in, so Kurt spent months constantly knitting, creating yards-long scarves and hats that grew wider and wider until they had no recognizable use. He eventually gave the knittings to a Chelsea gallery, causing a minor art-world frenzy—*a brilliant statement on the paralyzing results of an excess of material wealth!*—when they were exhibited, prices upon request. The show sold out before the opening reception, scandalizing half the art world and dazzling the rest.

Matheson loved the sound installation, as he loved everything that Kurt loved, and was sure that its effect on his brain waves was at least somewhat responsible for the decrease in his insomnia and less frequent migraines. It moved him to think about how enmeshed his well-being was with Kurt's, how dependent they were on each other.

For the last decade Matheson had been the executive assistant for all Kurt's affairs: sorting his calendars, e-mails, appointments, financial decisions, acting as a stylist for his public appearances, responding to event invitations, and almost anything else. Sometimes Kurt would call him in the middle of the night to sleepily relay a dream while Matheson typed it into a document forwarded to Kurt's psychoanalyst, and every weekday morning Matheson transcribed as Kurt rambled about whatever was on his mind—screenplay ideas; topics he wanted to research; studies to commission; random unfounded theories; books he might have written; love-life woes; childhood memories; complaints; inventions; career strategies; and possible structures, styles, or ideas for editing *The Walk*.

The few boyfriends who had passed through Matheson's life had all accused him of loving Kurt more than he loved them, and each time this accusation came, he would have to realize the bit of truth in it. He had more or less given up on boyfriends in the last few years and his obligations with Kurt soon filled any extra space left in his life, and even his small apartment near the Gowanus Canal began to feel more like a storage space for something that belonged to Kurt. Though this sense of possession was somewhat unconscious, a few times, in the purgatory of a stalled subway car or during those first soft minutes awake but still prone in bed, Matheson had realized that he was devoted to Kurt in such an encompassing way that there was no part of his life that he wouldn't change for him. Not so with any boyfriend he'd ever had. Not so with his own family.

But ever since he began organizing the GX, insecurities had crept in. What if this army of girlfriends began to take over tasks that belonged to Matheson? What if Kurt grew to prefer their company to his? (He'd long believed himself to be irreplaceable, that he and Kurt had been through so much now that there was no chance of their ever parting, but when he'd first read the responsibilities of the Emotional Girlfriend, he felt something in his body drop and spill.) Or what if the Intellectual Girlfriend replaced Matheson as a consult on *The Walk*? Or what if the

Maternal Girlfriend took over all his domestic tasks? Or what if he hired a girlfriend who ran his social life?

The screening process for hiring all these women had become even more time-consuming and stressful than Matheson had anticipated, and though he'd hired a temporary assistant, Melissa, even her presence began to unnerve him after a few days. Melissa—an acting MFA student, twenty-two, new to the city—came to work each day wearing a dramatic trompe d'oeil of makeup, and dresses bought on credit, worn with the tags hidden. And though he first thought her to be as harmless as any young person trying to seem older, he soon found her youth somewhat intimidating. She reminded him, horrifyingly, of the young man he'd once been, the young man he'd probably been when Kurt hired him, that early-twenties eagerness that radiates, potent and impermanent. He would never be that way again. He would never have the power of that specific kind of not-knowing. Matheson tried (and succeeded) in making sure Melissa never crossed paths with Kurt, but his anxiety that she might permeated his every interaction with her.

Just before on-boarding began, Matheson stopped by the Research Division's office to watch the live video of the women coming in, Melissa going through the check-in protocol with each woman, imitating an authority she didn't have. No one in the Research Division paid him any mind at all. He looked over their shoulders as they worked, typing and clicking and occasionally murmuring to each other as they pointed at one of the screens of moving numbers or lines squiggling across a graph.

The members of the Research Division—six men and four women, a somewhat androgynous bunch, a range of skin tones, all of whom wore glasses, some of whom were of average height and some of whom were slightly shorter than average, all lacking any particularly defining characteristics—were almost always silent. They often whispered to one another as they passed hand-written notes or clipboards thick with documents, but to Matheson they said nothing aside from what was absolutely necessary, and even then they were slow to actually begin sentences, as if they were always waiting on someone else to jump in with an answer. They had no obvious leader but seemed to take turns speaking for the group.

Where had they even come from? They had just shown up one day.

Kurt had given Matheson only a week's warning before they appeared, never revealing how they'd been selected. Suddenly they were setting up their office full of screens and odd machines, arriving by nine or earlier, covertly lunching at their desks, hard at work all day. Some would sit at computers, typing an endless script of numbers and abbreviations, while others read and reread documents, made notes, drew and erased and redrew diagrams on their massive whiteboard. Matheson noticed how, when they spoke to one another, they leaned together, as if for warmth.

Individually there was nothing imposing about the Research Division but taken as a whole their authority filled the room many times over. In their first week Matheson had stopped by their office with some regularity, saying he was just checking in on them, to see if they had everything they needed, but he soon realized they wanted nothing to do with him. They wanted to be left alone. They were here to complete a goal that Matheson would in no way affect, it seemed. His role in the GX was administrative and he felt this meant they didn't take him seriously. And of course they didn't take him seriously. The Research Division knew they were the ones doing the real work of the GX: designing the study, giving assignments, providing their custom-designed sensors that measured everything occurring within Kurt and the women during Relational Experiments, analyzing the data, producing reports. Matheson was merely a liaison between them and Kurt and the girlfriends. Anyone could have done this job. Matheson didn't even understand what the sensors were measuring, and as he stood at the center of their office, watching the Research Division's machines and monitors fill and flash with information, he felt much less crucial than he once had.

One of the displays was zoomed in on Ashley's face as a series of dotted lines made triangles over it, a shifting geometry measuring the distance between cheekbone and chin, between pupil and brow, outer edges of her mouth, tracking each infinitesimal expression. Beneath this image, a ticker tape of information went by, and Matheson watched the numbers and words for a while before giving up and leaving. From her data the researchers knew Ashley was physically fatigued and digesting a large amount of protein. They could also see that the part of her brain associated with deep memories was extremely active and that her baseline of cortisol appeared higher than average. A little sweat clung to her forehead just below the hairline.

But anyone paying enough attention to her could see Ashley was packed away in her head. Her legs throbbed from her morning drills and the aches had triggered a memory of a story she'd once heard of a man who had irrationally wanted both his legs amputated. The man had gone to doctor after doctor and all were shocked, then disgusted by his request. He should be happy, the doctors told him. He had a body that still worked and he should appreciate the years he had, but these doctors, the man thought, they weren't listening to him so he asked again—*Just, you know, theoretically, what would need to happen for a man to have both his legs amputated?* The doctors still refused his questions, suggested psychologists, suggested religion, a purpose, a hobby, anything. Even the plastic surgeons, accustomed to delusion, had him escorted from their buildings. This was a true story, Ashley thought. She still couldn't remember where she had heard this story but she could imagine the man so clearly, looking down at his legs, good legs, strong legs, but somehow sure that a legless life would be better, in a wheelchair, half his body gone. Ashley felt she understood him, in a way, though he was a stranger, or maybe a fiction. It was just a different version of the way she hated her own face, that burdening inheritance from her mother, the reason, she was told, she got groped three times on the subway and once on the bus before she was even fifteen. *No one knows*, her mother said in halting English, *how it costs so much to be beautiful*, though Luisa never said what prices she'd paid, just as Ashley didn't tell anyone she'd heard all this before: *Tits like that, face like that*, the man had whispered before leaving the train, disappearing into a terrible crowd. She wished for invisibility, wished she could just move around the world on her own, unnoticed, and that last night at Jason's house, she had wished he'd hit her hard enough to break her jaw or nose—maybe that would have imbalanced her enough to be invisible—but all she'd gotten were some bruises and a lump on her scalp, hidden. For years she waited to get busted in a spar, to chip a tooth or crook her nose, but it never happened. She was too fast, too graceful, and eventually it became a point of pride—that you should fear the scarless fighter more than those who've taken enough to be changed—but she still resented her looks in the street. Men would just stare at her sometimes, women, too, maybe thinking she didn't notice, but she did—her peripheral so wide and trained. Sometimes she'd sense a gaze boring into her from behind, and when she turned, some man was always there. Anyway, that guy who hated his legs, in the end he packed dry ice around them until the flesh was ruined, frozen and burned at the same time, and one of the doctors who'd said, *No, absolutely not, never*—he was tasked with the surgery, and while sawing through the man's femur, he couldn't help but notice the smell that came with this ending, like chalk but burning.

As Ashley stared out the window, Mary noticed her, felt comforted that at least one other person here wasn't trying to make small talk with the others. Beginning conversations with strangers had always seemed nearly impossible to Mary, a limitation that often caused her problems, especially abroad when she'd become lost and be unable to ask directions, and at its worst she would sometimes rather go hungry than go into a restaurant and have to ask for something. But soon Vicky had come in and noticed Ashley, the two of them embracing, making Mary, again, the only loner.

It had been fifteen days, she now realized, since she had seen or even heard from Chandra and she couldn't recall ever going that long before. As Matheson began his presentation about the sensors, handbooks, Relational Experiments, and Research Division, Mary felt increasingly puny in herself, dipping in and out of attention. Perhaps she should not be a person's Emotional Girlfriend. Perhaps she shouldn't allow her *neurological and psychological activity patterns* to be analyzed. Perhaps she shouldn't sign this *one last waiver*. She tried to make herself get up and leave and she tried to imagine what advice Chandra might give her in this moment, but that was just the problem—she couldn't give herself what Chandra would have given her. She could not be Chandra to herself. Only Chandra, it seemed, could be Chandra to Mary.

The GX is fully committed to uncovering the mysteries of limerence, and your participation is the first step toward a more emotionally evolved future, Matheson said, seeming sure this experiment would generate practical, usable, real information about love, making love last, decoding the mysteries of limerence—which was, he said, the psychological and physiological state of a body as it falls in love. (Paul had said this word to her on a few occasions—*limerence*—naming the feeling between them in those early days, and she'd first thought Paul had invented the word, since the feeling she had around him felt so incredibly new that it seemed impossible that there could already be a word for it—this heat high in the chest and bone deep and above her head at once—but later, when Paul had brought up this idea of limerence again, she became frightened because if this feeling had already been defined, then it was possible someone might be able to prove or disprove whether she actually loved him. It was possible she might not have the right feeling after all, that she wasn't in love, wasn't in limerence, but was in some unnamed place, alone.)

And by conclusions, Matheson continued, *I don't mean some sort of bogus self-help pseudoscience or truisms—far from it. The ultimate objective of the GX is to devise a scientifically proven system for making human pair bonding behavior more perfect and satisfying, to make the benefits of limerence persist over the long term. This system will involve technological therapies that we cannot yet explain to you, but the GX is a crucial first step—really more of an exploration than an experiment—toward this goal. You are at the forefront of the creation of truly innovative technological solutions to emotional and psychological problems that were previously thought to be just part of the human condition.*

The handbooks were distributed and Matheson explained them, page by page, the wardrobe and makeup requirements, the topics they should never bring up with Kurt, the prohibited words, prohibited actions, how they should never mention the existence of the other women in the GX, how they should say nothing to Kurt about his career unless he brought it up first, how they should never reference any part of his history or life that he hadn't told them directly.

I realize some of you know more about Kurt than others, but for the purposes of your work with him in the GX, we will need you to pretend, and be actually convincing, that you've never heard of him or seen him before.

There was a Pre-session Protocol, the sensor application with the Research Division, wardrobe and makeup, the guided meditation with Kurt's meditation counselor, Yuri. Then there was the Post-session Protocol—the exit interviews with the Research Division, sensor removal, and Yuri's compartmentalization exercises that would, as Matheson explained, *prevent any emotional bleed-over into your real lives.*

Then it was all over and everyone was leaving, some of the other women sharing cabs somewhere, going wherever they were going, and Mary wondered if those women were making the conscious choice to be like that, whether they had to intentionally start a conversation with someone they didn't know, or whether they just did, without thinking, because that's just how they were. Mary walked to the subway alone, slowly, rubbing at a strangely sore muscle in her back, anticipating her next appointment with Ed—two and a half days away.

The late-afternoon light was thick and orange and she passed four different couples taking photos of themselves on the same cobblestoned block, all their loves endlessly recorded and reviewed, ever and ever, a little archive of two. On the subway a tide of anxiety came in and her back began to ache and spasm, and as she tried to contort herself to ease the discomfort, the people standing near her inched away. She felt an urgency and a certainty that something was happening to Chandra, a kind of intuition that she'd never before felt, and when her stop came, she bolted, quickly weaving her way through the crowd though her back was still gripped by pain, and when she finally reached her apartment door, she found a note that seemed to confirm her premonitions.

> Going away for a while, not sure when I'll be back, don't worry.
> Make sure you keep going to Ed.
> Love & light, xC

She couldn't tell what hurt more: not knowing where Chandra had gone or that she had just missed saying goodbye. Was it possible that she and Chandra were so connected that they had been thinking of each other at the same moment? She sat on the cold, dirty floor of her living room and tried to justify the separation: Mary and Chandra were different people, and because they were *different* people, they needed different things and because they needed different things they sometimes had to be in places without the other, to go about their lives alone, and *sometimes*, Chandra had often reminded Mary, *some people need to be unseen*, to be alone, to be unreachable for a while. And there was nothing wrong with this. Everyone has a right to her secrecy. Of course they do. Of course.

4

Her first years in the city Mary still woke before sunrise each morning as Chandra slept in on the lower bunk. She went out wandering, walking in and out of grocery stores and pharmacies and all-night bodegas, trying to learn the foreign language of energy drinks and pregnancy tests and creams that could fight your age. She learned that 4:00 a.m. can bring anger or drowsy sweetness out of people and it was 4:00 a.m. when a drugstore clerk at the end of her night shift pressed a package of earplugs into Mary's hand—*Can't sleep, can you? I use these things. Sleep good now.* Mary hesitated, tried to give them back, but the woman, fatigued into a violent compassion, insisted, *Take them! It's a gift! I work crazy hours, crazy hours. That shit will fuck you up. Young thing like you shouldn't have nothing to keep her awake.*

So Mary thanked her, took the gift, thanked her again.

All this noise, the clerk shouted, laughing.

In the street Mary twisted two blue plugs into her ears and all that noise—subway cars screeching below the grates and garbage trucks chewing trash and the obliterating roar of an empty bus shooting down Broadway—all of it paled and muted and Mary could hear her lungs charge and drain, heart thudding, feel her veins flexing beneath the skin. The sun rose and the streets filled with the dusty light of another broken morning and Mary felt shielded, felt safer.

She began wearing earplugs nearly all the time, until that pre-dawn on a narrow, dim street when this arm came out of nowhere, clamping her chest (a stranger's heat on her back), and another arm looped her waist and this body took her body from the sidewalk and into an alleyway, beside some trash bins (banana peel, old beer, something putrid), and this body cornered her and a hand pried open her jaw (head feeling hollow) and a man's voice made noises muffled by the earplugs and his body pushed some of itself into her mouth (and what is a mouth and what is a body?) and the body held her head like it wanted and the voice told her what to do so she did and her skull bounced against the wall (and what are walls and what do they do?) and the earplugs kept the sound of all this deep in her head (throat seizing, gurgling, head drumming on brick) and it all felt impossible and too real and she kept her eyes shut (hard squint) and told her thoughts to swim elsewhere, and it all happened fast and slow at the same time and her skull felt it might shatter in her head (and what is anyone's head but a history, a house for all your history) and she was erasing the memory even as it happened, even as he finished (whatever he was doing, whatever it had done) and his hand held her mouth shut till she swallowed and he thrashed her head against the metal bin (a gong, almost holy) and was gone.

She was still for a moment, then retched until she spit up bile and something.

She stayed still, tried to exit herself.

The taste in her mouth was hateful and large.

No one found her.

The streets were quiet, the nonplace between night and morning.

She walked home, slack, lacking even the energy to tremble.

Chandra was away for the weekend. Their tiny dorm room, lit by dim yellow lamps, was silent. She took out the earplugs and threw them away. She took off her clothes and threw them away. She brushed her teeth until her gums bled and scrubbed her tongue and spat in the trash and threw the toothbrush in after it. She showered in scalding water and threw the soap away. She got back in bed naked though the sun was now coming up, a terrible orange dawn, and as she slept, her period came because bodies know nothing about timing, bodies, awful bodies. They put a Rorschach between your thighs and stain your sheets to remind you that all you're doing is bleeding and dying if you're not making more life.

That afternoon she went to the park and lay in some grass, stared at the clouds, thought of Tennessee, thought of the woods where she never saw a man she didn't know, never saw a man who wasn't her father, and she wept. She wept but her face did not move. She wept but she made no sound. She told no one until she told Chandra a year later, a secret that cemented them, made them family, and Chandra told her what you tell a person who tells you this: *This does not define you. You are not this.*

Four minutes of a life. Almost nothing, but there it is, recurring in her after being recalled by one smell or another, the quality of some light, the texture of a brick wall. It could have been so much worse, she sometimes thought, but it wasn't worse. Nothing's ever worse.

Chandra took her to a self-defense class—something physical

to do, a motion, a movement they could make together—and a women's circle in Park Slope, though they both felt too shy to say anything—and Chandra took her to a rally for survivors of sexual violence, but Mary felt overwhelmed by the crowd and had to duck into a department store and take the escalators up to a floor overlooking Union Square, watched the mob of surviving women from above, ashamed she couldn't withstand just standing with them.

5

Though she'd been trained by Matheson in what to say and how to say it and though she had been outfitted in exactly the right clothes and instructed how to apply the supplied makeup and though she'd done the guided meditation through the app installed on her GX phone and though Matheson had given her the Relational Experiment outline from the Research Division, Mary still did not know how to be around him.

It was 8:00 p.m. on a Tuesday, in the secret back room of an unmarked cocktail bar in the West Village—Savant House— full of mahogany and velvet and dead animal heads. The illusion of exclusivity made the patrons feel privileged to spend forty-three dollars on a single glass of liquid. The back room was nearly impossible to find, the last of three doors, the other two fake, down an alley beside the main unmarked door, and Mary had been instructed to press a doorbell three times before listening for the click, pushing the door open, going up the narrow spiral staircase to the right, heading down the hallway and down another narrow spiral staircase, through the blue velvet curtains, showing her ID to two security guards and a maître d'.

Of course Kurt wasn't there yet, wouldn't arrive until she'd been waiting for at least twenty minutes (*It's one of his things*, Matheson said), so as Mary waited alone at the only table in the cavernous room (*Mr. Sky will be with you shortly*), she tried to read a book but the light was too low, and though she didn't order anything, a wisp-thin man in an all-black suit placed a glass of pale pink liquid floating a cucumber slice before her. His eyes were so deep set and shadowed she could hardly see them.

From the Savant. A tonic for health and vitality, he said.

He kept standing there, watching her with the bored intensity of a child staring into a television. Savory and slightly effervescent, the first sip immediately deadened her nervy stomach, and it was suddenly so easy to be herself that she felt as if she were someone else. Mary looked back up at the waiter, still waiting, and not knowing what to say, she just nodded and he nodded and slipped away. Several empty minutes later she caught the waiter staring at her, half his face and body obscured by a burgundy curtain, but before she could even have a feeling about this, Kurt appeared, saying, *Hey, you*, and hugging her in a long-lost-friend way instead of the halting, protected way that strangers usually touch each other for the first time.

Did you find the place all right?

He smelled like campfire but somehow sweet and his face was so symmetrical it almost called his humanity into question. His eyes had this constant tension, as if he were looking into a bright light and forcing himself not to squint. One of her guidelines was to mirror his expressions, so she tried to smile in the alert way that he smiled, concentrating so intently that she didn't notice the waiter taking away her first drink and replacing it with two glasses of something clear and slightly blue and Kurt lifted his glass, so she lifted hers and he smelled his so she did and they drank—sweet, floral—and though he closed his eyes while swishing and swallowing, she kept hers open, watching him.

He explained how this place had no menu, that a bespoke cocktail artist—the Savant—made each drink in a hidden lab, creating the exact beverage that he believed that particular patron needed through methods that no one knew. Some thought it was hidden cameras; others said the waiters were in on it; a few claimed he was psychic. The drinks sometimes, but not always, contained alcohol, but they always contained medicinal tinctures and some hypothesized that the Savant dosed some with peyote or psilocybin, though this had never been proven or disproven.

It's the only place to ever earn a Michelin star without serving any solid food, Kurt said. Chandra had explained to Mary what a Michelin star was, though she couldn't remember now, but it didn't matter whether she understood Kurt. She wasn't expected to conduct any meaningful discussions—as there was an Intellectual Girlfriend for that—or to comfort him—since that was up to the Maternal Girlfriend. She only had to listen and respond to Kurt in the way she'd been trained, putting a hand on his hand or knee when he brought up a memory of his mother and putting a hand on his shoulder when he said anything about being stressed about his work. She spoke as infrequently as possible, always below the decibel level she'd been trained to never breach, and never using any of the words on the black list: *vibe, fiscal, underscored, kitty, literally, lactose, hashtag, hoopla, whatevs, vomit,* and several others. If he asked her a question about herself, she was to answer it as honestly and concisely as possible, but during this first session he didn't ask her one.

A fleet of liquids were brought out over the evening, some in cups as small as a thimble, some low and lonely in a wide-mouthed glass. They made Mary feel both calm and alert, a mysteriously clear feeling that seemed, almost, to originate outside her body, hitting her like a sound, like music.

My mother once told me that I would take the pacifier out of my mouth as a baby and I would cry even though I had the pacifier in my hand, that I could put it back whenever I wanted. But I would just look at it, crying, until I felt I was done with crying, then I'd put it back in my mouth and I'd be fine, totally content. Kurt paused for effect here, ran his finger around the edge of his glass, then looked above Mary's head. *I think it's because I've always wanted to feel everything there is to feel.*

He kept on with anecdotes like this, each imbued with some sort of lesson about him, something Mary should know about him, some wisdom, some clue. She kept nodding, making eye contact, paying close attention, as her guidelines had instructed.

The question arose—after nearly two hours of Mary's listening and nodding and humming a hundred hums of acknowledgment—of whether Kurt was just behaving in the way he'd been assigned to behave, or if this was just how he was. He never, not once, segued out of a story about himself by doing that thing she had noticed other people doing—by abruptly saying, *well, anyway*—a phrase it seemed that everyone said in exactly the same, rushed way, as if some level of self-exposure could trigger a need to send the attention elsewhere. Mary couldn't even imagine Kurt saying that phrase—*well, anyway*. She knew that the main priority of this Relational Experiment was for Kurt to talk and for her to listen, but it wasn't against the rules of the Relational Experiment for him to listen to her and wasn't he at all interested in what she had to say? Or perhaps he already knew everything he needed to know about her from the interviews and background check and everything. Perhaps she'd never have to say anything to him and perhaps that suited her just fine.

Mary couldn't tell from the way he was behaving, but Kurt had actually looked forward to meeting her—a thirty-year-old woman in New York who had *never even heard of him*. Yet he found it impossible to not mention the parts of his career that impressed people the most, craving, despite himself, the automatic awe he usually got from a stranger. He told her the story of his first film, *The Father Game*, how it was a huge critical and commercial success, and how his performance as a teen runaway trying to find his biological parents in Cleveland had earned him an Oscar and how it was only then that his real-life father, estranged throughout Kurt's childhood except in the form of child support checks, tried to reach out to him with this ridiculous letter that said he was, *more or less, somewhat proud*, even though Kurt's part *was overwritten and most of the characters were only moderately believable.* In fact the letter wasn't quite as harsh as Kurt remembered it but it wasn't as warm as it could have been, and since Kurt had endured his mother's cancer and death alone, he was sure he didn't need a too-late father now. Kurt never wrote back, and his father, now dead as well, remained moderately, if not completely, satisfied by only keeping up with his son through magazines and movies. When someone asked this man about his first short marriage and son, all he ever said was *People make mistakes*.

Kurt paused in the middle of the story. He bit his lip, tapped his fingernails against the table, and slowly smiled. (This gesture sequence had become so deeply ingrained in him, a reflex, that he didn't even know he was doing it, a tic that appeared in most of his characters, at least in his later films, and when someone impersonated him, this was always part of the act. A website even posted nothing but looping GIFs of this—the bit lip, tapped fingers, slow grin—and once Kurt found this page deep in some anxious Internet searching for himself, and for some time he couldn't look away from all those tiny hims, biting and tapping and grinning, endlessly.)

When strangers recognize you and know stuff about you, it makes things really confusing, he said, *and I couldn't tell when someone was genuinely connecting with me or when they were just connecting with the idea of me or something they wanted.*

Mary nodded.

This might sound crazy, but I'm tired of the attention. I really am. I want to be understood, not just wanted. (Kurt was quiet for a moment, thinking back to the girls in the early years—crowds of jumping girls, shaking girls, girls screaming, girls in shirts that said MRS. KURT SKY, girls who somehow didn't mind being packed shoulder to shoulder with all those other Mrs. Kurt Skys as they mobbed hotel lobbies or spilled over sidewalk barricades, girls reaching stick arms at him, girls in glittery blue eye shadow hoping the shimmer might bring his eyes to theirs, girls hyper-ventilating, girls breaking out in hives, girls stabbing each other with EpiPens, girls holding up fainted girls, girls dropping those girls to stampede him—determined and in some kind of love, these girls. (This odd moment before adulthood: biologically old enough to know desire, but young enough to believe in magic. Hormones and hope creating a fantasy as they shook with a fe-rocious love, or the idea of love, or the fantasy of a future love, or the love of the idea of the fantasy of love.) A few young women (women who had remained girls) even found his home address and occasionally stood at the front gate, screaming his name, watching his windows with a sniper's focus as they lit or dark-ened. Each time Kurt heard one of them standing out there, he felt a slight annoyance followed by a flood of pleasure, pleasure when he had to call Matheson to say another one was at the gate, pleasure to feel so wanted, to feel he had driven someone moderately insane. It was a dangerous power, and only years later did he wonder if this had ruined him in a way, if it had raised his tolerance for another person's desire to such a degree that he could never be satisfied by a normal love. Kurt would sometimes sit in his darkened living room before the police took one of those girls away, listening to her voice fray as she screamed his name. *I know you're listening*, one of them once shouted, *I know you can hear me!* and he almost felt found.)

The session was almost over when Kurt said, *We should really talk about what's happening*, Mary's cue to look down, inhale slowly and subtly, reach for his nearest hand with both her hands, wait for him to place his other hand on top of hers before looking up, her expression a sort of wistful-overwhelmed-elated, a look she'd practiced with Matheson for a solid hour the prior day.

Yes, she said.

She was thinking of how she'd been told to not think of her Emotional Girlfriend sessions as work or acting but to inhabit each moment as if it were a meditation, and though she knew that thinking of this instruction prevented her from following it, maybe that was the closest she could come to that hyper-unawareness, intentional un-intention. She'd been told the most important part of her job was to follow the instructions, since the instructions were scientifically designed to bring about the correct feeling in her that would bring about the correct feeling in him. Though Mary had studied her handbook intensely, had tried to push all the rules into a place of muscle memory, she was often unsure if she was being the correct way, an uncertainty that chaperoned her constantly.

This is so important, he said. *What you're doing. It's hard for me to feel like I can fully explain how important this is.*

Mary looked at Kurt with a blank expectance and it had been

so long since he'd seen someone look at him in such a way that he was immediately comforted, taken back to a time he was less filtered, freer, less observed. He remembered that naïve privacy he'd had, something he didn't notice until it was gone, until strangers regularly descended on him in the street, before hungry faces hovered over his restaurant tables saying, *Please*, saying, *Sorry, just saying hello.* They beamed at him—*I'm sorry*—half-embarrassed, half-certain, half-trying to back out of themselves—*I'm sorry to interrupt but I just had to say*—deeply needing to get these few words in—*I'm sorry but I had to say something because you, your work, you just*—decades of these people and he still couldn't decide how to feel about them—*I'm sorry but I had to say something and I'm not sure what to say, just that I'm a big fan, and I know you must get this all the time, but I had to say something and I'm sorry.* This *sorry/please/sorry/please*, these strangers asking for hugs or autographs or photos, wanting proof they once existed with him, already an artifact, already a memory. *Well, nice to meet you. Thank you so much. No, really. Have a nice night. Take care. Bye now.*

Kurt placed a hand on Mary's face, open and soft and relaxed, as instructed, and since the session was off-site, she didn't wear the facial sensors, just the bodily ones, which sat warm on her skin, between dress and waist, between bracelet and wrist, behind the ears, recording. Mary remembered that when he put a hand on her face she was to remain in silent eye contact for three slow counts before closing her eyes and pressing her cheek into his palm, the way cats will push into a petting hand, giving themselves to what's given.

It was still strange for Mary to be alone with a man (except Ed, which was strange in another way). She felt odd cramps and tensions in her body. She tried to force herself to be relaxed, and though she could never completely do so, she did manage to enjoy, somewhat, the spectacle and difficulty of being around him.

Kurt looked at her, said, *Thank you*, ran a hand through her hair, kissed her cheek, and left.

Mary sat there awhile, staring at the table, feeling herself being watched again by that waiter as he slipped between velvet curtains at the edge of the room. She was required to wait several minutes after Kurt left a session before she left. Kurt hated goodbyes, and she was never to make any goodbye-like gesture or even give the impression that she was ever leaving. She thought of this on the walk home, how she would always be in the places he entered or left. Still, she slept that night better than she'd slept in years or possibly ever.

6

Traffic was backed up for blocks, holding his car at a standstill in the neighborhood he used to live in, on his old street. The car rolled slowly past the door that had once been his and he found himself staring at it, waiting for his past self to come walking out. Still painted the same blue, he noticed, nauseated and annoyed by how much time had passed. Fifteen years already? He didn't want to do the math.

Traffic, the driver said, flicking his eyes at him in the rearview.

Yeah. Kurt rolled down the window, peered up at his old balcony. He could almost see it and began to feel wistful, almost weepy— No. He was being ridiculous. He raised the window, but the memory of his time with Alexi sat like a pill in his throat. They'd had a good run for a few months, hadn't they? Or had they? Maybe they'd even been in love for a little while or maybe it only seemed that way from a distance. A vague set of images cued up—Alexi across a room at a party they'd gone to, pretending to not be together. He and Alexi sharing a midnight cigarette on his roof—or was it hers? Alexi in the second row of some theater somewhere, staring neutrally at him onstage as he was interviewed for a film festival—though he couldn't now remember what it had been. Anyway. It had been a good summer, he thought. They'd had a good time.

But then a bomb went off—or at least what sounded like a bomb—a plane crashing into a building a mile away. Alexi had been at her place that morning, a microscopic two-bedroom she shared with another actress in a hazardous walk-up, and when she heard it, she immediately thought of Kurt, became increasingly frantic when he didn't pick up the phone, then terrified that something had happened, then certain that something had happened because he would have found a way to reach her by now, and her body went wild trying to escape itself—vomiting and achy and collapsing—and she thought of how tragic it was that this, potentially losing him to whatever had happened out there (so many rumors in the street), had finally revealed that their love had a real weight, real roots in her. Against her roommate's shouts and tears, she walked out into the ash-hazy streets, surrounded by a chorus of sirens as she dashed to his place, arriving coated in ash and sweat at his door, trembling. His first words to her: *You should take a shower.*

So she did, crying but keeping quiet, not wanting him to worry.

How was it that he seemed so calm? Hadn't he been worried about her? Hadn't he been afraid? Or perhaps, she thought, he was swallowing his fear to be steady for her, that his love had manifested not in mania but in solidity, that this was the way they balanced each other. This moment, this horrible moment, had made them see, she thought, how necessary they were for each other. She stood wrapped in a towel, feeling so changed and important.

Kurt gave her a change of clothes, jean shorts and a T-shirt that she'd left at his place that Kurt had put by the door for the last couple weeks, hoping she would take them home. He handled her toxic, dusty clothes with dish gloves, sealing them in plastic bags and disinfecting everything they'd touched.

This is all outside of our control, he said as Alexi clutched on to him, her hair wet, eyes red.

Her outsize emotions bothered him. The few people she knew in the city—her roommate and her two other real friends—had been accounted for. She didn't know anyone who worked in the Financial District. She hadn't personally *lost* anything. This wasn't her tragedy. She was reacting too much like a certain kind of actress would, taking any opportunity as a chance to perform.

They didn't speak much for the rest of the afternoon or night, just listened for a while to a radio that worked, turning it off to have athletic, wordless sex to which they each ascribed a different meaning.

Weeks later, when she asked him what he had been thinking of that day, she was unnerved (then upset, then repulsed) by what he said. It wasn't Alexi's safety or his safety or even his friends' safety (and did he even have any friends?) and wasn't even the staggering heaps of human life wasted only blocks from his luxury west SoHo loft. No. He confessed to Alexi that he thought of how the funding for *The Walk* would probably fall through now—and, *yes*, Kurt said, he realized she might think this was *shallow* or *detached*, and he realized that he wasn't experiencing the attack in the *emotionally penetrable* way that she was, *not that there was anything wrong with that, per se, but there really sort of was, if you thought about it, but listen,* he told her as she began to sob, *will you just fucking listen to what I'm saying for once instead of obsessing over your own emotional reality? Huh? For once? Can you do that for me?*

The way his beautiful face went hard—eyes molted with his young-man beliefs—this would be the image Alexi kept with her long after she left him. Maybe his heart had atrophied after being so publicly beloved, and maybe that's why he seemed unmoved by the shrines to the lost, the faded, photocopied portraits of the dead on every street corner—*Have you seen this person?*—a city of unashamed eye contact, millions of people now reverent with each other, seeing the holy in each other, and this man, this little monster, was worried about his fucking production schedule.

Everyone out there right now, he said, *all the volunteers and firefighters and everyone having their big come-to-Jesus, everyone crying over this admittedly truly horrible and terrifying thing—listen—no, listen!*

She tamped down her tears to hear the exact ways in which he was terrible.

You may think you're crying because all those people died and it's tragic, but you're still crying for yourself. You're crying because you know it could have been you. You're crying because life is not special and everyone dies and the complexity of your "self" is still going to vanish someday and there's no such thing as justice.

Her tears had stopped.

No one can cry for someone else.

She examined his face as if he were an object.

I'm not prone to ecstatic displays of emotion to get attention, but

I still feel things. I just organize that experience in a different way. I process it logically.

It saddened her that *this* was the man she had chosen to sleep with for a whole summer into autumn, a man so stingy with himself that he refused to witness another's pain.

When I realized what had happened, I thought, one, human life is temporary; and two, the only way I can cope with this fact is making something that outlives me; and three, the film I have been developing for the last three years is probably going to get delayed yet again if there are problems with funding; and four, yes, I could be so much as a pile of dust tomorrow and that's sad; and five, the only way that I can deal with that fact is by working, that I could make something bigger than me, something that has an effect on other people.

She felt nauseous as she considered the many ounces of him that she had sucked into her body. What was he really made of?

Do you understand what I'm saying? Or do you just want to think I'm a bad guy because I don't cry the way you do?

(She remembered him sipping a goblet of red wine in his living room the night of the attacks, after they'd had what she thought was emotionally potent sex. He was enjoying the most expensive bottle he had, alone, because Alexi was on a diet for a role, so he sat in the living room reading a novel—a fucking novel!—while she stayed in bed, the dust on the windows filtering the light all gauzy, her head swimming in the sincere enormity of the present, distantly wondering why he had gotten out of bed without explanation, why he didn't answer when she asked where he was going, why he wasn't in bed with her, warm at her side.)

I'm a different fucking person from you. I see the world differently, I process emotion differently. And there's nothing wrong with that. You just need to grow up and accept it.

(He had returned to bed that night with lips edged and breath heavy with Cabernet, and though Alexi's face was swollen red and salt-gritty from tears flowing, drying, and flowing again, he made no move to comfort her, just turned out the light and was snoring in minutes.)

I don't need to become more like you. Hell, you probably need to be less like the sort of person you are.

That was the last thing he ever said to her. He had trouble getting to sleep after she left mid-argument, and not because his call had gone straight to voice mail and not because she had tried to make him feel coldhearted, and not because he missed her, because he didn't, because he enjoyed being alone, really enjoyed it, and he didn't lie awake that night for two hours because of the World Trade Center, and when he later woke up crying, he knew it wasn't sadness for life lost or the victims' families or the bravery of people who risked their own insignificant lives for the insignificant lives of others. No. He must have just been crying for himself. Simple anxiety. He crossed his arms, felt his biceps, his chest, his belly, moved his hands down to his thighs. He was here. He didn't need to cry for himself. He didn't need to cry at all, he thought, and he stopped, fell asleep, slept until noon.

The traffic had finally loosened but Kurt hadn't noticed, had been completely folded into this memory. The car was crossing the bridge when he opened his eyes, night-black river below, people walking along the lamplit waterfront in pairs, staring at each other or at the skyline, all of it so much more fragile than it seemed, everyone on the edge of oblivion, as usual. He watched the bridge beams rush by outside the window and thought about something he read once about some tiny muscles in the human face that send signals to other brains while bypassing a person's awareness, skipping the eyes, going straight to their core. An unknown sonar, some language none realized they were speaking, an honest whisper. He wondered what his face may have said to her.

7

The Mundanity Girlfriend's handbook explained all the ways she should be silent, how crucial her silence was, how she shouldn't mistake her work for nothing—*Like sleep for life, mundane company is an essential part of any successful pair bond, even beneficial to one's health. It encourages the body into metabolic efficiency, lowers the heart rate, strengthens the immune system, allows damaged cells to regenerate more quickly. Your work as the Mundanity Girlfriend is an essential first step to understanding why and how certain neural activities occur when people do nothing together.*

The handbook told the Mundanity Girlfriend what parts of the loft were off-limits, the positions she should or should not hold on a chaise or sofa or armchair, how many times per hour she was allowed to move. She was allowed to read a magazine or book, but never a screen. She was allowed to stare absently out a window in a daze for up to three minutes at a time as long as she kept her expression neutral, placid—never disdainful or bored. She was not to nap or crack her knuckles or bite her nails. She was to do everything she could to conceal a yawn.

If Kurt enters the room, you will look in his direction, but not at his eyes. You will smile, slightly, as if you are thinking about something else. You should remain occupied by your chosen activity. You should not think of Kurt or let any of your attention settle on where he is in the room.

Lying there at her first session, Poppy daydreamed of those early months with Sam—how he'd gone to Ohio for two weeks of work and instead of talking or texting each other the trivialities of their days, they decided to communicate entirely in videos— two minutes, four minutes—of themselves doing almost nothing. In hers she was going about her life as usual—morning coffee, blow-drying her hair, practicing headstands in the living room— while in his he was usually reading in the beige nonspace of his room at the Days Inn—a book, a newspaper, a spiral-bound report on the efficiency of his company's data management software. She watched each one over and over, then let them play in a loop as she did something else, the sound track of his sighs, turned pages, a cough, or a sneeze keeping her company. She was sure no one had ever been more in love than they were in those weeks, consumed by such longing, wanting to just be alive beside each other.

The years that followed were often quiet, pleasantly at first, then less so—silent train rides to see his mother up in Boston, waiting in line for one thing or another, pitch-dark nights and dim mornings spent trying to fall asleep or wake up, overcast afternoons when it seemed possible the whole world had run out of things to say. Toward the end they had fewer slow dinners, fewer nights talking through the dark, more films and plays where they could quietly forget each other in a crowd. Still, when she overheard him taking a shower—the sound of water breaking against his body as he hummed or sang low—she felt the most pleasurable kind of loneliness, even toward the end. It was possible, Poppy realized, daydreaming during her first Relational Experiment, that she had loved Sam the best in his silence, as his life went and carried her with it, as her life took him, too. She did not miss his voice, which, in the end, carried so much abuse, and she did not miss his body, which had a few times been used against her, and she did not miss the history or rituals they had created, the mythology all lovers write, but she did miss the comfort of his life drifting beside hers. She missed his nothing. It had felt like something.

Kurt had been in Poppy's peripheral all morning, staring out one of the large windows at the bridges and seeing himself from the outside, seeing himself being so casually content while Poppy was over there, being so casually content. He wondered if his self-awareness would complicate the data from the sensors, though he didn't completely understand what they were measuring. Little, it seemed, had really been explained during the presentations the Research Division had given Kurt and Matheson weeks ago about their plan for the GX, or perhaps he hadn't been listening as closely as he could have.

Two of the researchers had led the presentation on how the sensors worked. Kurt had been sure these two men were twins, though they denied it. Still—they were nearly identical, same height, same haircut, even had the same glasses. *It's just the glasses*, one of them said, and the other removed his frames as if this would prove something, though it did not.

During their demonstration about the sensors, one of the not-twins had worn a set of them, while the other explained the various charts and graphs the data had begun to produce: information about the not-twin's mood, the concentration of various hormones and neurotransmitters in his blood, nervous system activity patterns, heart and respiratory rate, something called vagal tone, which is important to romantic love for some reason, skin conductivity (whatever that is), and other things, though Kurt stopped listening, just nodded and squinted at the numbers and charts on the screen, as if he might have been able to give them some great insight about what he saw.

So, this is how you'll be able to tell, Kurt said, *you know, what's . . . happening . . . internally . . . during the Relational Experiments?*

The not-twins said *Yes* in unison. A machine clicked and another beeped, then a woman's voice rose from the back of the room.

Feelings and emotions are not mysterious. They are merely attempts to respond rationally to an uncertain world, a series of neurochemical reactions that can be analyzed and traced back to their origins.

The not-twin who wasn't wearing the sensors spoke up, too—*Though we do acknowledge that this is an inexact science, measuring people's feelings and moods.*

Yes. We do acknowledge that, the woman in the back said.

But our methods are becoming more exact all the time, the sensored not-twin said.

Yes, all the time, the other not-twin said.

A human system merely responds to the data it is given and creates a set of data as an answer to that data, the woman said. *And the more deeply we can understand these matrices of information, the better we will be able to diagnose and treat medical, psychological, and even interpersonal problems.*

More was said but Kurt wasn't quite listening anymore, just looking at the Research Division in their starched white lab coats, pleased with himself for assembling these people to make the world nicer. The other members of the Research Division said nothing for the hour-long presentation; they did not even seem to move in their chairs scattered around the edge of the office. Some, it seemed, could have been sleeping with their eyes open. They were a strange lot, the Research Division—but he'd been assured they were the best.

Kurt wasn't a scientist and would be the first to admit that, but wasn't it sometimes the case in history that those who were not technically scientists—those who were, instead, *visionaries*, let's say—wasn't it sometimes the case that these visionaries predicted a scientific fact centuries before these facts could be scientifically proven? He couldn't remember exactly who, but there had been someone, not da Vinci but someone *like* da Vinci, someone of that era, some self-taught philosopher who had made an accurate prediction of something like DNA or the Internet. Some guy who was, like, *Hey, you know what?* Someone with a *hunch*. Anyway, Kurt wasn't saying—to himself or to anyone else—that he was da Vinci or anything, but he did have this hunch that people had been missing some key element of romantic love. He felt sure there was a way to decode our disorganized reactions to partnership, the way two people can make each other so tremendously happy at one point only to reach new depths of misery or boredom only years, weeks, or months later. And, yes, he had his personal reasons for wanting to put himself at the center of the study, but Yuri had suggested he do so, said this whole thing would be particularly healing to Kurt, but what he was really trying to do was help make a discovery that would help others, deeply alter the world.

And after years of thinking and theorizing and after months of planning and hiring and preparation—it was finally here, the first Relational Experiment held within his home. (For a while he had considered setting up a second apartment in which to run the GX, but Yuri had convinced him that having the GX in his home would be important to his healing.) He felt he was standing on a precipice, that he was witnessing himself begin what would become his legacy.

But it was a burden, as well, to make something this large. He'd woken at four that morning, wide-awake in the blacked-out bedroom wondering if what he wanted might be impossible. He knew, in some ways, that solving love was impossible, but the wanting of impossible things, the faith that the impossible could become possible, this was where change came from—he was sure. This was the whole point.

He shut his eyes, tried and failed to go back to sleep, his heart beating strangely in his chest. Somehow he felt that so much depended on this day, on making sure these first in-house Relational Experiments for the GX went well, and though he had the impulse to get up and make a note, he forced himself to remain in bed, to rest up for his work.

In a liminal state between sleeping and waking, memories of past love cued up in him, paraded by as if he were counting sheep. He'd fallen in love a few times, to various intensities, and he had seen the awful, horrible ways it could unravel—slow ends and sudden ones, that aching tapering off or a disastrous blaze. But how did he know, for sure, that any of these supposed loves had been actual love? How could a person measure this? Old love went blurry in memory, and looking back, trying to get a real count on how intensely he may have loved or whom or how many—he wasn't sure he could put anyone on that list.

He and Christy, his last real relationship, they'd had a nice few months together—steady and pleasant—but something had been missing the whole time and eventually he stopped calling her, and though he felt a little guilt over disappearing, it wasn't even guilt, just sadness over his not even *wanting* to call her. On paper she'd been perfect. How was it that off paper she was something else? But Camille—the first Camille, not the second one—well, that had to have been love, at least initially. In those first weeks they believed they had cracked some unseen code, found something that had long seemed to be a myth. But after some perceived slight, she lashed out at him, ranted about how she didn't have time for inconsistent men anymore—she really didn't—but she wasn't angry, she said (though she sounded furious), she was just sad, sad that she had mistaken Kurt for someone who understood himself enough to be kind.

Something about the way she spoke was a little too rehearsed, though, as if she reached this scene with any lover, and it made him wonder if she'd been enacting a script for their entire affair. Camille had always seemed more like a character than a real person—a little too perfect, a little too precisely the sort of woman he'd imagined himself with. Maybe it had never been what it had appeared to be. Anyway that was years ago now— four, five—he wasn't sure.

Staring into the bedroom's darkness, he tried to force himself to relax and stop indulging all this nostalgia, get another hour of sleep, but his mind wouldn't stop spinning. A year before Camille had been Melanie, five months that now felt a lifetime away. She was a few years older than him, an actress often described as a *formidable talent*, known for taking few interviews, for being recalcitrant and indifferent in the ones she did do, known for her graceful and brief acceptance speeches. Surprising even himself, Kurt bought a ring, booked a suite at her favorite hotel in the middle of the desert, proposed to her their first morning, still in bed. She said nothing, got up, put pants on, went topless to the patio to smoke.

You don't love me, she said. *You love the idea of me.*

He'd never seen her smoke before and noticed how she exhaled in a self-conscious, half-guilty way. She glanced down at the ring in his hand as if it were a plate she was waiting to be cleared from her table.

You can put that away, really. It's sweet of you to be so idealistic but this is just . . . this isn't that.

She was smarter than he was—he knew that, had always known that, had always loved that about her, but it meant she had more control of him, was able to leave him with such self-assured ease. He went over the girlfriends he'd had before Melanie—Sara, Martina, Jenny, Kate—each relationship marked by some kind of frenzied beginning and a long decline or a sudden souring. He thought all the way back to his first love or first maybe-love—Alyssa. He was sixteen, she was two years older, both of them fools. Spring of his sophomore year, her senior, they would make out endlessly, pressing against each other, faces mashed together for hours upon hours, but they never had sex, never even talked about it, and as he looked back as an adult, this baffled him—it wasn't a religious or a moral issue; all their friends were fucking each other; they had condoms from sex ed; her parents were never around. Hadn't they both been healthy teenagers? And didn't Kurt feel as if his body were dissolving when he was around her? He remembered shivering on a warm April day and she said when she was with him she felt as if she were standing at the edge of something high, how a body feels when it fears a fall, and sometimes they'd just stare at each other in a trance of feeling and at night they'd tie up their parents' phone lines by staying up for hours, listening to the other's breathing finally soften toward sleep. But if they had been in love, completely in love, wouldn't they have been unable to not have sex? Wouldn't it have been inevitable? It wasn't for lack of opportunity or attraction or hormones. They just hadn't. When Kurt lost his virginity to a college girl at a party a few months later—pretty, distant, inconsequential—he was mainly just relieved to have done it at all. Alyssa had graduated and gone off to Vassar and had probably already met someone else, he thought, and he felt oddly fine about that, too. He sent her one letter and she called him once or twice, when she'd heard his mom was sick, but that was all. So perhaps, he thought now, that whatever he felt with Alyssa was not a complete love—unless the sexlessness of their desire indicated a purity, a vapor-distilled, uncontaminated joy in the other's being, not some sort of procreative impulse or lust renamed devotion, but the real thing, a feeling that needed nothing.

After Alyssa there were others, but no one he'd been so content to just stare at. In those months his mother was in chemo he did kiss one girl—Nicola someone—but he had felt so troublingly empty that when she moaned, pulled him closer, put her hand in his back pocket, all he could do was remove her hand, back away, shake his head, and say he had to go. He remembered a brief look of sadness in her face but it faded and she returned to the birthday party they had ducked away from, and later he'd even seen her roller-skating, arms linked with another girl, laughing. He sat on a bench intentionally far away from all the other kids and brooded over a fountain soda until someone's mom came by and asked him if he wanted anything to eat and he could tell from the way she had looked at him that she knew about his mom. He said he was okay. She patted his shoulder and left. Why did he remember all this so clearly?

In his dark bedroom now, sun still hidden in the east, he indulged himself in dwelling. He always thought of that day at the skating rink as an important part of his mythology, a narrative he'd projected over all his sceneless, arcless days. He felt he could remember the exact thoughts he'd had while watching Nicola skate in circles, smiling, fine to be around these other people, lacking nothing. He remembered thinking that no one needed anyone in particular—that people just generally needed other people, but probably no one ever irrevocably needed someone above all else, and in realizing this, that no pair carried a patent on a feeling, Kurt feared he may have broken himself, that if he believed this idea, then he might have just vaccinated himself against ever being in love. And even if he did let himself be in love, he would always know that beneath any theater of romance he might perform would be this thought: I could be anyone else. She could be anyone else.

But he'd still managed to do it, hadn't he? Managed to fall in love a few times? Maybe he had. And maybe it had been best that summer with Alexi. He remembered time with her as always feeling easy and calm and their sex had always followed some innate choreography, while still feeling improvised and urgent. When their eyes met for the first time after an absence, it seemed every color around them grew brighter and sounds sharpened and their attention poured into each other as easily as smoke blending into the air.

That September it all vanished. Lots of people were breaking up then as everyone had been loudly reminded of their approaching death and reacted accordingly, quitting habits or starting habits, quitting jobs or people or versions of themselves, having realizations—anything to stop the suspicion that everything, *everything*, was completely outside one's control. Perhaps it was a helpful delusion to do what one could when faced with the enormity of how little one can really do. It was necessary to find a way to push against the world, to forget what was helpful to forget.

And forgetting, too, was necessary to falling in love, a drink from the river Lethe, all past love was renounced for the present.

Maybe this wasn't completely a delusion, but a form of evolution, that the brain might somehow be chemically altered by the experience of falling in love, and that any love that came after that love would have to be more enormous than the last in order to register in that chemically altered brain.

He resisted, again, getting out of bed to write this down or speak it into a recorder for Matheson, thinking if this thought was true, it would return.

But how did a person, how did a brain or a body, measure the old love against the new? Was there some inner barometer, some switch that had to be flipped? And if there was—and Kurt felt blindly sure there was—he wanted this barometer to be located and set, like a thermostat, to keep someone in love, to transform an unconscious activity into a conscious one.

Then, on that thought, as if on cue, the blinds and curtains of his bedroom began their automated opening with the sun's rise, light seeping in on Kurt, giving him the sense, the euphoric but delusional sense, that this was some clear sign to him.

Later that day, in the middle of his Relational Experiment with the Mundanity Girlfriend, Kurt stood at the large window and stared at the bridge, feeling the sensors on his body warming and cooling and warming again as he watched a single jogger making his way through the crowd of tourists. Shifting his focus, he caught Poppy's reflection in the glass. She lounged on the sofa on her belly, wearing the loose, neutral clothes the Research Division had determined appropriate. She read a magazine, her hair tied up in a knot. He felt comforted in her ambivalence toward him, this absent presence. At the thought of this his eyes flooded, though his face hardly moved, just flushed red. It startled him—he rarely cried—but here was this woman, a stranger he had never once exchanged a word with and would never speak a word to, whose merely being here seemed to have given him such a deep solace. And, true, you could say Kurt's actual connection to her was so shallow that it was nonexistent, but Kurt rejoiced and was moved by its meaninglessness, its total lack of complication.

Hours later, after the experiment was over and Poppy was gone, the researcher removing Kurt's sensors told him the Research Division had a short presentation to make about an important feature of these sensors, something they hadn't been able to tell him before and needed to explain to him immediately. A screen was pulled down, lights dimmed, a projector turned on, and another researcher appeared before it, cleared her throat, and began.

As you know, the long-held goal of the Research Division has been to optimize human emotions, to discover ways that we can use technology to better understand our decisions, our mistakes, to make the human mind and body healthier, more logical.

Kurt looked over his shoulder and realized the rest of the Research Division had gathered behind him, as if they were watching a movie together.

Now, we want to explain to you an extremely sophisticated and unparalleled feature of our sensors called Internal Directives.

A series of windows appeared on the screen: a small spreadsheet of digits changing and changing, the glowing green line of a cardiogram, a pie chart with slices that grew and shrank, what appeared to be an MRI of a brain, and a surveillance video of Kurt standing at the window just hours ago, staring at the bridge. His eyes went straight to the video, accustomed as he was to seeing himself on-screen, and he quickly concluded it was a good shot, well framed, his stance unaffected, natural—only then remembering this wasn't a film set but was part of his home, his experiment, his Research Division.

This, as it may be obvious, is the feed of information that you produced today, as measured by the sensors and cameras. As you already know, the data produced by each subject within a Relational Experiment is being collected and run through our analytic software, creating a nuanced portrait of yours and the girlfriends' physiology and mental temperament over a period of time under a given set of circumstances.

The researcher gestured to the screen.

For example, today you entered the Relational Experiment feeling rather peaceful, contemplative, though mildly underslept, just a little dehydrated, and occasionally distracted by a stray sexual thought—but on the whole, rather content. Would you agree?

I suppose so. He couldn't be sure what he felt. Exposed? Impressed? Glad that the Research Division's sensors could so easily capture him? He wondered what the sensors would have gathered now, had he been wearing them.

Now, suppose I could tell you, for absolute certain, that having even a passing sexual thought, even an unconscious fantasy in the back of your mind, suppose I could tell you that this was having a catastrophic effect on your creative output—

Is that what—

Just suppose that were true. I'm not saying it is, but just suppose it was. I'm only giving this example to prove a point and it in no way reflects our actual research.

One thing Kurt had asked the Research Division to focus on was whether there was some relationship between one's romantic and sexual life and one's creative output, as he'd long wondered if his inconsistent and unfulfilling relationships with women had been sapping his energy, stopping him from completing a full cut of *The Walk*.

What if I told you—it's very simple, Kurt, if you just stop thinking about sex unless you're actually having it, then your creative energy will be completely unhindered and within your control. Do you think you could do that very easily? Do you think anyone could?

Well— He noticed now that of all the women in the Research Division she was easily the most attractive, fortysomething and graceful, milky-brown hair to her shoulders glittered with whitish gray, but now that she was asking him to not think about sex, he was gripped with the image of kneeling at her feet, pushing up her lab coat, pulling her hips to his mouth . . . *Well, no, in fact, no, I don't think anyone would be able to do that.*

Exactly—controlling one's own mind is nearly impossible for most people. Yet even more basic, conscious tasks—exercising, eating well, remembering to drink water—people have such a problem doing even these things that are within their control, even when the benefits are obvious and often immediate. People, in fact, are the main thing that stop themselves from their own well-being, and circumventing this self-sabotage, we've decided, is the only way we can effect actual change in making the human experience more streamlined and harmonious.

All the data and images on the screen vanished and a different set of graphs and images took their place.

To this end we have developed a feature of the sensors called Internal Directives. Instead of merely recording the bio-information of a body wearing the sensors, Internal Directives allow us to transfer information into the body, telling it how to behave, which hormones or neurotransmitters to increase or decrease, shifting the body's vagal tone, raising or lowering the heart rate, and so forth.

It would take too long and frankly be too boring to explain precisely how Internal Directives work, but essentially it uses a series of something like electromagnetic pulses to send data into the body. Now, what we have here on the screen are the graphs measuring your Emotional Vulnerability Quotient, EVQ, during today's Relational Experiment with the Mundanity Girlfriend. Again, I can't completely explain the exact mathematical formula we use to calculate one's EVQ, but essentially we take all these different data points that your sensors are generating and run them through a complex algorithm that then gives us a measure of how willing or able a person is, in any given moment, to experience their surroundings and their internal state in a meaningful way. Essentially it's a measure of how closely you're paying attention to the outside world, your emotions, and the emotions of others.

The researcher turned on a laser pointer and aimed it at the graphs on the screen.

So, about midway through today's Relational Experiment we administered an Internal Directive to you intending to raise your EVQ. And you took to it quite well. You even teared up a bit, which you can see here—

She used a red laser pointer to circle a spike in one of the graphs.

She paused, looked at him in wait of some kind of reaction, but all he could do was squint at the screen. He tried to think of something to say, but just stammered, *So you . . .*

Right, we caused that to happen.

He could have felt angry, he knew, to have been marionetted like that, but he felt strangely fine about it. The researcher giving the presentation was still looking at him, waiting for something, but he couldn't think of anything to say, just shook his head and smiled, confused.

She continued, *Often the way a person treats someone they love is contaminated by past relationships or grudges or things they may have had little to no control in creating—the way they were raised, unconscious biases and behaviors, even the epigenetic effect of the quality of a person's grandparents' marriages as their parents were conceived. For most people, it's impossible to dismantle these unconscious behaviors and deeply embedded systems of logic, yet our intention with*

Internal Directives is to train a mind out of these unhelpful habits. Hence the example I gave you earlier about sexual thoughts—everyone has them of course, to a greater or lesser degree—but trying to not think of something as entrenched as sexual desire won't get you very far. By using Internal Directives, however, one would be able to decide how to spend their mental energy, to choose how to be.

Kurt looked over his shoulder again. Every member of the Research Division was looking at him, all with that same expression.

I realize you may have concerns, the researcher standing at the head of the room said as he turned back to face her, *about safety perhaps? Or the ethics of using such a technology on those who are not aware?*

And, yes, theoretically, Kurt understood there would have been ethical and safety concerns about such a thing—yet he felt no concern or worry. Even though he knew he had in some way been violated, he didn't *feel* violated. His unbothered state might have been a result of this thing that had already been used on him, but Kurt's calmness belonged to him completely and he couldn't manage to question it.

One of the not-twins rolled his office chair up to Kurt's left side and said, *We've been testing Internal Directives on ourselves for almost two years now.*

Kurt smiled at the not-twin, almost wanted to hug him. It was marvelous—wasn't it?—marvelous what they had discovered, what this could mean for the world.

Our intent, in its simplest terms—the not-twin lowered his voice to a firm whisper—*is to create a treatment that can allow people to feel what they want to feel and to not feel those feelings that are unhelpful to them. And though we hope that Internal Directives could be used as an alternative to psychotropic drugs or electroconvulsive therapy, this psychotechnology could also be useful to anyone who might like their life to be somehow improved, not just those with major mood disorders.*

The not-twin smiled at Kurt.

Feelings are a kind of energy, a kind of matter, the other not-twin said as he rolled his chair to Kurt's right. *They cannot be created or destroyed.*

True, the first not-twin said, *there's really no arguing with feeling, now is there? There's just repression or self-deception.*

Weren't Internal Directives then a kind of repression or deception? Kurt wondered distantly, but didn't ask. The researcher who had been leading the presentation was speaking again, telling him something about how they wouldn't use Internal Directives on Kurt as much as they'd use them on the girlfriends, but that it was important to the study for Kurt not to know when they were being used and when they were not being used. There were more graphs, more lasers pointed at different points of these graphs. Kurt kept listening to her for a while but everything had gone hazy in him. He excused himself for a nap, and this day blended into his dreams like years blended into a life, unseen but still felt, the line between memory and present always bleeding.

8

Ashley looked at her plate, large and white, a gallery for these lonely slivers of raw fish, so recently dead they still seemed a little alive, and being this close to this edge of life and death made her wonder which of the people in this restaurant, thousands of dollars in their mouths, had the fewest days left to live. She was wearing a dress someone else owned, these weird sensors hidden beneath it, and makeup someone had put on her face. So as she ate all this money, and knew her bank account held less than half what she owed this month, the invisible time limit everyone had, the wealth none could accrue, was the only thing that made her feel even with the people in this room. Ashley felt sure that she was the only diner in the restaurant who had mopped a floor in recent memory, though she wasn't sure what that fact indicated, if anything.

High above her head were massive light fixtures that looked

like jellyfish riddled with diamonds, and Kurt was still discussing the merits of unfiltered sake with the sommelier. The seriousness of their tone annoyed Ashley. It was fucking juice. A pinched ache moved across the sommelier's face, as if he knew so much about rice wine that it had become painful to him, that his knowledge created pressure in his skull. Ever so slightly, the jellyfish swayed.

This was Ashley's first public Relational Experiment, during which she was supposed to seem unanimously interested in everything Kurt said for the first hour of the date, then to turn slightly sour, to insist nothing was wrong when he asked what was wrong, but to begin subtly undermining everything he said, then to berate him for how long he was taking to finish *The Walk*, storm out before the dinner was through, wait in the backseat of his town car, slap him when he got in, let a tense silence grow between them before wordlessly getting out of the car, hailing a cab, and disappearing into the night.

At her apartment and looking back on the evening, she'd been surprised by how easy it had been, that one night's work had earned her as much money as she could make in a week of good tips—more than a few sessions with her trainer.

Slapping Kurt had felt less ridiculous and happened more intuitively than she'd expected, and as they sat there breathing heavily for the required twenty seconds of silence, she felt the same elation she had after a good fight, the sensation that her body somehow contained additional bodies. There is likely a way to explain this feeling from afar—the activation of certain neurotransmitters or a chug of adrenaline—but from the inside it was mythic, as unmistakable as it was addictive, that sense of being more than she was.

The *omakase*'s foams and drizzles had left her hungry, so

a can-shaped congeal of chicken soup softened in the pot while she watched one of her favorite fights between Kit Kimberly and Shauna Matthews on her GX phone—she'd never had one of those things before—playing and replaying as Kit's left hook took Shauna down. On the fifth or sixth loop a text came in from Matheson—the Research Division was pleased with how the assignment had gone, her activity patterns had been promising, and her next assignment would be written and sent tomorrow.

She played the fight again, and once more, and drank the soup without tasting it. That night she dreamed of her father, Omar, sitting on the high branch of a tree, his skin, for some reason, light purple. It had been years since she'd dreamed of him. He said he was sorry and asked her if she knew why. She did and said she did, then they sat there silently for a while, letting the unsaid expand between them. Then he asked her about her training schedule, and everything was mundane for a while, as dreams sometimes become—even the unconscious mind wants a little routine. He abruptly climbed down the tree, and though Ashley was aware it was her dream to control, she let him go. She woke to a silent room, morning light coming in at a serious angle.

Any day now, Omar used to tell her, *any day now we're going to get a call that'll change everything. We don't belong in this place. You'll see.*

But they never did see. Her mother had been a slightly successful model in São Paulo, but no one in New York seemed to care. Luisa was told she had a commercial look but she never got any commercials except that one for an ESL school that paid in a course she didn't want to take. Omar had been a boxer who'd had a strong beginning to his career but had never rebounded after breaking his leg in a fall (he would never say drunken fall, but it was a semi-drunken fall) down the subway stairs at Eighty-Sixth Street. The only calls they got were from bill collectors or telemarketers or Luisa's mother or sister back in Brazil, family Ashley couldn't remember having ever met, their voices a little familiar but less so with every passing year.

How Omar and Luisa got together was a long story, one Luisa always recalled in Portuguese, as if the memory couldn't be translated. Omar told it in the same clichés—how he *just knew she was the one* and how *she was the most beautiful woman* he'd ever seen. Their native tongues were different, and even now, decades later, Ashley still wonders if this is the reason that their love seemed to persist so much longer than the average couple's—that having a language barrier set a realistic expectation, that they might never completely understand each other. The unknowable, perhaps, had kept them together. But other times Ashley remembered the nervous way her mother would stare at Omar, the same way those tiny dogs look at their owners, a fearful love.

Their one-and-a-half-bedroom in the East Bronx was supposed to be the starter apartment for the young family, *just until things take off*, her father said, but the longer they were *temporarily* there the clearer it became that the temporary had become the forever. Omar kept their hope alive by pointing to certain cars and saying, *That's the one we're going to get*, and Luisa kept the Sunday paper's real estate section on the kitchen table all week, but then Omar spent most of their savings on a used Lexus, and when he drove up outside their crumbling apartment, Luisa quivered for a minute before cursing him. She just didn't understand, Omar said. You had to appear to be whomever you were *trying* to be.

We're going for a drive, he told them, *get in the car. We're going*.

They drove around Rye that afternoon, looking at all the massive and pristine houses from the car.

Nice family, nice car, and one of these days a nice neighborhood like this one, a nice house, a pool. You've always wanted a pool, haven't you, Lu?

Luisa wept steadily and quietly in the backseat. Ashley was seven and just happy to sit shotgun. *Your mother worries too much,* Omar whispered, but eventually he sold the car and stopped talking about leaving their neighborhood and even stopped praying for it at Sunday mass. *It's nice here,* he said.

By then Ashley had grown into a teenage beauty that left a trail of craned necks, and since being grabbed on the bus and subway, she'd taken an interest in the fine art of beating the shit out of people. Luisa had suggested modeling classes instead, but Ashley was tired of people looking at her. Omar thought the headshots and everything would be too expensive anyway, and she could train for free at the gym where he coached. It put him at ease to teach Ashley how to defend herself since he and her mother sometimes had to leave her alone to work longer hours. The older she got, the more beautiful she became, and though she tried to hide herself in jerseys and baggy pants, there was no hiding her face, no getting out of her body.

Sweat drenched after her training, waiting for her dad to finish with a client, she met Jason, and though she usually didn't talk to guys she didn't know, he got past her filter somehow—he didn't have that knowing smile, that unhidden agenda, when he looked at her. Smiley, white, well dressed. *Maybe he's gay,* she thought, and this thought warmed her, gave her permission to talk easily with him. He was almost eighteen and in acting school and soon he was going to get an agent and everything. He didn't ask anything of her, just talked and talked. He'd just gotten this award that meant he got to meet with some famous actor. *Sort of like a coach,* he said, *because being famous is tough, you know. You got to have someone show you how to do it.*

He wasn't exactly in acting school but in a mandatory pro-gram as part of his juvenile probation after he busted in that kid's head at the foster home where he'd lived since he was thirteen. His behavior had been good for the last two years, and compared to that of the other students, his acting was almost promising, so he'd been picked for this mentorship program for teenagers with a juvenile offense. But he abbreviated the story: acting school.

When he asked her how she got into boxing, she said it was her dad's idea, nodding to Omar, who was tossing a medicine ball at one of his trainees, who did agonized crunches with the weight—a soft-bellied banker who still had a *Rocky* poster tacked up in his living room.

That's your dad?

Omar. He's a coach. Only then did she realize she wanted to seem parentless to Jason, without or beyond an origin.

Will your dad beat me up if I ask for your number?

She wrote it down, smiling, feeling somehow significant and uncomfortable, a nervousness that stiffened her face.

They started meeting after the gym. He said he liked to see her all sweaty in those baggy clothes, that she was beautiful no matter what she wore, and though she had come to hate that word—*beautiful*, what strangers hissed at her on the street—hearing it from Jason gave it a purpose. She had only kissed two boys, that guy Brandon (last winter after the first and only school dance she'd ever gone to) and Tracy Simpson's older brother the summer she was twelve and he was seventeen, and though she wanted to replace these memories with something better, she had not exactly been looking forward to it. Her father's only advice had come two years ago—*The boys, they're all trying to get the same thing*—which she already knew much better than he did.

She kept her meetings with Jason secret and brief, at first reluctant to even let him touch her waist while they kissed, not even entirely sure she enjoyed it but curious, looking for something in it. He was both annoyed and pleased by her modesty, said a lesser girl would have put out by now, said he could wait *his whole life* for her. But Ashley wasn't looking for her whole life and didn't think of Jason as someone who meant *everything* to her, the way she'd heard other girls talk about their boyfriends. But he was something. He was enough. All the cliques at school had reset with puberty and she'd been left out, her silence and good looks seen as stuck-up and bitchy. Jason, her only friend, gave some continuity to her days.

On nights her dad was out of town for a tournament and her mother had the night shift, Ashley would spend the night at the apartment in East Harlem where Jason lived with his cousin. Half the time a handful of other guys hung out in the living room. Ashley hated the way their presence changed Jason—his voice lowered, he grabbed her ass in front of them, said stupid shit to sound tough, and sometimes he got stoned and sometimes he got a little drunk and sometimes he'd try too much with her even though it had only been two months, but he kept saying, *It's been two month*s, as if that were the longest time that anyone had ever waited for anything ever.

One night he was already half-drunk when she got there and something about the way Jason looked at her told her to leave, but she didn't. She watched him and his friends play a video game, and two of them were jumpy and strange and Jason's cousin would not stop laughing this constant and terrifying laughter that went on and on, even after the games were over and the jumpy guys had jittered away. After everyone had gone, Jason picked Ashley up and carried her to his bedroom and tossed her on the bed, which seemed like a joke so she smiled, even as he pinned both her hands down, even as he wouldn't look her in the eye. Soon it didn't seem like a joke anymore (the pitch of the cousin's laughter cutting through the walls) and soon her dress was pushed up—a dress Jason had bought for her, a fitted basketball jersey—and everything was still for a moment, a half second she later scrutinized, wondering if that was the moment she could have done something—the moment she realized he was not kidding as he held her still and not kidding when he forced himself inside her, his hand smashed over her mouth, and she went as still as she'd been as a child during hide-and-seek (if she couldn't be found, she couldn't be hurt) and she could still hear the cousin's stringy laughter in the other room but nothing felt funny, nothing had ever been funny in her life. He rolled off and she tried to hold it together, tried to be tough, tried to put all her anger into her clenched jaw—this was nothing, this meant nothing, he was nothing, meant nothing—but she couldn't stop herself from crying.

Don't be one of those girls, acting like you don't want it. I know what you want. You've been begging me for this all week.

To this her eyes went hard and dry. She stood slow, felt a warm trickle down her thigh. Something of his was in her now, something of his terribleness. She leaned over and hooked him in the jaw, but he reacted faster than she expected, jumping up and pushing her down, smacking her skull against the bedside table, a water glass smashing off, spilling and breaking, and he got his face close to hers, held her arms down with his knees.

Don't you ever— He didn't finish the sentence, just slapped her hard in the face, and she spit in his eye and he slapped her again.

You like it, it's not my fault you've been begging me to get fucked like that.

He made her sleep on the floor but she didn't sleep and in the morning he locked her in his room from the outside so she pulled out his AC, climbed down the fire escape, dangled from the ladder, and dropped herself into a bush. When she found the dank alleyway out of the courtyard, she started running, slowly at first, floating, keeping something at her center solid and still. She weaved through the bodies on the sidewalks, dashed past bodies sitting on stoops. She ran past a group of boys her age who whistled and she was angry that they didn't know what had happened to her though she didn't want them to know what had happened to her, and she felt vaguely afraid of them and she felt angry that she was afraid of them and sorry for that fear, then angry again, angry as the city woke up, as the streets became full and loud. She was furious at mothers pushing strollers and at children swarming the playgrounds, and even more furious at men in cars, all the men in trucks and cabs, all the men in all that metal filling the streets with danger and the air with sickness. As she neared her home, she felt the cartilage and tendons knotted in her knees, a throbbing low in her back. She felt the pavement jolting through these flimsy little sneakers, felt sweat making that terrible dress stick to her body.

Her apartment was dim and silent (Luisa was sleeping off her overnight shift and Omar was still out of town) and Ashley moved quietly through it, keeping the lights off, stepping lightly. She took a shower, threw up on her feet. She opened her mouth to the shower stream, swallowed scalding water, her body hot and nauseated and hungry and repulsed. With her hair still wet she took a twenty from the emergency cash and went a few blocks over to the cheap, bad restaurant pretending to be a good restaurant. She ordered a steak and sat in a barrel-backed stool with her legs splayed open under the bar, taking up all the room she could. She went at that steak feeling that if she could destroy it, she could destroy everything that had happened, destroy that moment she had had a chance to say something but said nothing, destroy the memory of his face above her, conquer all of it, be done with it, be fine. A man at the other end of the bar was nursing a beer and watching her from over the edge of a newspaper.

What? she shouted at him.

He lowered his paper. Smiled at her.

What do you want? she said, louder, and she didn't recognize this voice, lower now, more of her body in it, more powerful.

You like that steak, sweetie?

Without thinking she cut a piece and flung it at him. It hit his chest and landed on the paper, making a puddle of grease, and he smiled at Ashley, but she wasn't looking. He watched her the way adults watch children, entertained by what they think is naïveté, and it seemed to Ashley that boys grew up to be men, but girls just stayed girls as long as the whole world agreed to treat them this way, liabilities, precious objects, things to be protected or told what to do. Omar had once taken the neighbor's kid to a parking lot to teach him how to drive, and even though that boy was two years younger than Ashley, Omar wouldn't let her try, said she didn't need to know, because not even her father's love could override that when he looked at a boy, he could see the man he would become, but when he looked at Ashley, he still saw the little girl she'd been.

She ate all the meat. And the pale chunk of broccoli, still part raw. And the potato with all the sour cream and butter, skin and all.

9

Ed's office was dark when Mary arrived, the door slightly ajar. She knocked, pushed the door open, saw Ed propped on a *zafu* facing the altar in the corner. He made no signal that he'd heard her, but she knew that he knew she was there, knew he was inviting her in. She closed the door. The faint light from the waiting room vanished and the dark hardened around her, broken only by a warm pool of candlelight before Ed.

Sit, he said, and she knew where to sit. He remained facing the corner. She knew he meant for her to sit on the plain wooden chair in the corner opposite him. But how did she know? She knew this so completely, so assuredly, that she did not even ask herself how she could know, didn't even notice how she didn't have to ask herself the question of how she knew. And Ed may not even have said the word *sit* aloud. He might have said nothing. There might have been another sense, another kind of conveyance between them now.

They were silent, minutes that accordioned into years, and at some point Mary became aware she was lying on her back on the table, her clothes folded into a neat stack atop the chair, though she didn't remember the actions between sitting and lying. She felt she was falling and rising at the same time, as if water or air were rushing both up and down her body, or that gravity and a lack of gravity were acting on her at once. Though she thought she could hear some music, she couldn't tell whether it was a recording or an instrument Ed was playing or whether it was possibly emanating from inside her, that somehow her body had become an antenna. She knew she did not need to say anything. It seemed each pore on her body had become a mouth and was breathing in great gasps, and this breathing covered her, and she felt it in her face, in the spaces between her fingers, the heavy skin along her thighs, papery backs of hands, soft lobes, all of it. Her eyes went watery and loose behind the lids.

Ed draped a thin, white sheet over her body to the chin, and only then did she realize she didn't have on the usual shorts and bra, that she was bare in the solid darkness, and she sensed Ed was unclothed, too, though she couldn't see him.

We will do something very large today, he said. *A surgery. We know you are ready for this, though it is also impossible to be ready.*

A tremendous silence overtook both of them, and one candle extinguished itself and another flame doubled its light.

Mary felt Ed's body had gone back to the altar, but she also felt two heavy hands pressing her shoulders flat against the table. Some intangible thing began to fill her, beginning as a coldness in the fingertips and toes, warming as it moved up her limbs, hot as it met her chest, then filling the space between her body and the part of her—the part of anyone—that is not a part of the body. Pushed from herself, the boundaries that held her from the world were broken and her skin seemed to uncoil, spooling out around the room. Language vanished. Any comprehension of suffering or desire vanished. Her memories vanished. Her life meant nothing. And there was no peace like this, being unaware, even, of the idea of peace. This cold wave, this force—it began to multiply, became a small crowd of something like ghosts, working within her as she was supine in her own periphery, watching. These ghosts, it seemed, were her ghosts. They belonged to her. They had already lived her life and died for her. They carried her. They ate her like termites. They fed her dreams and she dissolved into them, saw an island with a rocky coast, saw herself as a child, saw her eyes made of polished silver, her hair tangled with kelp, neck deep in an ocean. She saw a man lighting and extinguishing matches in a pitch-dark room, his face appearing and vanishing, appearing and vanishing again.

Then she returned to her body. She felt she was crying but there were no tears. She felt as if she were bleeding light, that her blood had been replaced by an endless supply of light and it flooded the room. A home had been created where there had been a homelessness and all at once it became clear, like finding lucidity in a dream, that this loss of herself was so simple, that it was the purest form of love, both visceral and transcendent, and it shook within her like a kind of sex with nothing, sex without a body, sex without sex, an unbodied love that reached far beyond the *I love you* and the *I love you, too*, a love that was pure nothing, erasure, completion, a joining, a god, the only reason anyone breathes.

She woke up wrapped in a sheet damp and sweet-smelling, her lungs aching and her heart beating slow, as if they had been forced to end and rebegin. All the candles had burned out. The room was silent and so dark. Ed was there, she could feel him somewhere in the room but she didn't know where. Her legs were sore. Her arms were so heavy. There was a memory, slipping from her like a dream at daybreak, of Ed ripping her body apart, of his telling her there was no such thing as anything and that she could destroy and remake herself, destroy and remake herself or just remain destroyed, that there was great power in being destroyed, that her debt meant nothing, her past meant nothing, she was free to live in this world in whatever way she could, that she owed no one anything, that no one owed her anything, that all was uncertain and there was great darkness and great light and no such thing as people. She might have fallen asleep again or this might have all been some kind of dream, too, levels of a dream, layers of places and times she was slipping into or from.

Eventually she was Mary again. Mary in a body. Mary living in Mary's body in Mary's clothes, and Ed became Ed again. He was lying on the floor in front of her; she was sitting in the plain wooden chair again. She looked down at Ed's body, only now noticing the pale freckles that cloaked him. He had cut his hair, and though it was unevenly done, it followed a sort of logic, like a plant. His mouth was thin and wide, his forehead short, his eyes small and shaped in a way that made his kindness clear, unmissable. She looked at his eyelids, little flaps of skin we depend on for darkness, for sleep, for remaining alive. She had an impulse, almost, to touch them, to lean over him and touch his eyelids, those little veils. He held a small black stone in one hand, and a clear crystal hung on a chain above his heart. She did not touch him; she did not need to touch him. They were already one thing, she knew, and the empty space between their bodies was filled with a substance that cannot be named, a substance that was not a substance, not material nor immaterial, invisible yet undeniable. It was only love, she knew, but it was also larger than that, something that had always been, would always be, not love for a person but love without people. He sat up suddenly, eyes still shut, and sang a song in a language she didn't understand.

Later, on the street the world regreeted her with its usual ambivalence but also, it seemed, an acceptance of how she'd been changed. She walked to that small, neglected park nearby, sat on a bench, lowered her gaze to her knees. Being among all these bodies rushing around—all so urgent over money to make or spend—made her feel even slower and slower still, a stoned feeling or the feeling of being a stone.

When she looked up again, after some time, she saw two familiar forms, a woman and a man she recognized from her neighborhood, on the bench across the park from her. The woman's head was bent into the crook of the man's neck, the two of them warming each other like cats. Her hair could no longer be untangled, and she wore dirty sneakers coming apart at the seams. The man wore a navy uniform and was freckled like Ed with a wild clot of dark hair. Their little smiles had a secrecy and she could feel the tenderness between them radiating, a palpable and encompassing heat. Mary had often seen these two embracing on street curbs, in doorways, under awnings. They always seemed to be saying hello or goodbye, but when she looked at them now, she could see that they could never really leave each other, that they were always in that love.

And she knew now that what they had, she had it, too, only she had it alone somehow. It was clear then, so painfully clear, that people fell in love to find something in themselves that they'd had all along.

10

Mary stood in the large white room, beneath high ceilings. Whatever had changed during yesterday's work with Ed still felt palpable and large. Time had slowed. She felt every molecule she pulled into her lungs, felt she could almost count them. She stood at the window, watched a ferry ripple through the river. Speaking felt impossible, as contained and enclosed as she was, a longing that went on loop, a longing for nothing at all.

But the script for today's Relational Experiment would require her to speak. She wasn't sure what she would say, whether she could say anything, or whether Kurt would be able to see that even in just the few days since they'd met, she'd been irrevocably changed. Had it shifted the meat in her face, reformed the bones? Had it removed something or installed something in her eyes? She felt sure it must have done something visible, changed her in some undeniable way, only she couldn't get far enough from herself to know what it was.

She heard steps approaching and saw a hazy reflection of Kurt in the window. She turned to see him, walked toward him as she'd been instructed, smiled as instructed, put her arms around him and let him put his arms around her. He touched her face, stroked her hair not unlike how a person might stroke a cat, firm and methodical.

He was already talking as they sat, beginning the Personal History and Opinion Sharing Relational Experiment. She didn't feel any of the awkwardness she'd felt at the Savant House, but it had been replaced by a sense of being near and far from herself, as if she had just moved into a new home, and everything was still hidden in boxes.

Kurt sat in front of her. Kurt's mouth moved. Kurt's voice told stories he wanted her to hear. There were his eyes meeting her eyes. There was his hand reaching out sometimes to hold her hand. All she could do was be kind to him. Kindness would be her only compass in getting through these sessions, these alien rituals, acting out a feeling she didn't have and didn't want to have.

Did she know, he asked, that this building used to be a lampshade factory?

He seemed thrilled by this and she couldn't understand why. She wondered if her face was reflecting his in the correct way. She tried to concentrate on the protocols and rubrics she'd memorized, but they all felt misplaced. *Be kind*, she thought, *just be kind*.

When he'd bought the building, he said, it was totally decrepit, and all these reams of fabric were leaning in the stairwells, deteriorating. Production had stopped in the seventies, and the building's owner had converted it into artists' studios, with cheap, thin walls turning each floor into a dozen crumbling units, which some people started living in full-time as their art careers floundered. But Kurt hadn't realized this—he hadn't been told there were tenants—so when he began renovations, he didn't know he was evicting people not just from their studios but from their homes, and unfortunately someone at the *Observer* found out that a few of these displaced artists were now on the streets, and in an unfortunate coincidence Kurt's latest film, *Trains*, featured him as a rail-hopping, green-haired gutter punk named Pitt. And though Kurt never directly and publicly responded to the artist eviction thing, he did feel kind of bad about it, so he spent the guilt on volunteering his name to a housing nonprofit, making an appearance, signing a check, and giving a heartfelt speech at a benefit gala.

(Mary tried to listen to him as if she were reading a book, the way she dropped out of herself, displaced.)

But the more Kurt thought about his donations to the housing nonprofit, he told her, the more he worried that it wasn't enough, because his mother had told him years ago, just before she died, that the only way to stay sane on this earth was to make it your priority to care for others. That otherwise you'd go crazy and cold. And maybe, Kurt said he thought back then, maybe he *was* going crazy and cold. All he thought of at the time were the renovations and tile choices and lighting fixtures and all kinds of marble. These are the sorts of concerns, he said he thought at the time, that might make a person truly go crazy and cold, and around that time he was asked to volunteer for New Stage, a mentorship program that paired at-risk youth with professional actors. Though Kurt had barely talked to a kid since he'd stopped being one, he said he would do it, be that person who could care for others, be that mentor actor to these kids.

(Mary remembered what Ed had told her just before she left his office—that she would need to be careful, that she might have too great of an effect on people, might draw them closer to her than she intended—but she was uncertain if she was re-membering him saying this or if he was somehow speaking to her now, whispering this into her head from far away.)

One kid had stuck out to Kurt as potentially talented, though Jason was also the only white kid in the program and Kurt felt weird about giving him any extra attention, though Kurt was genuinely sure (or almost genuinely sure) that he wasn't being subconsciously racially biased, that he was responding to what he thought was genuine talent, a capacity. After Kurt stopped vol-unteering for New Stage, he and Jason kept up infrequently, some-times just phone calls but other times over an expensive lunch, Kurt thinking highly of himself for fulfilling his mother's ask, for having found a way to care for someone else. At times it seemed his mentoring hadn't done so much for Jason, whose career suf-fered endless near misses, making Kurt wonder if he'd either mis-judged Jason's talent or been ineffective in his help. Maybe Jason would have thrived with someone different, someone better, a Clooney or Damon, one of those actors who impressed people by being *people*. No one ever talked or wrote about Kurt in that way. He believed that people respected him as an actor and artist, but he wasn't *beloved*, and it bothered him, and it bothered him that it bothered him. Then Jason started to get a few roles, commer-cials, a few TV parts, and for years it seemed that he was on the perpetual edge of a breakout. Anticipating that he would soon be genuinely proud of his protégé, Kurt started inviting him to the occasional party he held at the loft, until the third one, when Jason brought some blow, not at all unusual for the crowd, but it unnerved Kurt, seemed like a warning sign of Jason's impending failure (though when Kurt's rich, famous friends got high, it was just a symptom of their success). Jason, his face bulging, his hands fluttering, told Kurt he couldn't wait until people bothered him in the street, until he got recognized anywhere he went, until it was difficult, really fucking difficult, to go out in public. Jason had chewed a cocktail straw into splinters and he inhaled and coughed up a shard.

You want it to be difficult, Kurt said, *to go somewhere? You want to live in that kind of prison?*

Prison! Prison! You're gonna talk to me *about prison?*

Jason wasn't angry, but he was shouting, eyelids stretched taut. He laughed, slapped his leg, took Kurt's face in his hands, and kissed him on the lips.

Ha! Prison. I'm not getting locked up, motherfucker. People are going to know me. People are going to know who I am.

And as Kurt reached this line of the story, he was struck by the softness of Mary's gray eyes, how she looked at him like she knew him already, knew him deeply, knew a part of him that even he didn't know. This, he realized, was why he had been telling her about Jason, about Jason's desire to be known. It was a way of telling her that he felt she knew him in a way he didn't even know himself yet. No one, it seemed, really understood how terrible it was to feel unknown beneath a costume of being known, and this was why it hurt so much to see Jason begin to suffer from a desire that Kurt knew so well, only from the other side.

(And as he said all this to Mary, he felt some kind of dawn breaking in him, his thoughts moving with a new agility. Tears gathered as he looked at her, so placid and plain. He was sure she had done something to him, something dangerous and necessary.)

They'd fallen more or less out of touch, Kurt and Jason, but Kurt still thought of him often and still had this old photograph of them hanging in his office—a reminder of how Kurt had perhaps failed in some ways and succeeded in other ways of trying to care for someone. When he saw that photo, Kurt sometimes wondered if Jason would ever find the fame he'd wanted, though

Kurt knew it would have solved nothing, just reframed the problem, as all successes or failures do.

They continued this Personal History and Opinion Sharing Relational Experiment for another two hours, alternately speaking and listening, and though Mary was mentally distant from Kurt, he felt that she was with him, completely. She still met all her cues, recited her lines, followed protocols, and it was unclear to her if she was just impersonating affection, or if this impersonation had changed her from within, synthesized a kind of love in her.

Kurt told a long story about going on a whale-watching trip on a boat with his mother when he was a child, during which they saw no whales but it was the most relaxed he'd ever seen or would ever see her, and as he told this story, his voice began to rush, as if he and Mary only had a minute left together, though they still had plenty. He remembered that she'd bought him an ice cream cone beforehand, then leaned over to bite a chunk out of it while snarling like an animal so that he would laugh, and he couldn't stop laughing and his laughing made her laugh so much that people waiting on the boat turned to stare so she held him close to her, tried to squeeze themselves quiet again. He remembered how she had her hair wrapped in a scarf with little red flowers, and a man in a corduroy jacket had kept trying to talk to her, and when this man, in what seemed like a last-ditch effort to charm her, called her beautiful, she smiled a go-away smile and told him she was with her son. A person may never be loved more than he was that afternoon.

As Kurt told her this memory, he held Mary's hand with both his hands, and when it was over, she noticed how his eyes were low and scattered, troubled, as if he hadn't meant to tell this story. He asked her to tell him something like that, tell him about a day she'd live again if given the chance.

(Immediately she thought of but didn't tell him about one of the first days she and Paul spent together, meeting in Bryant Park, finding two hundred dollars of rubber-banded twenties in the street, which they immediately spent on an elaborate dinner. She'd never felt a desire as strong and mysterious as she had for him then, her body a constant flutter, always near fainting, but she didn't tell Kurt this story because she couldn't tell him this story, not really. Past love is as good as a past dream, intangible, impossible to share.)

She told Kurt about a day she'd spent alone on a beach in Majorca, how the ocean was the perfect temperature and the sand was silky and no one spoke to her. She felt so calm, nearly nonexistent, all day till sunset, light fading into oranges and pinks so surreal she wondered if this could even be the world. Near her two women dozed on their backs, careless and half-naked, and it seemed most of the bodies around her were exposed and asleep. But then some shouting in Spanish broke the silence, which Mary ignored at first, since it seemed joyful or drunk, but soon it was clear that someone was drowning and four or five men were running into the water, diving, swimming, shouting, and soon a body was being brought out, limp and small, a child, a woman, she couldn't tell. One man hunched over it, breathing into it, until this body removed the ocean from itself, began again.

Mary told Kurt this story as she had been instructed—by speaking steadily with unbroken eye contact, not censoring herself, not allowing herself to labor over which details to include and which to leave out—but the moment she stopped speaking, she was overcome with all that was happening all at once, everywhere—a man quietly sobbing in the shower, a woman screaming through childbirth, a child happily caking himself in mud, and lovers in airports dropping their bags to embrace each other, and men being shot in the gut, and girls combing one another's hair in the dusty towns, preening in cracked mirrors, and two people could be sitting in an empty church in some large city, unnoticed, holding hands, ungoverned by the idea of God but still reverent with each other as two red cardinals flew in circles just beyond the stained glass—and how could Mary, how could anyone, go on doing anything when you could feel all this happening, out of sight, out of earshot, but happening all the same, happening to someone, someone you could have loved, someone you did love, someone you love still, deeply, without thinking.

Kurt noticed that something large and meaningful was going on beneath Mary's eyes, and he claimed that significance, believed himself to be her mover, fell into a sort of love with the version of her that he chose to see. He didn't question his feelings for Mary in this moment, didn't wonder what Internal Directives might be coursing through his sensors or hers. Later Kurt would pore over the reports, try to understand exactly what happened to him that day, but in the warm center of this feeling, there was no explaining it. He never found out if the Research Division had been using Internal Directives on him, but even if he found out they'd caused the feeling he had that day, it wouldn't have mattered. The feeling was his. It had happened.

After her compartmentalization protocol, Mary declined the car service and walked back to the train, lost in useless thoughts of Paul (What had they had together and how real had it been?), when she noticed a window a few floors up a building, light glowing through thin curtains. From that low angle she could see a fragment of a life—a framed photograph, a hanging plant, a figure walking by—and she ached for the unscheduled feelings and random lives that person might have had.

11

In the loft that night, Kurt felt idle and restless, sent Matheson and the Research Division home early and put on an old album by instinct. The third song stilled him, forced him to sit and do nothing but listen, something he'd rarely done since he was a teenager, when music had meant much more to him than it did now. How was it that this song—a woman and a guitar, half morose and hopeless, half romantic and hopeful—had broken through to him? When it ended, he played it again, then again, indulging himself.

Thoughts of Mary circled him. She paced in his head. This whole situation was perplexing, disruptive.

Was it that simple? That if you sat with someone for long enough, told them enough stories, that if you looked at them and they looked at you, then this feeling could occur? She wasn't beautiful, or at least not in a way that he found beautiful, but there was, Kurt thought, something beautiful *about* her. Maybe beauty had been part of the problem all along. So often love began in the visible. Maybe that was always the beginning of the end. Because what use did a person's beauty offer another? It was a signifier of the genes, sure, a suggestion of procreative abilities, but beyond that—what could it add to the time spent with that person, especially when procreation wasn't the goal? Some kind of mutual desire was important to a relationship, and this desire so often came from one's instinctual response to the aesthetic beauty of the other, but within any sexual encounter, the attractiveness of either lover served no purpose. The body of the other became a collage of sensation and shape, an invisible composite of both bodies feeling and being felt, sensed but not seen, eyes held shut to sink into feeling. And yes, the path leading to the moment two people became lovers was often a pageantry of appearances, but sex itself was not a primarily visual experience, and Kurt felt sure, considering it now, that the pageantry of seduction was the first place people went wrong in choosing what they thought was love. Love at first sight, that lie, a confusion of lust and aesthetics with something deeper.

As the song ended its fourth repeat, Kurt resisted playing it again. He felt he was sitting in Mary's gaze, that faraway peace, and the thought of her compelled him to his editing room to work. Launching the GX had been draining, and though he kept his regular working hours on *The Walk*, those afternoons had been going badly. He'd been making decisions in circles, deciding something only to undecide hours later, a cycle of sabotage that had been going on for a year, since he had impulsively and somewhat accidentally broken his self-imposed rule of not watching any films until he was done working (the practice, he'd been told, of a certain award-laden editor).

He blamed this misstep on an aspiring actress he'd met at a

party who had never seen *8½* (*A crime*, he said), but midway through screening the film Kurt realized his error and jumped from his chair. The actress asked if he was okay, but Kurt insisted everything was fine and she should keep watching, that it was *a fucking perfect work of fucking art*, that Fellini had *just enough self-awareness to complicate traditional filmmaking and enough cultural isolation to preserve his aesthetic vision*, and Kurt was overcome with a certainty that no one would ever make a film anywhere near the brilliance of *8½*, that we all knew too much now, had seen too much now, and everything was lost, hopeless.

The actress noticed the struggle between Kurt's eyes and skull as he spoke, as if his sockets had to somehow clench to stop his eyes from bulging out. She watched the rest of the film alone—at first a little rattled and antsy, then overtaken by the film's dreamy beauty—while Kurt went to his editing room to delete his most recent cut of *The Walk*. Then he found and deleted the raw footage, then the second and third backups, and he wept in anger until he realized that Matheson had a fourth backup at his place, then he wept harder and more pathetically because he realized he didn't have the nerve to delete those files, that he had to make something from the years of imperfect work he'd already put into it, the life he was wasting on subpar art. And he knew it would be inferior to the sort of work that outlived its maker and he knew he would have to live with that, that he had no easy way to bridge the distance between what he wished he could make and whatever he'd made so far. All he could do was salvage the scraps, finish it, and move on—though even that was proving impossible. It had been *years*. He didn't like to think of how many.

But that actress (he couldn't remember her name now) had been contaminated with her awe of *8½* and wouldn't stop talking about it even after Kurt tried twice to change the subject.

What was it he said . . . ? she asked. *No, I remember, he said,* I have nothing to say, but I still want to say it. *I loved that part! It's like acting, sort of, that I really want to say something but I want someone else to tell me what to say, you know?*

She went on like that for a while until Kurt said, *Let's call you a car,* and he noticed a look of momentary confusion in her face, then a visible calculation over whether she wanted to leave without having the sex they had both assumed would happen, then a look of relief when she realized she'd actually gotten the intimacy she wanted, a little late-night attention for being alive, and for a few minutes they talked about almost literally nothing (a rumor about a casting director they both knew), before she took the elevator down. He never saw her again. He called Matheson immediately to say that it had just occurred to him that the inconsistency of his sexual and romantic life was probably the real culprit of his constantly derailed creative process, an idea that eventually led to the GX.

He had tried to explain his theory of the relationship between the creative and the romantic to the Intellectual Girlfriend, but he could tell from the way she looked at him (always a yawn in her eyes) that she didn't believe or adequately understand what he was saying. Thoughts of Mary flashed like spliced film—her relaxed gaze, the sense he had that she understood him so clearly—and surely, he thought, surely there must be a way to measure and prove and replicate that feeling he had with Mary, to make it occur at will between people.

The Intellectual Girlfriend, though—perhaps she was *too* intellectual. Perhaps that was her problem—taking herself too seriously. She always had so much to say, spoke in complete sentences, seemed to intentionally use words Kurt didn't understand, undid his ideas with the ease of slipping a button through its eye. Listening to her—which it felt like most of his sessions were since she talked over him if he tried to interject into the conversation, bulldozing over anything he could have added, though if she would ever have given him the chance, she would likely have found his ideas to be relevant—listening to her filled Kurt with a heavy dread. She had a Ph.D. in something, in the aesthetics of something or the psychology of something, a degree so specific and pretentious sounding he was sure it was fake (though Matheson assured him it checked out), and she was always taking a stance decidedly against anything that Kurt said, and she didn't seem to respect any of his work as an actor, which he believed had, in a way, earned him a sort of honorary doctorate in psychology— *from experience*, he said, *I've truly experienced other minds in a way that most people don't get the chance, spending months in a character's head, an immersive sort of knowledge that psychologists probably don't even get*—but the Intellectual Girlfriend was having none of it and went on some rant about anecdote and experience versus data and observation and she even had the nerve to call the whole GX into question, which was the last goddamn straw for Kurt. That was it. He was done.

She's out, he told Matheson, bursting into his office, *send her home, I'm done*.

It rattled Matheson to see Kurt so rattled, but Matheson tried to keep it together, flipping open to the index of his handbook and finding the Proposal to Alter the Experiment Protocol.

We're not doing that, Kurt said. *Just send her home*.

And Matheson understood (he did, he really did) how stressful it can be to build something this complicated, to take risks the way that Kurt was willing to take risks, to do something that had never before been done (and Matheson admired him for that), but the truth was (and Matheson knew this and he knew that Kurt knew this) that rules and structures and protocols were there for *a reason*. And that reason was *this* reason. Times like this.

I'm hearing that you're stressed, that you're upset, so if you could just give me a Complaint Statement, you know, that might ease some of that stress. And I can put it on the Incident Report for us and we can send an Amendment Proposal over to the Research Division, and this should all be—

Just send her home, Kurt said, and the silence that followed this quietly crushed Matheson, who knew that Kurt knew that Matheson was really, really triggered when Kurt cut him off mid-sentence. They had been through this. They had been through this several times. They'd even had a few mediation sessions about this with Yuri, and Matheson had *really* thought Kurt had changed, and it hurt and exhausted Matheson in this moment to feel all the work they'd put into their communication just vanish. Matheson looked at Kurt, waiting on the inevitable apology, but he got nothing. Kurt turned to stare out the window, folding his arms, holding his ground.

Silently, Matheson rehearsed a rebuttal: that he was already managing all the girlfriends, all their changing schedules and million little questions and that half of them seemed allergic to reading their handbooks and some of them came to their sessions five, ten minutes behind schedule and a few times not at all, and he was working nearly twice his usual hours and it was really, when you got down to it, not really a part of his fucking job description to have to manage Kurt's sudden scientific whims, not that he was complaining, Matheson said to himself, in his anger, but was it so much to ask for Kurt—Kurt of all people—to just follow the fucking protocol?

It's just that, you know, Matheson said to Kurt, exerting all possible energy to keep his tone respectful, *it's actually really important that we respect the division of the personal, professional, and scientific boundaries of the GX. Don't you think we have a responsibility to maintain the integrity of the Research Division's work?*

This was the second time in a day Kurt had been directly challenged by someone he was *paying*, someone who was not even adequately listening to him, and though Kurt theoretically respected Matheson, his assistant of many good years now, a part of Kurt right then had also run out of the energy to respect anyone at all. He stared through Matheson, said nothing.

I'm sorry. I'm only trying to do what's best for the GX, Matheson said, *all the work you've put into it, you know?*

He knew it sounded as if he was groveling, which Kurt hated, but all Matheson wanted, like any misunderstood love wants, was to be understood again, to be in the same reality as Kurt again, so Matheson hit the emergency exit, the way we all try to return, immediately, to a better place: he said, *No, I'm sorry, you're right.*

When Matheson entered the Research Division office a moment later, everyone was hunched over scattered papers or making calculations on one of the whiteboards or watching numbers and graphs shoot across the screens. Matheson cleared his throat to get their attention and at once they all stopped, as if by some secret choreography, stilling their hands, turning to face him.

Ah, excuse me, we just wanted to let you know that we've decided to let the Intellectual Girlfriend go.

In pairs, they turned to each other, some of them whispering too quietly to be heard, others consulting each other wordlessly, until one of them, a hollow-chested man with closely shorn hair, said, *That would be fine.*

And we've decided in this case not to go through with the Experiment Alteration Protocol as outlined in the handbook, Matheson added with an unnecessary sense of authority, *and we're just going to send her home, the Intellectual Girlfriend.*

But they had all returned to their work, no longer listening to him. One or two of them looked up briefly, as if to let him know that he could leave them now, so, dejected, he did, returning to his office to find Kurt still standing where he'd left him, thinking, thinking. What was he always thinking of?

I think you're overworked, Kurt said, his back still to Matheson, whose body loosened with relief when he heard this.

You're probably right, he said, trying to seem strong.

So let's skip our Tuesday meeting.

About The Walk? *But—*

No, I think—I've decided to have Research do an experiment with Mary and my editing process. It makes more sense, especially since we've let Intellectual go. So let them know for me, will you?

And Kurt was gone.

Matheson looked at the shut door and replayed what Kurt had said again and again. He considered going after Kurt, telling him he wouldn't let this happen, that he was worried about him, really worried, that he couldn't just make such a large decision this quickly, but he just sat, staring at the door. How had Kurt just disregarded Matheson's years of experience for the sake of an experiment? He imagined what he would look like as he made this speech to Kurt. Perhaps Kurt would begin to cry stoically because he would know Matheson knew him so well, better than anyone else.

But Matheson didn't go after him, instead sat at his desk and quietly considered all the ways it might go if he did go after him. What if Kurt had never much liked Matheson's ideas? He caught himself chewing on a pen. He put it down, pulled at a cuticle until it bled. He thought about getting back into therapy, but immediately discarded the idea and instead drifted off, as he did so often, to that moment that happened a few years back—Matheson had been heading for the elevator after a long day's work when Kurt initiated (*really, went out of his way to initiate*) a hug that was much firmer than usual, and as they released from each other, Kurt sort of lingered (*no, he definitely lingered*) just ever so slightly (*or more than slightly*) near Matheson's face—and Matheson had long been attracted to Kurt but had always dismissed this attraction because Matheson was a professional and nearly everyone on the planet was attracted to Kurt Sky and of course there was the power dynamic between them and basically there was nothing but reasons (*so many reasons*) why Matheson should not read so much into being attracted to Kurt, to not be so stupid to fall for his boss (*his most likely mostly straight boss*), and even though Kurt seemed to intentionally linger in this hug (*more of an embrace, really*) for long enough that there seemed to be a suggestion in it, Matheson could not let himself believe in this suggestion because it was too painful to wonder if this had been his chance to change everything and he'd missed it.

He had quickly said good-night to Kurt, eventually resigning himself to never knowing what (*if anything*) Kurt had been trying to covertly convey. Sometimes Matheson was certain that Kurt had been trying to begin something with him and it had been Matheson who'd put up a boundary, remained professional, rejected him, and though there was some power in seeing the moment that way, there was just as much sadness.

12

Sometimes I think I can't edit this film because I can't feel anything about it anymore.

Everything was black in the editing room—black walls, black floor, ceiling, computer, all the furniture—everything except the white tabletop hovering above imperceptible black legs. It dizzied Mary to be there, as if she'd been set loose in space. Kurt sat at the table, facing the three large screens that hung in a triptych, each paused on slightly different close-ups of his own face. Hours could easily pass like this—Kurt staring at three images of himself, clicking a keyboard and a mouse to make tiny adjustments to the same few seconds of film, trying to decode something in the scene, figure out what was *off* about it, maybe the color, maybe the cropping, or maybe it needed a few more pauses, or a quicker cut between frames, or maybe he needed to go back to the raw footage to find something that had been lost somewhere, and maybe he'd overlooked the better take, lost something along the way. Always, it seemed, something had been lost along the way.

Everything is in the details—his back to her, speaking as if he were giving a presentation to a large crowd, but there was only Mary. The room was so insulated and small she could hear every key and mouse click. He was playing and replaying three different takes of himself saying, *Everything else has failed*—and as he played and replayed the clips for almost an hour—*Everything else has failed*—the pitch and tone and rhythm of those words became lodged in her head like a song—*Everything else has failed*—another pause of a few seconds, another adjustment to the frame, and again—*Everything else has failed*.

The Relational Experiment required her not to say anything unless Kurt faced her or asked her a direct question. She was supposed to remain attentive, alert, to always *have* something to say but never to say it unless asked.

Sometimes he would tell her this scene was a reference to a certain director or film or style; she would never have heard of this director or film or style, he knew, and sometimes he would turn around and explain it to her, but other times he just said, *Incredible*, and kept working.

You're completely uncontaminated. It's so incredible. You're the only person I've ever met who can see a work for what it really is.

From the floor she watched him work, her back against the wall, trying to discreetly readjust herself when her leg fell asleep or back went stiff, but when she came in the next week, a small chair was in her spot at the back of the room. It seemed like a child's chair, almost, and something about this felt insulting. She was still standing, staring at the chair, when Kurt entered the room.

I had Matheson get you a chair.

Oh, thank you.

Because I noticed how last time the floor didn't seem very comfortable.
She tried to keep her expression neutral.

Is everything okay?

Oh, yes. Of course.

You know, I have very specific ideas about the . . . aesthetics of a room. I'm very influenced by it. Every room should have a function and everything in the room should serve that function.

They were some weeks into the GX, so this wasn't news to Mary, but he spoke with a kind of confidential seriousness.

It may not seem like much, but this is . . . an important . . . moment. For us.

She looked at the chair and at him.

I had the chair put in here because I want you here. His heart rate was elevated, though Mary did not pick up on his nerves, just heard that familiar tone of a man telling a woman something he believes she should already know.

What I'm saying is that you're a part of this process now. And I need you to be here. Because, you are . . . significant . . . to me.

She thought of something she'd studied in a history class—years ago, the facts all foggy—something about a king who wouldn't allow those in a room with him to have their head higher than his head, all the chairs built low to the ground, maybe only inches, and anyone who was taller than him had to crawl in the king's presence.

I care about your comfort. I really do.

She put her hand on top of the hand he'd put on her shoulder, a protocol, until she remembered another protocol—that he was waiting for her to sit down so that he could sit down, so she did. She sat in the tiny chair.

It was unclear to Kurt why Mary's presence made him feel things differently, deeper, more clearly. The only other person whom he could remember this sort of feeling with was William, though the significance of that friendship was hard to untangle from the significance of that time in his life. Kurt was sixteen, his mom had just been diagnosed, and William was the son of a woman Kurt's mom had met in her support group. The four had these sleepovers during the worst parts of chemo, the women taking care of each other, the sons taking care of each other, a sudden, short-term family for the eight months before Kurt's mom passed. William and Kurt often stayed up late playing card games, almost never talking (what was there to say?) and Kurt pretended that it wasn't weird when William would put his head on Kurt's chest (in the middle of the night when they had to share a pull-out couch) because (Kurt reasoned) he didn't want to embarrass William, but, really, Kurt didn't have to pretend it wasn't weird because it wasn't weird—it somehow made sense. The two of them were twinned by seeing their mothers unravel like this, and together they became younger and older at the same time.

After the funeral Kurt had left for L.A., drowned his grief in saying yes to every job, in making no room in his days to stop and hear the absence of her voice. Success made the world strange, as he could never tell who was smiling at him and who was smiling at what they wanted from him, and it made him think of William, how their need and use for each other was so simple, like a spoon. Sometimes Kurt considered calling William's mother, but was too afraid she might not answer, that she might have died or moved, or that if she did answer, he wouldn't have a good excuse for all the years he hadn't called. He didn't want to be that person who found his own success more interesting than the people he used to know. As time went, it became harder and harder to imagine himself calling. Then it was impossible to imagine himself calling. Then the memory of William was just this warm press on his chest and the feeling of not having to explain or protect himself. But wouldn't a better person have stayed in touch? Wouldn't a good friend have remained a good friend? All of this sat quietly in him, large but far-off, like a mountain seen from a distance on a clear day. Matheson reminded Kurt of William (just a little, in the eyes, in certain kinds of light), which was at least part of the reason Kurt had hired him all those years ago, but Mary reminded Kurt of that feeling he'd had with William, that easy intimacy.

From her tiny chair Mary watched Kurt working, clicking and squinting and watching and rewatching the same clip. She tried to feel, in her body, the little tendon Ed had told her about at her last session, just below the ribs, a rare and tiny tendon that most people don't have. Something had made this rare tendon grow in her, and something else had made it scrunch, become the crumpled root of all her problems. In the dark, as Kurt played the same clip over and over, Mary tried to put her awareness on the tendon, but she couldn't seem to find it in her body. She wondered how Ed could be so certain about what was inside her.

Kurt swiveled around to face Mary in the dark, the three screens behind him all paused on different close-ups of his face in profile, the difference between the angles almost imperceptible. Kurt had been playing and replaying each take, having great difficulty choosing one.

I just thought of something, he said, backlit by himself. *Do you think love is the measure of how sad you would be if someone died?*

Without pausing she asked, *How do you measure sadness?*

Kurt recognized her expression (lit softly in that low light) as the same one she'd had in the last moment he saw her during their first session, at the Savant House. It was painful and peaceful and made him want something, and at the same time it made him feel he had everything he needed.

I like having you here, Mary. I don't think I've ever gotten so much done in a day as I have on the days that you've been here.

He hadn't answered her question and she got the sense that she might ask him a lot of questions that he would never answer.

Do you ever have that feeling, that you need someone else to tell you how you feel? That you need to see your feelings reflected back at you?

All the time, she said.

They sat in the dark for a while after that.

I think I've lost something, Mary. It seems I want my privacy more and more, but I also want, more than ever, to be understood. And somehow I think this film is what will make people understand me, but I've been working on this edit for over a decade now and I can't seem to make it as complete as I can see it in my head. And you know— wanting someone to be in your head, wanting everyone to see what's in there—that's the opposite of privacy. It just doesn't add up. I feel like there was something in the middle that's been taken out.

He turned to the screens again, looked at the large images of himself, then turned back to face her. His hair was chaotic and placed, an abstract painting, the edges of it glowed while his face was blacked out with shadow.

But it's not enough to just tell a story anymore. I'm so tired of stories of people pretending stuff on camera, plots and acting and effects. The world doesn't need any more nice films or stories. I want to make something bigger than that, something that changes people, you know, becomes a part of someone. Not a product, a fifteen-dollar ticket and ninety minutes of your life. I want to make a whole life, something huge.

Maybe it's this. Maybe you're doing it now.

She meant this film (though she'd seen less than a minute of it), but Kurt thought she meant the GX.

You really think so? His voice jolted at the affirmation, his needs laid bare. He was his most genuine in the dark, as anyone would be, and if she had struck a match at that moment, she would have seen his real face, the one everyone has and no one shows to anyone.

At the end of these sessions Kurt always left first, but sometimes he lingered awhile, staring at Mary, saying nothing. He liked the way the screen light coated her face in a strange blue.

13

2:23 a.m.
FROM: chandra@onelight.com
TO: mparsons@universaltravel.com
SUBJECT: THE WHAT AND WHY

It must be strange to hear from me like this, but I believe you can
   understand.
You of all people.
Sometimes people die while they're still alive.
It's all so clear to me now.
It must be strange to hear from me like this.

The first one came two weeks after the GX began—probably just
a misunderstanding or sent by accident, a note for herself now
out of context. Or it could have been some other Chandra, not
her Chandra, because Chandra had never mentioned anything

called One Light and she always told Mary about the healing circles and women's communes and whatever else she joined. The fact, also, that Chandra hadn't returned Mary's last two calls probably meant that she'd gone on a technology cleanse. So most likely, it wasn't her. It couldn't be. It must have been nothing.

A week later, two more.

3:14 a.m.
FROM: chandra@onelight.com
TO: mparsons@universaltravel.com
SUBJECT: RE: THE WHAT AND WHY

My mind has become too powerful, Mary.
Dying was the only way I could serve the other Devotees.
We are all in the light now.
My mind is a meeting place, and everyone is inside me, speaking.
It's so beautiful. Soon you'll see.
We all understand what is happening to you.
We have seen everything.

3:56 a.m.
FROM: chandra@onelight.com
TO: mparsons@universaltravel.com
SUBJECT: RE: RE: THE WHAT AND WHY

It must be strange to still be alive.
But you'll soon die the way I did.
Soon, you will see.
It's almost over. You're almost here.

Mary remembered Chandra had taken a writing class one semester and had become serious about it. She began spending all her free time speed-reading the books her peers mentioned casually, the things it seemed everyone had read years ago. She learned to refer to the writing faculty by their first names, even the ones she'd never seen. On weekends she nursed tepid beers at the dive where the writing majors hung out, their notebooks and paperbacks scattered across soggy tables as they debated whatever novel was getting the most polarizing reviews, some lauding it, sure it was pure brilliance, genius, others certain of its inauthenticity, warm bullshit in hardback. They spoke with the kind of passion that only the young try to get away with, all so sure there was a right idea to have, that they either had it already or needed to find it and show it to the others.

But Chandra ultimately decided against switching her major, claiming she couldn't get over the falseness of the other writing students, the falseness of fiction itself. Mary remembered a conversation they'd had about it sophomore year, the two of them drinking burned coffee in the student center. Chandra said she wanted to make something more immediate and less oblique than a story—*you know, something where you can't tell where the line is between regular life and art*—so maybe, Mary thought now, these e-mails were an attempt at that, a sort of performance.

It's all so artificial, you know? I don't want to make something that is so separate from life. (Midmorning light glowed in the frizzed edge of Chandra's hair, wild curls flopped to one side.) *If you're picking up a book or a magazine to read something—I don't think people really . . . I don't think they really . . . I just don't think it's the best way to really have an impact on someone. It can't just be, like, once there was this person and they did these things and felt blah blah blah. Or I don't think I want to do that anyway. I want to make something that changes people.*

Mary sent a reply to chandra@onelight.com—*Hey C, just wondering where you've been?*—but it bounced back.

Delivery to this address failed permanently
ERROR CODE: 550-No such user—psmtp

Three days later, another.

4:37 a.m.
FROM: chandra@onelight.com
TO: mparsons@universaltravel.com
SUBJECT: RE: RE: RE: THE WHAT AND WHY

I always knew. You never had to tell me.
I saw your father bury you and I watched you crawl out of the
    ground.
We've reversed time, the devotees and I, we've fixed everything.
Soon it will all make sense.
Tell Ed not to worry.

She dialed Chandra's number before she even realized what
she was doing. Nothing. She redialed. Nothing.

They hadn't spoken since before Mary started the GX, and
every day since then had been tightly scheduled—weekdays at
the agency, long lunch breaks with Ed, half her nights spent
catching up on the work she was perpetually behind on at the
office, as the other half of the week she had to leave work early
to go through wardrobe, makeup, and sensor application protocols before a session with Kurt—but still, despite the fact that
every minute of her life had been rented or given to someone else,
Mary knew she was still the person inside her body, the little
monster in herself that had let all these people (these people she
loved) disappear.

All she ever seemed to be doing was drifting from people—
Aunt Clara, her parents, even Paul, in a way. Chandra being gone

became everyone being gone and Mary increasingly felt her body was made of something else, of metal or glass, of insects or small animals. She went to the office bathroom and threw up—quickly, efficiently—threw cold water against her face, into her mouth, her eyes, her nose. She braced herself against the sink for a while— fluorescents buzzing above her, water dripping off her face, cool sweat on her scalp—then lowered herself to the tile floor, counting her fingers, one to ten, over and over, into the high hundreds. No one found her.

14

A younger version of Rachel would have been too offended to take this gig with Kurt Sky—playing the Maternal Girlfriend (what in the fuck?) to this white guy who was a year *older* than she was (typical)—but paying off her half of the kids' orthodontist bills, she decided, was worth it. If nothing else, just to get Chris off her case about it. All she'd had to do so far was hang out in that loft for a couple hours each week, scratch his back, make him grilled cheeses, run her fingers through his hair, fold his laundry, receive flowers from him on his mother's birthday, wear linen tunics and those weird sensor things, rub a spit-smeared thumb across his face sometimes—and, sure, it was a little strange, but it was no weirder than some of the adult-baby stuff she used to do. It wasn't hard to imagine the appeal in returning to a time you knew nothing.

But what had seemed straightforward for the first few weeks became, during the fifth session, just too much. That experiment required her to sit in the living room and listen to Tchaikovsky, slowly getting drunk on white wine in the middle of the day, first vacantly staring out the window and ignoring Kurt, then weeping inconsolably, moaning and clinging to him as he asked what was wrong, to which she was supposed to shake her head, remain silent.

It was a reenactment of Kurt's last memory of his mother before the chemo began, a sort of drama-therapy experiment that Yuri had come up with, though Rachel hadn't been told any of this, just felt something was weirdly fucked about the scene. During her exit protocol Rachel overheard Kurt crying in that athletic, frantic way—and, sure, nothing was inherently wrong with crying—but she sensed something wasn't right, and maybe because she was so full of chardonnay or maybe because all that Tchaikovsky had pushed her nerves up to the surface, she finally lost control and asked Matheson, *What the fuck was that all about?*

One of the not-twins who was removing her sensors stopped for a moment, asked if he should leave, but Matheson insisted they were fine—*There's no problem here.*

But what in the hell is all this, really?

Your Relational Experiment went well, and we—

No, this was fucked up. It's like . . . am I supposed to get beat up by his abusive dad next week? It's like—I don't even know what the fuck . . .

She was out of breath, half-drunk and sweaty. All her thoughts scattered.

I understand you're concerned, but Yuri is with Kurt now, and he's fine. You'll feel better after your compartmentalization meditation. I know it might not always make sense, but you just have to trust we know what we're doing.

But I don't know what you're doing.

Done with his work, the not-twin let himself out quickly and Rachel said, *Fuck this*, left without changing out of her wardrobe, and not until she sat on the floor of her living room after her four-train commute back to Jersey did she finally look down and think, *What in the fuck am I doing in a tunic?* She got up, fixed herself a cup of tea, threw the tunic to the floor as the water boiled. She tried to laugh at her day, that she had just made six hundred dollars reenacting some old childhood scars with a famous actor. What was her life? What was she doing?

She sat for a long time in her dining room letting the tea sober her, surrounded by the detritus of her sons—an upended toy truck, G.I. Joes spilling out of a repurposed plastic container, a thin layer of broken crayon bits and dirt tracked in from the yard. The boys were with their father for the next three days, and the absence of their endless screams and bickering suddenly weighed on her. They could fight for any toy or object—even a fucking spatula—that the other had, which soon became forgotten, misplaced, or crammed in a storage bin somewhere. How strong they could want something and how dissatisfied they were with having.

Why was *having* never enough? And why did wanting always feel so real? Rachel knew she wasn't exempt from this cycle, just larger and older. She longed for her sons when she was alone and hated to see them go, but when they were with her, the having did not shine as brightly as the wanting had, though she'd long known this was just how parenthood worked—fuzzy weeks of thrall and sleep deprivation punctuated by moments of joy and wholeness, a satisfaction stronger than any drug she'd ever known.

Her boys were getting older at a rate that almost nauseated her to think about, these little beings, once mushy and soft skulled, now larger, firmer, faster—people. Neither of them would let her hold him anymore and sometimes she found it painful to notice their faces maturing, especially Felix. Over supper sometimes she caught him clenching his jaw and staring at the far corner of the dining room's ceiling, as if trying to push some unyielding philosophical question along in his head.

He was twelve.

She assumed he'd learned this look from his teenaged stepbrother, Nevil, whom Rachel only knew from a distance, that boy who sometimes kept watch from the porch when she dropped her sons off at their dad's house.

The stepmother had her own jewelry business—handmade necklaces, delicate silver lattices that sat close to the neck. She had single-handedly brought back the choker look, a fashion website had said. She was an artist, had a gift, a skill. Rachel found herself sometimes just staring at the images of the necklaces online—and, yes, she knew she was jealous, but not because this woman had married her boys' father—Rachel had never married him herself and never wanted to—but Rachel envied how this woman got to have time with her sons that Rachel could never get back. She imagined Felix and Jay being freer and happier over there, in Nevil's company, Nevil and his cool mom, and she knew that Nevil would probably have more of an effect on her kids than *she* could for the next few years, as her children drifted through their teens, away from her. She wished Felix and Jay were babies again, though they were never babies at the same time, and she wished she could have been a baby with them, too, that they could all lie in a thoughtless baby lump, void of all responsibilities and knowledge, without history, just soft skin and fat, piled on each other like puppies, mother and children, impossibly all infants at the same time.

She stood before her open refrigerator, looking for something but only finding an old jar of tahini and a deflated peach. She sat on the kitchen tile, drank from a lukewarm juice box with a tiny straw, and wondered if the love she had for Felix and Jay had always contained this sense of compromise. It wasn't about the sacrifices she'd made to have and raise them—the daily chores, the financial constraint, the places unvisited and experiences never had. It was something larger. She finished the juice and the straw howled in the empty box.

15

The idea came to him in a dream—an experiment in standing someone up, to have a member of the Intimacy Team wait for him in public, some place popular enough for her embarrassment to be felt, as his lateness became a complete absence, her texts and calls unanswered, her waiting increasingly pathetic, a supplication. There was something to learn from this—Kurt was sure—this mixed state of guilt and power in making someone wait, the humbling that came with abandonment.

Lisa was the first to be assigned to this experiment. She arrived at the restaurant five minutes early, took the barstool closest to the windows, and waited as Kurt watched her through the mirrored windows of an SUV parked just outside. She thumbed her phone for a while, ordered a drink, feigned annoyance, sent the requisite texts at the predetermined intervals. The information her sensors collected—easy heart rate, steady breathing, the usual peak and flux of her emotional state—blurred across screens in the Research Division's office, but none took note. They'd humored Kurt in letting him think this was even an experiment at all. It wasn't.

Kurt's adrenaline spiked when a group of suit-y, cuff-linked dudes crowded into the bar near Lisa. One offered to buy her a drink (*I've got one*), offered to keep her company (*I'm good*), asked her name, to which she said nothing, to which he said, *It's just your name*, to which she said, *It's just get the fuck away from me*.

Kurt relished this moment from the car, watching a woman reject the company of another man for the pointed absence of his, but a moment later an old friend of Lisa's recognized her from the sidewalk and came inside, the two women seemingly ecstatic to see each other, which meant Kurt was no longer watching a woman being stood up by him, just two women enjoying each other's company. And what was the point in that? He told the driver to take him home. Lisa was informed her services were no longer needed, and the next IT Girlfriend put on this assignment was given a longer list of Relational Experiment Behavior Specifications, including not talking to anyone for longer than three minutes.

Rosa was sent to a different restaurant on a low-traffic block of SoHo on a dreary night. She brought a book to read and seemed not at all bothered by sitting in the bar, nursing her wine, occasionally looking up at the door as if she didn't particularly care whether anyone showed up. Eventually it began to rain and the window of the bar fogged up, obscuring Kurt's view, though by then he was already too disappointed by her contentment to care about what he couldn't see. Matheson suggested the women be given even more specific emotional directions—to be disappointed by Kurt's delay and absence—and even though Kurt worried instructions would ruin the authenticity of the data, he agreed.

But Mandi, the last IT Girlfriend on this assignment, overdid the role, checking and rechecking her phone, visibly jolting each time she heard the restaurant door swing open, staring out the window, trying to grimace out tears. Kurt left before a half hour had even passed, calling Matheson on the way home to tell him to cancel the experiment, that Kurt wasn't sure why he wanted to do this in the first place.

In their office the next morning, Matheson noticed something different about the mood of the Research Division, though he wasn't sure what, exactly, had changed. It seemed there were more of them than usual, or perhaps fewer, or something about their uniforms had been altered—had their lab coats been laundered? He stood there awhile, studying the room, searching for what was amiss, but nothing became clear.

But Matheson was right—there was trouble in the Research Division. They had once been united in a single goal: to endure the requirements of this actor's vanity project in exchange for the time, funding, and test subjects needed to develop their sensors, but their unity had been dissolving.

The disagreements were petty at first—their uniforms, their official titles, whether they should name themselves as a group, something more specific than the Research Division. Then there was the ongoing question about what to name the sensors—some believed they shouldn't be named until the development was further along, that perhaps they did not yet know what they were making, and others believed their research would be stymied if the technology remained nameless and some suggested possible names and others shot those names down but didn't offer any of their own and eventually someone would point out how much time had already been wasted on this debate and could they please table it and move on?

Data collected had been either inconclusive or overly conclusive. There were disagreements about statistical analysis, hypotheses formulation, approaches to software coding, ethical concerns, and so on. Some of the subjects responded immediately and clearly to the Internal Directives, while others seemed to have a more disorderly response. One of the women hired on the Mundanity Girlfriend track began quietly weeping when they sent an Internal Directive meant to synthesize limerence. Matheson reported that she'd quit on the spot after this experiment, which made no sense—they'd used the same Internal Directive on Jenny, during an Intimacy Team Relational Experiment, during which she and Kurt were alone in an unlit room monitored by infrared as they each used small devices to convey to each other, through a sort of Morse code, what level of physical intimacy they each consented to. Though Jenny had first only consented to kissing Kurt, once the Internal Directive was administered, she gave him her full consent and moments later broke the Relational Experiment Behavior Specification that required her to be silent.

I'm in love with you, she shouted mid-experiment, to which Kurt said nothing, finished, and left the room, leaving Jenny to quiver, ill with love. She was fired on the spot and two Research Division members had to escort her from the building.

There has to have been some mistake, she said in the elevator, eerily calm, *just ask him, he'll know. This is different.* (She seemed *brainwashed*, one of the researchers later said to another. *Don't call it brainwashed*, the researcher said in response, and the other wanted to know why. *It just sounds dumb, don't call it that.*)

In the lobby Jenny locked her knees, braced herself into a

corner, and held herself there for several minutes before flinging herself at the potted ferns, ripping the plants up, throwing them across the room, then dashing from the building.

Since then, everyone in the Research Division had been more hesitant with the Internal Directives. Perhaps they needed to re-write all the coding, some suggested, or employ a screening process. Subtler experiments were attempted, turning up someone's heart rate to see how it affected her mood, decreasing or increasing one hormone in tiny increments.

The Jenny Incident, as it came to be known, was referenced often, though each member of the Research Division had their own interpretation of it. Some thought it proved the efficacy of the Internal Directives to create a feeling from scratch in a person, but others were sure that Jenny must already have been in love with Kurt of her own accord, and the Limerence Internal Directive had just let that feeling be revealed.

You can't feel something you don't feel, the least-liked researcher said, though he was in the minority.

Feelings are just data, not mysterious, not immeasurable, another said. *This is the entire point of all of our research. You can't possibly think that a human feeling is anything more than information, electrical currents, controllable under the correct circumstances.*

That's not what I said, the least-liked researcher said.

That is what you said.

That's not what I meant.

I'm going to have to ask you to only say what you mean and mean what you say when you're in our lab—is that clear?

Of course. It was a mistake. I won't let it happen again. The least-liked researcher had long hoped that he might one day be able to discover a sort of special neurochemical reaction that only could happen in the brains of people who were really in love. He imagined it might be like mirror neurons, but much more rare and strong, something almost holy, though he'd never use such a word in the lab, and wouldn't dare tell anyone of this desire. He was a very romantic, almost silent person. He tied his shoes very slowly.

In meetings many complained the experiments had become overly cautious, that the results were pointless, that the inquiry would have no direction if no one was willing to take a risk. One researcher, the one who often suffered from sudden nosebleeds, spoke up quietly and slowly, about her fears that perhaps the Internal Directives were flatly unethical, that perhaps the means did not justify the—but someone else spoke over this meek voice, persuaded the others to turn against her.

Factions began to form. Some believed that some of the Girlfriends' data was so inconsistent that those Girlfriends should be let go, or that their files should be thrown out, but others believed that collecting the widest sample of data could only help the analytics. Some thought that the Internal Directives were to blame for the symptoms some of the Girlfriends had complained about, but others held that there were too many factors to draw a causation. Some thought Kurt's uninformed and self-serving ideas for Relational Experiments shouldn't be tolerated and some thought letting him think he had an impact was strategic. Some believed they could come up with some statement or discovery that could at least appease Kurt, but most were sure they never would, that they were working on borrowed time until Kurt figured out his objective—to solve love—was impossible. Most believed that Kurt and Matheson were at least a little sociopathic, but only a few thought this was a problem.

One of the not-twins had been developing a theory—that a brain in limerence believed itself to occupy two consciousnesses, that falling in love was, in some ways, a temporary suspension of the limitations of being one person—but he feared the others would find the evidence he'd collected in forming this theory to be strange, so he just kept quietly collecting his data.

As a test subject, Ashley was particularly divisive among the researchers. The least-liked researcher had the idea to do a case study on her, something about the interaction of love and hate in a brain, something that might prove how compassion was more powerful than anger. But others shot it down as too sappy, reductive. The physiological states and biometrics of compassion and anger would vary greatly among people and over time and Ashley was only *one* person. There couldn't be much to learn from this.

But this was only intended to be a case study, the least-liked researcher argued, *a starting point*.

Others wondered how he'd even been allowed to join the Research Division to begin with.

Ashley's resting data showed that she had a baseline disdain for Kurt, he continued, *a consistent hostility, no physical or emotional attraction to him whatsoever, and her assignments were always to attack him, nag him, pick emotional or physical fights with him. What if an Internal Directive could soothe her enough to make fighting him not worth it?*

Those opposing the idea cared so little that they didn't even dissent, and the least-liked researcher covertly began a series of experiments the next day. The Anger Girlfriend had a Relational Experiment that required her to burst into Kurt's bedroom as he was waking up, then pelt him with an armful of his shoes, one after another, screaming that she knew what he'd done, that he better tell her exactly what had happened, that she'd know if he was lying, that if he lied, it would all get worse. From their office, the least-liked researcher gradually sent her an Internal Directive meant to mimic the compassion and kindness of a long and well-built relationship, but Ashley's activity feed didn't change in the way he'd expected. She didn't soften or smile or stop screaming at Kurt and instead became louder, threw the shoes harder, breathed more erratically. Later that week during a Relational Experiment that had Ashley verbally abuse Kurt, the least-liked researcher found that the more he increased the concentration of her Compassion Internal Directive, the more vicious her attacks became, as if loving him a little had increased her ability to insult him.

In outgoing interviews that week Ashley reported a lingering nausea after each Relational Experiment, almost as if she'd had too much caffeine, she said, but otherwise she was fine. She didn't report how she woke each morning thinking of Kurt's face, thinking of his little expressions, the way he pronounced certain words, the hard/soft place where his neck met his jaw. She began mindlessly using the GX phone to look up pictures of him, a habit she sometimes began before even getting out of bed, her eyelids barely parting. At all hours of the day she would think, neither lovingly nor hatefully, of that mole on the right side of his neck. She would wonder where that mole was at that exact moment. She felt sometimes haunted by it—flat and dark, a perfect circle. No matter how absurd she knew it was to fixate on such a thing, she thought of it constantly. That fucking mole.

Yet she still felt sure that she hated him, hated his pretension, his vanity, hated that he'd hired all these women, hated that mole, hated the neck under the mole, hated the voice that came out of that neck. But this was unlike any hate she'd ever felt before. It was gleeful and all-consuming, an unlikely companion through her days. He was every character in her every dream and sometimes he sprouted out of walls, and sometimes every surface was covered with his image, and sometimes she dreamed in circles of nothing but the mole.

At the gym she felt stronger and faster, felt her body move with more urgency and strength. One afternoon she accidentally clipped some guy in the shoulder who was standing too close while she did drills, and the hit surprised him enough that he tripped on something, fell to the floor, and busted his lip. He bounded back to his feet, acted as if he were fine, though his eyes were rattled and wide. But Ashley didn't even apologize to him, indifferent to the pleasure or suffering of anyone but Kurt. Though the Internal Directives were synthetic, even a synthetic love, it seemed, had made her a monster.

At dim sum with Vicky the next week Ashley avoided speaking of the GX entirely, though they'd spent half the previous month's dinner talking shit about Kurt. But something was different now and Ashley didn't want to see what Vicky's face looked like when she mentioned Kurt. She wondered what Vicky's experiments might entail, wondered if her work was more or less important than Ashley's work and how could you even measure such significance and she felt her stomach seize, all appetite gone, and wondered why she was even wondering this. In the back of her head, the mole bounced along, taunting.

Is something wrong? Vicky asked, noticing Ashley's full plate, but she just made something up about the gym, about her training, a strained muscle, an upset stomach.

Yeah, you don't really seem like yourself, Vicky said, to which Ashley nodded, a constant *No* and a constant *Yes* running in her.

What a danger it is to love, how it warps a person from the inside, changes all the locks and loses all the keys.

16

Ed lightly pressed an elbow into Mary's back, asked if she'd
been using a cell phone.

I can tell from this little knob right here. And here, too. He rested
two fingers, just barely, in the slight hollow behind her ear. *You
should try to limit how much you use it, or stop using it completely, at
least until our work is done.*

I can't, she said, her face mushed in the cradle, *it's for work.*

For the travel agency?

New job—second job.

Doing . . . what exactly?

A personal, um, assistant kind of work.

Anything strange about how this person behaves toward you?

She knew *usual* and *unusual* didn't apply, so she said, after
some consideration, *No.*

Are they reliable?

I guess so, sure.

Pay on time?

Uh-huh.

Mm.

They were silent for a while. Ed had her flip over and she stared at the ceiling while he rolled a wooden sphere across her belly. The lights were low. He placed a small green crystal on her forehead.

Heard from Chandra recently?

No.

She lied without even considering the truth, not wanting to think about the way she had been hearing from Chandra, refusing to believe it *was* Chandra.

I think she may be traveling.

Ed nodded, moved the crystal to her chest. It was exactly as Chandra had told him it would be—an energetic contamination.

And you're still not involved with anyone . . . romantically?

No.

Not dating or sleeping with anyone?

No, nothing.

You do understand why it would be important to our work that I know that, right?

Of course.

That I need to know about any psychic cords that could be interacting with your pneuma in order to best prepare and protect myself from the aura displacement?

Ed had that neck cramp again, and a discomfort deep in his left wrist. He kept having visions of Mary without eyes. Possibly he'd become too emotionally involved with her, but in meditation the previous night, he'd gotten a clear message from Chandra about Mary's secrecy and self-destructiveness, that he had to be careful, that she was more energetically poisonous than she might realize.

Okay, he said, *just let me know if anything changes*.

Mary nodded, got up, got dressed, and tried to understand what, if anything, all her time with Ed meant, when you added it all up, when you smushed it together: all these hours they'd spent together, half-clothed, trying to make life better. What was that if it wasn't a relationship? Did love have to be declared to exist or was it just as real when it was a silent belief? It seemed to her that people could call love whatever they wanted, but it was really just a long manipulation, a changing, a willingness to be changed.

Perhaps all the time she'd spent working for the GX had confused her, she thought, had made her try to quantify a thing that couldn't be quantified, but, still—had she grown to love Ed or was she just dependent on what he did to her? And what was the difference between those things? Did she even want to know? He stared at her so neutrally sometimes she couldn't help but wonder what he might be hiding and sometimes she wanted to ask him what he was feeling about her, what he would call it if he had to give it a word. This might be what a marriage felt like, a puzzle, a staring contest.

As she left Ed's office her GX phone had three missed calls, four texts, and a voice mail, all from Matheson.

—confirming you for 5pm, quick meeting b4 wardrobe
—let me know
—call me as soon as u get this
—important that u call
—Hi, Mary, this is Matheson. Okay, so, I'm having a little
  trouble reaching you and it's been over an hour so just
  make sure you call me as soon as you get this. Okay.

Mary called as she walked up Broadway, sidewalks dense with slow tourist traffic, and just as Matheson picked up, she passed a man bulging in a navy suit, shouting into his phone . . . *can go to hell, he can just eat my dick.*

Mary?

Hi, yeah, I'm just walking back to work. I had a, um, doctor's appointment and—

That's not on your conflicts and commitments sheet.

I didn't realize I needed—

Mary, do you really understand how your position in the GX requires you to be reachable at all times?

It's just—

And it's very simple for you to let us know ahead of time when you have something like a doctor's appointment. Unless it was urgent—was it urgent? Sudden? Are you dying of something? Are you contagious?

No, I just didn't realize I needed to tell you.

Maybe you should have read that part of your handbook a bit more carefully. Jesus! Doesn't anyone read their fucking handbooks?

Mary ducked into one of those metal shells that used to hold a public phone so she could hear him more clearly. Everything smelled like urine and dirty hair and the man who'd suggested someone could eat his dick was down the street now, buying an ice cream cone from a truck, vanilla, rainbow sprinkles.

And actually, Matheson continued, *the reason I needed you to come in earlier is that we want to bring you on full-time, so you need to quit your other job as soon as possible.*

Oh.

But do you really think you're ready for that?

She knew she was barely ready to be alive, but she also felt she didn't have a choice, that circumstance had whittled her options, that her body needed PAKing and PAKing needed the GX and the GX needed her, now, all her hours. It seemed possible that she'd never made a choice of her own. It seemed that all her life she'd been moved by circumstance instead of desire, that she'd never had to consider the possibility of being ready or not ready for something. She heard herself saying, *Yes, I'm ready, I can.*

In the office Mary taped a note to her computer screen—*Quit*—and though she had no sentimental attachment to this job, and though she never looked forward to work, quitting felt somehow like a loss, as if she had to do it quickly, quietly. But then, as she was waiting for the service elevator to arrive, she noticed a stack of boxes—extra copy paper and office supplies or whatever—and just as the elevator doors opened, she pushed it all over, a rumble and a smash and a few loose sheets of paper sent flying up and floating down.

The elevator descended. She smiled.

17

They ate blossoms and mosses, saps, uncommon pickles, thin slices of flesh.

Fiddle-fern mousse, petrified hake, reduced algae, Chef Breton said, as if reciting a prayer, gesturing to the plate just placed before them.

Mary stared at a lump of something coated in green jelly as Kurt told her Kandinsky was Chef Breton's main inspiration for his plating technique, that he had won an award just for the way he put food on a plate. She looked at these award-winning smears, at Kurt, back at the smears. The dinner was supposed to be a celebration but it felt like an ordeal, a fuss to honor her going full-time. Eating it was half-pleasant and half-unpleasant, the same as almost everything lately—the uncomfortable relief of PAKing, the interesting annoyance of being around Kurt, the lonely contentment she felt in her apartment, earning all this money but immediately giving it to Ed or throwing it into the debt pit. Kurt kept talking about whatever he talked about, and Mary listened in the way she'd been taught and when he finally stopped talking for a minute, closing his eyes while chewing a walnut-oil-vaporized golden heirloom beet, she wondered if this was how he came to be how he was—always being seen and never seeing.

That night she was to replace, for the first time, the Sleeping Girlfriend. Matheson had gone through the sleepover protocol just before dinner: the meditation, the showering with precise amounts of certain soaps, the facial regimen, the gray silk slip, the bedtime determined by Kurt's circadian-rhythm tracker and the schedule of the sun. She was to be in bed first, waiting for him with her eyes open (*very important that you have your eyes open*), and that night, as he did most nights a week, Kurt had a forty-minute session with an IT Girlfriend in a room on the other side of the loft, followed by a shower and an evening meditation before joining Mary in his bedroom.

She was to be on her left side, facing west on the west side of the bed, and he slept beside her, each of them with their knees bent to 140 degrees, his knees bent behind her bent knees, his right arm curved around her waist, forearm against her forearm. They lay like that for seventeen minutes of silent holding before Kurt rolled onto his back, his left leg stretched out close to her so he could feel the heat of her sleeping. She was to remain on her side or, if necessary, turn onto her back or belly at the same time he turned onto his back, so her movement wouldn't disturb him. In the morning the curtains, automated, slowly parted to wake them, at which point Mary was to resume her initial position on her side, knees bent, waiting for Kurt to roll back to her, resuming the silent holding position for seven minutes until Kurt got up and left. Mary was then sent away until three, told to go wherever and do whatever she pleased as long as it was something she could later tell Kurt about, though he never asked.

She went home wearing the makeup and clothes the GX had supplied—*You'll only wear pieces from our wardrobe from now on*, Matheson explained—and she noticed how this made the city move around her in new ways. People held doors open for her everywhere, smiled at her for no particular reason, told her to have a nice day. She felt eyes drift toward her, and the sort of women she'd felt invisible beside started giving her knowing glances or asking *who* had made this *piece* she was wearing. Everything had become a *piece*, not a dress, a *piece*. She never knew who had made it, so she just shrugged. This seemed to be impressive—this ignorance—though she didn't understand why.

In her apartment she'd always take *the piece* off, hang it up by the door, and put on the same musky sweatshirt, trying to think of something interesting to do that Kurt wasn't going to ask about anyway. Usually she settled on nothing or went for a walk up the river, where she would sometimes read and reread e-mails from Chandra on her phone, enigmatic lines that arrived at all hours. Somehow Chandra had gotten her GX e-mail, and though Mary wasn't sure how that could have been possible, nothing really seemed possible or impossible anymore.

I want you to know that your communications are being received.
We realize you have been taken hostage.
We're all very proud of you. But you must remain on alert. Do not trust them.

Sometimes Mary tried to resist opening these messages, as she knew nothing was to be gained but more confusion, but she always gave in. She had been indifferent about the GX phone at first, would sometimes misplace it or not hear its alerts, but now that it was her only point of connection to Chandra she never let it out of her sight and sometimes, when she couldn't find it for a moment, she'd frantically search around her apartment, only to realize that she'd been intensely clutching it the whole time. Mary caught herself curled around the phone at all hours, checking and rechecking for word from Chandra (or "Chandra" or someone, or something). Sometimes Mary sent a reply, and even though they bounced back, she still held out hope they might somehow be going through.

During her sessions at the loft, Mary felt a constant, stymied impulse to check her phone. She was half-removed from the room, there and not there.

It's been almost four months, Matheson said to her one day in his office. She didn't understand what he was saying. *Four months. Remember what you were supposed to do at some point after three months? We had been so hoping it would happen organically, you know. Saying you love him? Remember?*

It had always been unclear to Mary why saying these words in this order—*I love you*—had been made into such a spectacle. In college she had listened to other girls debate the reasonable amount of time two people had to spend together before it could be said and whether it was better to do the saying or the hearing for the first time. And she remembered Paul saying it for the first time to her, his palm sweaty and so much terror in his eyes. Mary wondered if hearing himself say these words made him doubt their substance. (But they were in love, weren't they? Weren't they?) It seemed that everything that had to be done and felt before these words became true, the daily vulnerability, the ever-increasing risk, the sustained nerve to look into the same face each day (as if to say, *Still me? Still you?*), all of this meant so much more than a sentence. (Subject, verb, object. Subject, verb, object, modifier.) Once two loved each other, it had already been said, just as when the love was undone, she thought, neither had to speak it. It simply became clear.

If she loved Kurt, she didn't love him in a way she recognized, but by enacting the evidence of love she had noticed some amount of strangeness in her. She might have loved the strangeness, she thought, and that might have been enough. Anyway, saying some words wasn't hard for her, so the afternoon Matheson reminded her of this task, she said them. It was the middle of a Personal History and Opinion Sharing Relational Experiment, and when it was her turn to speak, she said she loved him instead of answering whatever he'd asked.

Kurt stared at her, or above her or just over her shoulder. Sometimes she couldn't get a good read on where he was looking, what he was seeing. He smiled, looked down, widened his smile, looked up, said, *I love you, too*, and embraced her. But later he complained to Matheson that Mary had picked a sort of stale moment to say it for the first time.

I thought so, too, Matheson said.

But I do believe her, Kurt said, though he didn't believe himself when he said that he believed her. Yet, she must have loved him. How could she not? The perfect environment had been created, Kurt thought, to create a pure and unwanting love, untethered to sex, without obligation, beyond a community—a love that asks for nothing. Or this is what he thought had been created, until a report came from the Research Division advising they let Mary go.

Disorganized attachment, they said. *Pretty typical. Sure, she's doing all the protocols, but the data sets she's creating are inconsistent.*

Some days it seems she's in love, but on those days her activity patterns reflect a sort of nostalgic state, like she's reliving a memory instead of being in the moment.

Are you saying she's incapable of this, Kurt asked, *is that what you're saying?*

That wasn't what they were saying, but they knew enough now to not always say what they really meant to Kurt.

It's not yet clear what we're saying, they said.

He told them he'd consider it.

(In truth, Mary's involvement in the GX was simply getting in the Research Division's way. She didn't respond to Internal Directives in any way that made sense to them—she hardly responded to them at all—and her data, in general, was boring. They hadn't even been able to run any significant tests on Kurt in their sessions and those who had first been interested in the Mary-Kurt dynamic had moved on to more interesting problems. She was dead weight.)

That night Kurt dreamed about the Girlfriend Experiment as a kind of city, with each girlfriend being a street that ran parallel to the others, no intersections, so the city was impossible to traverse. He wandered this unpeopled city, trying to climb over buildings or squeeze through narrow alleyways to reach other streets. In the morning he was completely convinced the GX needed some kind of integration—especially with Mary. Perhaps if she better understood her role within this larger project, if she understood the importance of her assignments, then she would be able to feel more for Kurt. Yes, Kurt had known all along (hadn't he?) that something had always been just under the surface with Mary, just out of reach. He felt sure there was some depth, some greater thing that could exist between the two of them if only they could reach it, if only they could shock it from themselves. He felt more urgently about Mary than he ever had, an urgency that paced around him, had no place to go.

What was it that she was missing or not letting herself feel? What was it? How could he reach it? How could he show it to her?

18

You're a terrible person, Ashley said, *a horrible fucking person*.

Kurt and Mary stood at the elevator, which shut and sank behind them. Kurt moved toward her, said *Ash* as if it were his pet name for her, or maybe just because her punch stopped his mouth.

You bitch, he said, hunched over, his hand muffling his words. *You fucking bitch*, he said, louder, as if she'd asked him to repeat himself.

Ashley was silent for a moment, smiling, cracking her knuckles.

Right . . . I'm the bitch, I'm the bitch, yeah, keep telling yourself that.

Over dinner earlier that night, Kurt had told Mary about an experimental theater group that staged their work for unsuspecting audiences, blurring the line between life and performance, and when Ashley first began her attack, Mary watched with a kind of presence that would have been impossible if looking at a stage or a screen; it wasn't until later that she wondered if the conversation at dinner had been intended as a clue.

She knew she wasn't allowed to ask what Ashley and Kurt might have done together, what she might have meant to him, what he had promised to her, but something in Ashley's face made Mary wonder if this anger was her own, not assigned. Mary had a strong desire to comfort her, to push the hair from her face, to hold her still and feel the muscles release under her skin, but soon Ashley had punched Kurt again, then kicked him hard in the knees, and as he fell, Ashley bolted through the emergency exit, the alarm swirling on, leaping down the back stairs and bounding into the night.

Kurt was shaking, ablaze with two women in heightened emotional states over him, that contrast, the sense of being caught. A rush of cortisol and adrenaline had wordlessly bonded him to Mary as he looked at her now. She brought him a dish towel to sop up the blood, and he could tell the experiment had already worked, that something had intensified between them.

Mary remained silent though she could tell he was waiting for her to say something. Her long silences unnerved him, and in this silence, he felt he finally understood this strange feeling he had around Mary. It was doubt. Something about her made him question himself and he wasn't sure if he wanted to feel this way.

In the bedroom a little later, their night rituals all thrown off, she sat on the bed beside him and petted his hair and felt whatever she felt. It wasn't that she loved him. It was something else. She didn't know what it was.

This man is my employer, she reminded herself. *This is my job. This is my workplace.*

But she didn't know where she was or who he was or whom she had become.

The next time Ashley showed up, Mary believed Kurt when he insisted it had been unplanned, that something was wrong with this woman, that he didn't know why she was behaving this way, but by the third or fourth time, Mary suspected the attacks were now a part of the design. Ashley would arrive suddenly and attack him or just scream at him or break something and threaten him with the shards. The looming possibility of her arrival made Mary and Kurt's time together feel stolen and special.

You're a good person, Ashley shouted at Mary one night as Kurt let his nose bleed over the sink. *He wants us to hate each other, but fuck him. He doesn't own us. I won't play his games.*

After throwing a wineglass at Kurt that shattered on his shoulder, Ashley left in a rush, setting off the alarm, as was her pattern. Other times she was all insults—he was a hack, a fraud, a truly awful person, unredeemable, a shitty artist, he'd gotten everywhere on his looks and nepotism and under it he was nothing. He was nothing at all.

And after nights like that the silence of the apartment had a luxurious quality to it, like silk against clean, warm skin. He'd stay silent for a while, then cry, heaving violently against Mary in bed, and she could do nothing but lie there and let him. Sometimes she'd cry, too, but she didn't know where it was coming from or whom it was really for. Those nights they slept the way children sleep, exhausted by feeling a full range of emotions in a single day, but faithful that someone would take care of them tomorrow.

19

In Ed's waiting room that Tuesday a small potted tree was on the receptionist's desk and behind the tree a laptop and behind the laptop a small receptionist. The door to Ed's office was shut. It was never shut before Mary's appointments. Ed was usually standing there, waiting for her, each time she arrived. But Ed was nowhere and the lighting seemed harder now, brighter and somehow flat.

Excuse me, your name, please? The receptionist spoke in a hurry, looking past Mary instead of at her.

I have a PAKing session.

With whom?

With . . . Ed.

He's actually unavailable at the moment. May I take a message?

But—this is my regular time and he didn't say anything—

Oh, well, let's just see— The receptionist flipped through some papers on her desk without any discernible goal. *Actually your appointments have been canceled. Ed won't be seeing you anymore.*

Mary waited for the receptionist to realize her mistake.

You've completed your PAKing series.

But I have at least four more sessions—

There's been no mistake, Mary. Ed cannot work with you any longer. I would be happy to leave a message for him, but I can't promise you that he'll respond.

Mary's mouth went dry. Several muscles in her back spasmed.

Tell him I can explain everything, and that I just need to . . .

But the receptionist wasn't listening, had gone back to reading a magazine about yoga. Mary stared at Ed's door, straining to hear if he was in there with someone else, but all she could hear were his white-noise machines. She was too surprised to move for a moment, then too embarrassed to stay, rushing from the room and into an elevator, suspecting that even the deliveryman in his brown uniform and that stranger draped with that thin lilac sweater could tell that she was a liar, that she'd done something horribly wrong, her shame creating a stink around her. She went home and immediately to sleep in an attempt to avoid or stave off the avalanche of symptoms she felt certain were rumbling in her body, ready to upend her.

She woke at three the next morning, her body empty and dry, and picked up her phone, hoping for a word, no matter how confusing, from Chandra.

Mary, you are trapped by the present moment.

Some people will try to tell you that the truth lives in the present but it doesn't.

It is a weakness to live in the present. Lies live there.

You are now entering the future.

Chandra had taken her to a dance class in college, and Mary had lurched through the moves—the graceless lumber she'd learned from a childhood of farmwork—while Chandra glided in them. It seemed she had extra seconds in her counts, a private circuit of time, and Mary wondered now, as she read this e-mail over and over, if Chandra could still pirouette and leap as easily as she once had, if perhaps she'd had this control of time all along. The only time Mary had felt that sort of easiness had been in those dreamy hours just after PAKing. Now, without Chandra and without Ed, she felt the absence of all these people who had come to and gone from her, people who had meant something, done things to her, changed her, made her who she was now, alone. She waited in her clammy bed for dawn to come, tried to figure out what she felt, scanned her body as Ed had taught, looking for any tender place, a feeling, a message from some core of herself, some place she couldn't reach.

In the dark she used the GX phone to search for *PAKing New York* but there was nothing, then *PAKing*, nothing, then *Pneuma Adaptive Kinesthesia*, and still nothing. There was no evidence of what had happened to her, no proof but her memory, that flimsy appliance.

Voices from the street slipped in the window above her mattress. A sad woman was telling a story, voice thick from weeping, half her words too melted to hear, as another woman soberly consoled. Mary put the phone down and tried to listen—it was something about a guy, something about two weeks ago and Facebook and *it's like she doesn't even know me* and a text, a lost sweater or some lost days or something else lost—Mary couldn't be sure. Did her listening have any effect on the woman? Did the woman feel how her story, however incomplete, was landing somewhere? Something about listening from a distance, drowsy in bed and in the dark, made Mary's caring feel so pure.

A car drove up. The voices stopped. Doors opened, slammed, the car motored away, and the silence came back heavier.

Then, lulled into a half sleep, Mary vaguely remembered someone using Facebook to track someone else down. She'd never used Facebook (or *had* it or *been on* or *in* it—a person's grammatical relationship to Facebook had never been clear to her) because it had seemed, in college, to be a display case for friendships (of which she had few) or a document of one's past (which she didn't want to believe she had) or a way to keep tabs on the people who had receded from one's life. So she had never joined until now, thirty years old, entering no photographs, no hometown or job or interests, no hobbies, political or religious views, just this blank blue-and-gray receptacle with her name (*a* name) on it. It was alarmingly easy to find her, the only Chandra Broder, a little square photo of her taken from behind—full lotus on a beach, facing a sunset. Add Friend.

She stared at the tiny photo of Chandra until she fell asleep, and when she woke, she found nothing had changed except daylight had come back, that ambivalent turn. Her apartment was as empty as it had ever been. She wouldn't be needed at the loft until the afternoon so she stayed in bed for the next few hours, copying and pasting the same message to Chandra's friends.

You don't know me, but I was Chandra Broder's college roommate. I have been unable to reach her lately and I am worried. Also I have been getting distressing e-mails from someone who claims to be her. Any information would be helpful. Thank you, Mary Parsons

It read stiffly. She wondered if she should lighten or darken the mood of it, make it seem more or less urgent, friendly, distressed, but she gave up revising and kept sending it out, without variation, to each friend on Chandra's list.

The first reply was from someone who couldn't remember how he'd met her. Another hadn't heard from her in years: *Sorry*. Another: *Dude, weird*. Another said she would try to get in touch, but that even though she didn't know Chandra that well, this didn't sound that weird to her. *She's flaky*, the message said. Mary deleted it.

All the while a blank white box on Facebook kept asking, *What's on your mind?*—and telling her to upload a picture so her friends could find her, to add her schools so her classmates could find her, to complete her page, explain herself, but Mary kept on her task, sending the message, reading the shrugging replies, until a page came up with a blue thumbs-down: *Sorry, something went wrong*. Everything was gone and she couldn't get back in. She threw the phone across the room, hoping it would break, but it landed on a towel, perfectly fine.

Eventually she got out of bed, took a long shower, gargling and spitting mouthfuls of water, then screaming, just a little and quietly.

It seemed her whole life had been a series of waves, that everything and everyone she'd ever known had come at her with a force she couldn't fight, rushing in, roaring, sucking her down, nearly drowning her before spewing her out again, leaving her alone on a shore before another wave came for her, another force from some unseen center.

20

Love is a compromise for only getting to be one person, Mary said, her pupils huge and deep, her whole life, her entire history, Merle and Clara, that tiny dorm room shared with Chandra, whatever happened in that alley, the Paul months, every fact she'd ever learned, every word read or written, every exhale, every blink, every ounce of her pressed forward, pressed her into the present, this patch of grass on his rooftop's garden, the sky awash in a pastel summer sunset, her hand in Kurt's sweating hand—the ordinary (hand in hand) turned so remarkable and terrifying, a whole other consciousness trapped in flesh touching flesh, touching the flesh holding her consciousness—and her brain was every ocean and every sea combined and her eyesight impeccable as she felt she could see every ridge of every brick on any building across the river, that she could count each spoke on the bikes spinning across the bridge. Every fiber and cell of her pulsed against the air and she felt true.

Wait, Kurt said, his eyes as doll-like as hers. *Wait right there.* Mary watched him retrieve his phone. *Say it again, say it exactly as you just said it.*

She closed her eyes and opened her mouth, forgot everything she'd ever said, forgot all language, forgot her life, and as she opened her mouth, lips untouching slowly, her vocal cords shaking words from her throat, she could feel every slick tooth and muscle in her mouth in the highest detail, and she was filled with wonder over the perfect construction of her mouth, of all mouths, all those wet tongues lying behind lips, beside teeth, between roof and bed of mouth in so many skulls and it was the tongue where all this had begun only an hour before, when they had licked a white powder off a glass plate in his kitchen, chased the bitterness with grapefruit juice and seltzer before splaying themselves on the grass of Kurt's rooftop garden, every living green blade coming alive against their backs as the drug hit, nerves pulsing under the skin, around the heart and gut, in the spine, behind their eyes. She could feel the fire in everything, more alive than ever.

All this time, she thought, *all of this was here and we didn't see it. How could we have missed it? How did we forget?*

After he had recorded her saying the sentence (*Love is a compromise for only getting to be one person*) and after he had replayed it several times into the air, smiling and manic (*Love is a compromise for only getting to be one person . . . Love is a compromise for only getting to be one person . . .*), the two stood, locking hands, unable to look directly at each other without overwhelming and being overwhelmed. They walked to the edge of the roof and looked at the skyline for what felt like hours but was only a few minutes.

The meat around my skull can't stop smiling, she said, and he laughed so much she was afraid he might never stop, and when he did, she was so relieved that she hugged him with the intensity that a parent would hug a child previously feared to have been kidnapped, and they held each other quietly for some time, feeling the bones and tendons in each other's back and thinking about nothing but the simplicity of their bodies pushed together, life against life, all there is. The sun was setting and below them and some blocks away a street fair had lit up with lights strung between posts and the noise of carnival games and the smell of fried dough wafted up in the hot air and it filled their noses and mouths and ears and sinus cavities, reminding Kurt of summers long past, of the child he no longer was.

We should go down there, Kurt said, a boy again, *we should go see what it is*. The drug had burned away some of his fears, as drugs will do, and though he had an intense dislike of crowds and fear of being photographed with anyone in public, he felt that his sunglasses and hat and Mary and this incalculable awe would keep him safe.

A block from the loft they noticed a couple under some construction scaffolding, arguing. The couple seemed resigned to their dissatisfaction with each other, as if it had been going on this way for such a long time that they had committed themselves, moved into it, signed a lease. The man appeared to be exerting all his energy into the skin around his skull, and the woman was shouting, leaning toward him, both her hands held out with the palms up, pleading. Then she covered her face and began to shake. He moved toward her, put a hand on her arm that she shrugged away. She uncovered her face, a ruin of red and tears, and threw some hard words at him that Kurt and Mary could barely recognize as English.

What are they saying? Kurt asked, not expecting an answer, but Mary took his question seriously and began to translate the argument in a state of revelation.

Why are you not me? Why are you not doing life like I would do it? I thought being in love meant getting to be two people. How could you do something I wouldn't do? This is impossible and insane. I can't be only one person. I need to be you, too. Let me be you. —And she is saying, Shut up, you have it all wrong. I am you, not the other way around. You don't get to be me. I get to be you. I am you. There is no you, only the other me.

Kurt stared at her as she spoke, believing her to be some kind of genius or saint, though he couldn't get any words out of his throat, just stood there, until he finally said—*Yes, that's it! That's it!* Then even louder: *YES!*

The arguing couple looked over at them and Kurt shouted *YES* again and that yes echoed between the tall buildings, leaving fragments of itself everywhere until Kurt added, *Hey! We just solved all your problems!*

The woman shook her head and muttered something as the man shouted, *Hey! Fuck you!* He put his arm around her and they stomped down a darker part of the street, united in their dislike of this stranger. They later made fun of his baseball cap.

Kurt and Mary watched shadows shift across the couple's backs as they walked away but found the couple's anger didn't bother them. They walked toward the street fair, transfixed by its distant glow, weaving their way into the throngs of people, women with their hair tied up in scarves, men eating funnel cakes, children engulfed by neon-yellow and hot-pink stuffed animals, fuzzy dogs and puffer fish with fur and plastic eyes bulging bigger than the children's heads, these prizes, this synthetic joy.

Somewhere a mariachi band played, the horns and guitars distorted by distance, melting in the heat, and as Kurt listened, he realized he'd been in public, just out here, for maybe two full minutes, but no one had noticed him, and no one had asked to take a photo with him or to sign his name on something, and no one had asked him to listen to whatever the person needed to say to him and no one had grabbed him and no one had given him a headshot or a card and no one had told him an incredibly sad life story—and instead everyone had let him exist without being reminded of himself, to exist as part of a crowd, a person, and his eyes were so joyful behind his sunglasses, unobserved, a gift these people didn't know they'd given, and he cried.

He stood still for a while longer, until he noticed that Mary had let go of his hand and he turned to find her standing a few yards from him, staring off, mesmerized by whatever she was mesmerized by, alone in whatever she was thinking. Kurt wished he could be in her head—though this is not to say that he wanted to know what she was thinking, and this is not to say that he wanted Mary to tell him what she was thinking—no, he wanted, more than anything, so painfully and impossibly, to feel her thoughts and feelings at the same time as she was having them. He wanted to feel this moment exactly as she felt this moment, not to observe her life through the lens of his life—no, he wanted to inhabit Mary completely and he thought this must be love, that he had now reached some state of pure love. He felt, with a blinding certainty, that the feeling he had about Mary in this moment was truly permanent, but the permanence he felt was not the permanence of his love for her—as none know which loves can survive a life—what he felt was the permanence of love itself, outside of people. Yet he also felt doubt and protectiveness—how could he ensure this feeling would never leave him in this world so full of endings—nights ending, people there, then gone, melted ice cream, drugs making their finite journeys through a body. He ached to find a way to make this feeling last for at least the short duration of his life—was that asking for so much? Couldn't there be a way, he thought, to convince this feeling to keep him company, unwavering, to death?

Mary was scanning the crowd, searching for something (for

him, he thought) and Kurt came close to her and she smiled, but only a little, and he buried his face into her neck, took in the perfect animal smell of her, wrapped his arms around her waist, and she whispered, *I need water. I can't find any water here*, and he was overtaken with urgency—anything she needed, he needed even more desperately for her.

The crowd suddenly seemed sinister, impatient, perverse. Everyone was standing in a line going somewhere terrible or talking to an angry child, little dictators with huge eyes and chocolate or dirt ringing their terrible mouths, freakishly colored animal corpses hanging on their backs. The vendors were all screaming—screaming orders to each other or advertising their cheap games or flimsy shit for sale. The scent of burning meat was everywhere. People dug their sharp teeth in cones of red ice. People were moaning, were covered in sweat, and no one seemed well.

We have to get out of here, Kurt said, taking her hand, running them through the awful people, this last place on earth they needed to be. They ducked into a juice bar and confronted a large cooler of bottles—green, yellow, milky-white, and red juices—and Kurt was paralyzed by the colors, the mystery of all these liquids, the impossibility of even imagining putting a liquid like this into his body at this precise moment, this sensationally complicated and overdetailed moment, not noticing that Mary was talking to the boy behind the counter.

I'd like a water.

Totally. What kind?

Of water?

We have coconut water, aloe water, ginger water, vegetable water, herb-infused water, yellow watermelon-juice-enhanced water, turmeric water, and deionized apple-cider-vinegar agave water.

She felt dreadful and dry.

Oh—and honey lemon water. And maple water.

I couldn't— Don't you have water?

We have waters.

Regular water?

We offer micronutrient-enhanced hydration.

Why can't you answer me?

The boy behind the counter stared at Mary, smiled, caught on to her high, then saw and recognized Kurt, who was still captivated by all the bottles of colored liquids. A previously unnoticed man in a white apron smeared with beet juice switched on the metal juicer, this death machine, and he scowled as he forced carrots and celery stalks into this contraption and his hair may or may not have been made of worms and the boy at the register now had a look of utter derangement and he appeared to be a human carrot, a vegetable cannibal. Kurt and Mary bolted out the door, ran all the way home, hand in hand, down a less crowded street to avoid the fair again, and they rushed past his doorman Jorge, not even saying hello, frenzied and determined to be alone in the perfectly calibrated comfort of Kurt's loft.

Why did we ever go anywhere? Kurt asked, breathless, in the elevator. He held her to his chest and she clung to him and for a moment they were happy and peaceful enough to not wonder how they might keep this feeling forever, how they might cheat the system.

They spent the rest of the night doing the secretly magical things that people on psychotropics do—locked in unashamed eye contact, talking in slow truisms that whittle all the world's problems down to a single sentence or word, weeping over mundanities turned profound—water falling from a faucet, a pen rolling across the counter, pillow prone on the floor.

The comedown came slowly and as Mary drifted in and out of some half-asleep dream or half-awake trance, she couldn't tell what was the drug's trick and what was her own perception. She was faintly aware of something happening to her body. A pressure was on her feet, then her legs, between her legs, against her belly. She felt almost paralyzed but she managed to reach out and feel Kurt sleeping on his side of the bed and she tried to move her legs but she could not move her legs and she reached up, and felt Kurt's shoulders hovering above her but at the same time she could not reach up, was not reaching up, and her body spun inside itself and it was hot and cold at once and she felt she was safe but locked up in a very small space and she couldn't tell if she was being held down or held still or had somehow become nothing at all.

She looked toward the window and Kurt was there, looking at the skyline, and she looked at the bedroom door and he was there, too, backlit and leaning against the jamb and she felt his legs against her legs and his arms wrapped around her and she felt something inside her body, and she wondered if all she felt inside her body was just more of her body, and she wondered if she had somehow come unstuck in time but she also felt stuck in time, unable to get away from the feeling that all the time she'd spent with Kurt was somehow circling her, sieging her.

Every memory she had of him flashed by—from that first session in that hidden bar, to all the silent afternoons in his loft, to their dinners together, the hours in the editing room, the black cars he sent her away in some nights or the black cars they shared on others. She remembered Kurt laughing with her or serious with her or smiling at her or crying and she remembered the tender shock on his face the first night the Anger Girlfriend appeared, and the way his panic seemed increasingly performed with each visit from Ashley. She thought of the night he told her about his mother, about how she lived and died, about what happened to him after, and though Mary was still mostly thankful that he asked her nothing of her past, she also vaguely resented that he'd never asked and felt his lack of curiosity must have meant he cared for her not at all— And wasn't that okay? Since he was her employer? Since this was all some strange experiment or therapy or game?

But as the drug wore off like a season's snowmelt, she found a plain sadness. She had lost her family, a preventable loss, and taught herself to not even miss them. But hadn't it been their responsibility to not lose her? Or did children eventually become the parents to their parents, as she'd once heard someone say, and if so, had that already happened to her? At what age did you lap them? Had she missed her chance? And what happened to parent-children without their child-parents? What could she do now?

As another day broke, Mary stared at Kurt's sleeping face, marveling at how he could be asleep while she was so awake, her eyes and mind clear now, and she knew she loved him in a way that immediately required her to hate him, a little, for how he had never asked her what had happened to her. But would she have even told him about the cabin, about Merle, his manifesto, her little lonely beginning? But this was what people in love do, isn't it? Give each other their stories as a way to re-hear them, as a way to re-understand their histories, what those histories did to them, what they do to them still?

Though losing his mother was the most painful thing Kurt had ever felt, he almost enjoyed, in a way, telling the story of her loss more than twenty years later because her death was the most human thing that had ever happened to him and it sometimes seemed to be the last truly human thing that had happened to him before his life became surreal, and before he began taking that surreal life for granted, floating somewhere near himself, watching himself become more known—but when he told the story of his mother, when he recalled the way she looked at him in those last days when they both knew she was leaving her body and he was staying in his, Kurt became, again, a whole person, a human on the earth, but when he stopped telling this story, he floated back up again, went away from himself, watched himself almost live.

As Mary stood in the bathroom that morning, she thought of what she'd seen in Kurt's face the few times he had spoken about his mother, of how his face became softer in a way, as if some system of tethers that had been controlling him from the inside now went slack.

If you take everything for granted, then you're blind, but if you take nothing for granted, you're paralyzed, she said, aloud, watching her mouth in the mirror.

And as she said this, some of that paralysis fell away. She still had a vague sense that something had happened to her body in the night, but when she searched herself for evidence of something, a bruise, a sore spot, she only found a soreness deep in her head.

21

Neither Kurt nor Mary had noticed they were being photographed through the juice bar windows, didn't see two paparazzi keeping pace with them across the street as they ran home, hand in hand, but by morning the photos had been sold and published and republished and a dozen reporters had spoken to the cashier and juice-maker, and a few thoughtless think pieces had been written overnight, each making guesses as to who the extremely *normal*-looking girl with Kurt was and why they hadn't bought any juice and what were they running from or toward? All the while Kurt and Mary were oblivious, sleeping, living low to pay for all the high they'd had. Mary returned to bed from the bathroom and he held her with the intimate remove of a child holding a blanket.

Kurt Sky isn't even my birth name, he said later, as midday light began to make their late bed seem strange. *It was Kurtis Joel Kerensky. And no one knows. Not even Matheson. Only you.*

If he had told her this while they had been high, she might have felt the significance of his giving her something of himself he'd never given anyone else, or she would have seen how this made them similar—both born under names they'd shed—but she wasn't high anymore, and she couldn't see the world from that angle. Back on the heavy earth, this didn't feel like much at all, so as he told her the story of how he changed his name, all Mary could think was how she would never tell him what her first name had been, that protecting her history was the only way she could control it, that if no one knew the way her childhood had been taken, then she had, in a way, taken it back.

Kurt took his time telling her this story that supposedly no one else knew, how it had, at some point, involved his mother signing something while she was on her deathbed, and though Kurt made some expression in the dim bedroom light that this was an emotionally significant detail to him, his expression didn't—and this embarrassed Mary—seem genuine to her. She tried to make a face signaling to him that she had registered this story as emotionally resonant, that she could almost feel what he felt, but he didn't seem to notice, kept talking, and she began to wonder how she'd ever survive another day in his company, how she'd ever made it this far. Of course it was just her job to care, to listen, to be available, and she knew this was employment, not a relationship, that she was merely participating in the worldwide tradition of dreading one's work, but she felt a new difficulty in getting herself to cooperate, to go along with it all. A tide, it seemed, had gone out.

Kurt, I need to speak to you for a moment please.

Good morning to you, too, Kurt said, but Matheson just turned and walked back toward his office. It was two in the fucking afternoon, Matheson thought. Kurt followed, shrugging at Mary as he left her alone.

Midday, the loft was filled with sunlight in bright, holy quantities. Mary felt something she often felt during PAKing, that she wasn't sure if something was really happening to her or if she was bracing so much for something to happen that she had made something happen. It could have been the drug still leaving her system or the lack of sleep or it could have been that she was worried about not seeing Ed, waiting for her body to go wrong again. She lay down on the big white couch and almost fell into something like sleep, waking only when she felt Kurt sit beside her.

What was it?

Nothing, just some photos on the Internet that Matheson is paranoid about.

She was dizzy and breathing hard. He didn't notice, didn't say anything, just ran his fingers through her hair and stared out the window. As she looked up at him, his face seemed somehow different, an uncomfortable comfort.

You know, Shia LaBeouf's paper bag made so much sense to me. It seemed like the most sane thing to do, maybe the only sane thing to do.

She stared at him, totally unsure of what he was talking about.

See that's what I like about you. You don't know about any of this stupid Hollywood stuff.

He went on to explain this stupid Hollywood stuff, how this other actor had been fucking with it, somehow, rejecting the viewer, rejecting the industry, then he ranted for a while about identity and self-perception, about being misperceived or overperceived by others, about self-scrutiny, about mass scrutiny, about surveillance and access and intimacy and the loss of the intimate. He talked so much that Mary forgot she also had the ability to say things and her mute watching fueled him.

There is no intimate space left in my life, he said what felt like an hour later, on the edge of tears. *Everyone needs privacy, a sense of the intimate. You go crazy without it. I wish people understood.* And for a little while Mary did see him as a person, just this little man with the same confusions and exhaustions as anyone, desperation, a wish for some better way to be, though she hadn't really been listening to what he'd been saying, just the way he'd been speaking, his tone, his trouble. It was possible, she thought, that's all anyone could really do for another.

What do you think I should do?

What do you mean?

Kurt's face scattered, eyes welled. He'd broken a sweat. *About all of this? How I've put myself into a place where I can't—I can't—*

He pulled Mary toward him, held her head that way her mother had all those years ago. She thought he might be crying.

I think you should quit everything, she finally said. He stroked her hair. *If you don't like it.*

They parted and she stood by him and he looked at her, hesitating, noticing for the first time that she did have some grim beauty about her, something that couldn't be seen so quickly. She was right, also, that it was time to change everything, that he was long overdue to enter some new phase. He began pacing the room, wondering how he would make his exit from the Kurt Sky that everyone had come to expect into the version of himself that he felt he was. The Gala was a week away, an event that had increasingly become a media spectacle instead of what it had once been—a fund-raiser for one charity or another, though Kurt could never remember which one. He'd always gone unaccompanied, and each year he vowed, with increasing certainty, that he would not return the next year, as the event seemed increasingly false and performatory, a large-scale publicity stunt, a cry for attention from the people who already had everyone's attention. Every year he went back and every year he regretted it. But this year he would go and not regret it. He would use it as his stage to make his exit, to make a statement about falseness.

That afternoon he had Matheson commission a custom gown for Mary, a simple black silk slip dress with a headpiece, a cape that obscured her whole face. It hung on her with an inevitability, as if her body had created it, grown it off her skin like a thin pelt, capping her crown to clavicle, the drape perfect.

Kurt issued no statements and took no questions as the pair made a slow walk down the red carpet, camera flashes epileptic—Kurt Sky and this cloaked woman, her stride not exactly elegant, both her hands gripping his elbow to steady herself on heels. In minutes several blog posts had run alongside the eerie pictures of them—Kurt with an alarmingly mundane expression, Mary invisible except for her bare, pale arms. The first site to post about it crashed from the traffic, the head of a peloton taking the brunt. A hashtag immediately sprang up (#baglady), gathering reports from inside the Gala. (Some speculated it was botched plastic surgery, while others thought she might be an android, as she was robotically motionless for the entire evening, and for a while it seemed to echo a stunt by an emerging L.A. performance artist who had, only a few weeks before, sat in a gallery for fourteen hours a day with a similar bag over her head as every episode of every season of *Game of Thrones* played and played and played.) Some were amused and others annoyed at what a spectacle Kurt and his bag lady had created, usurping all their lesser stunts, their translucent gowns, their unlikely dates, the just-divorced power couple each arriving as a part of a new power couple. The Gala itself consisted of a dinner no one ate, a series of presentations no one listened to, then a lot of standing around, everyone looking around to see everyone else looking around.

Kurt and the bag lady made their exit just as the presentations were beginning, a trail of paparazzi following them from the venue, following their car to Kurt's loft. The photos were so valuable now that some charged into the apartment lobby, the flashes reflecting wildly off the mirrors and white marble, Jorge screaming, threatening to call the police.

Ashley had been in the loft for two hours, ready for a session that had been long ago scheduled, a Relational Experiment that Matheson hadn't moved (intentionally or not, it was never clear) after Kurt had come up with this Gala stunt. Bored and furious at the long delay of Kurt's arrival—which would mess up her sleep and potentially thwart tomorrow's training—Ashley began roaming the loft, slightly tilting the frames on the wall, going through his desk, disorganizing his closet, leaving thumb smudges of lipstick on white bedsheets and towels, until a cluster of framed photographs in his office stopped her—Kurt with his first Oscar, glowing and delirious and so young, and a candid in a restaurant taken by a friend who went on to become famous for photographing his famous friends—and a teenaged Kurt with his mother, scarf tied over a bald head (her fearful face, flattened out by a flash, smiling at days she'd never see). Some of Ashley's anger dissolved, or stalled for a moment, until she looked at the last photograph: Kurt with his arm slung around a younger man. A familiar face. A terrible and familiar face. She threw it across the room, smiling though she wasn't happy.

The Research Division crowded around her video feed, some of them trying to analyze the data, baffled by the rise and fall of her activity patterns, how each photograph had done something drastically different to her. None of them knew, as Ashley's background check or brain scans could tell them nothing of it, what seeing that face had meant to her.

If she'd been a more superstitious person she could have seen a conspiracy, a plot against her, but she didn't believe in such things. What she knew then was that this job was no longer worth it, that she could no longer rent herself to this man and his experiment, and with this attitude she began to storm around the loft, to all the rooms that had been deemed off-limits, the rooms without surveillance, and though one member of the Research Division stood, made a move to the door to bring Ashley back, Matheson told him to sit, to let her go, that it was fine. Why he permitted Ashley to go where she liked is also unclear, whether he had an intent, whether he planted what Ashley discovered in the editing room.

The room was in an unusual state of disarray, the screens still on, the desk scattered with notes and photographs and files. The middle of the screen triptych was paused on an image Ashley recognized, an evening last week when her assignment had been to interrupt Kurt and Mary in the middle of a dinner. She tried to find a way to play the scene, but the computer seemed to be locked. When she looked over some of the papers—an outline of scenes, a script, photographs of various women taken from strange angles, Ashley among them—it all became clear and sickening. She ripped up the pages and photos, pushed the desk over, threw anything she could at the three screens, stormed from the room, and heard the elevator arrive just as she turned the corner, Mary blinking in the light after taking off her hood.

Hardly anyone can remember how this attack happened—Mary and Kurt and Ashley each have their own accounts, incorrect and incomplete. Mary screamed at some point or perhaps did not, and Ashley was silent or may have said something to

Kurt as she did her work. One surveillance video did capture a shot of Kurt as he staggered into a room and fell, his arm flopping out of its socket, the emergency-exit alarm blaring, Ashley gone, blood drizzling from Kurt's nose and smeared across his white tuxedo shirt, the black jacket heaped aside like roadkill.

Mary hardly remembers anything about the ambulance, only that she didn't think she'd be allowed to ride with him to the hospital because she wasn't family, but Kurt had insisted, pain drunk, and the EMTs let her in, and as they sped through the night, Mary felt an emotional vertigo of looking backward and forward at once, seeing a younger version of herself look at this older version of herself, a dizzy confusion over how her life could have gone this way. There was no real path, it seemed, no logical way to live. Everything was a broken, blood-filled mess.

Still in her Gala gown in the hospital's waiting room, she glimpsed a television screen hanging in the corner and finally saw what everyone else had seen: a faceless woman hanging stiff on Kurt's arm. The manic editing (four seconds here, three seconds there, a zoom-in on Kurt's face, a pan-up shot of the whole gown, a zoom-in on the silk bag, back to a split screen of commentators, back to Kurt, the gown, and back again) was dizzying and she could only watch for half a minute before she had to close her eyes. *How does this world survive itself?*

The waiting room was full of the bandaged, the moaning, the sleeping, the angry, the despondent, the anxiously hopeful. None of them had noticed her or Ashley, all of them stuck in their personal emergencies. This was a good place, she realized, to be invisible. She felt a hand on her shoulder and expected a nurse to be there; when she looked up, it was Ashley, radiant, backlit, saintlike. They didn't say anything and Ashley eventually lowered herself into the seat beside Mary. The muted television played the same images of Kurt and the bag-headed Mary on a loop and Ashley watched for a moment, eventually turning to Mary.

We don't know each other, Ashley said, almost whispering, *not really, but in some ways we know each other completely.*

Mary wasn't sure what to say, wasn't sure if there was anything she could say and wasn't sure if she still had the ability to speak, this late, this tired, this bewildered.

In a way, Ashley said, rising suddenly as she spoke, *we're practically sisters—*

She left quickly then, and for a moment Mary considered running after her, dashing into the night, throwing her dead phone into a sewer, walking whatever distance between this hospital and home, forgetting all of this had ever happened and just leaving, quitting, finding some other way to be, but just then a nurse did appear, brought her back to see Kurt, and if any of these midnight nurses knew who he was, they didn't let on, treated his body as if it were any body, though he wasn't alert enough to notice.

His shoulder and arm had been mashed back into place but would be tender and bruised for a while and he had a concussion, someone explained, some young man with heavy bags under his eyes, and Mary was told that concussions are both common and mysterious, might mean nothing and might mean, days or weeks from now, Kurt could suddenly fall dead to the ground or maybe just have a headache or mild vertigo. He was probably still in shock but he knew his own name, what year it was, the president, so all he needed now was to rest.

Nothing we can do about it, the doctor said, *nothing I can really tell you.*

When they got back home, Kurt was zombified on painkillers, still in his tux pants and bloodstained shirt, leaning heavily on Mary, but Matheson had been waiting and began barking at her—

Why didn't you call me, I can't believe you didn't call me—I didn't even know what hospital they'd sent you—a massive oversight, Mary, totally unprofessional. I have to hear from Jorge *about the paparazzi and you won't even pick up your phone! What the fuck?*

She squinted at him, felt the day had lasted too long.

Go home. Don't come back until I call you, Matheson said, leaving her in the lobby as he guided Kurt to the elevator, arm around his waist, limping together.

Awake alone, early morning, does a person ever wish for instructions on how to best love the other people sleeping in their home—their children or partners, blood and chosen families?

And if that person overhears those people clinking glasses and mugs in the kitchen—asking about coffee, are we out of juice, and what about the weather—does that person wonder if they're loving their people correctly? When those people yawn or sneeze or when they're silent as morning radio tells them everything, where exactly is the love between the person and their people? Is it a scent in the room? Is it located in the memory? Is it, like out-of-season clothes, in the basement?

And when the people cannot find their shoes, their keys, their wallets, and when they ask the person if they've seen them and when the person says they haven't, is there a part of the person that wishes they had? Does the person wish they knew where everything went? Does the person wish they knew, for certain, for absolute certain, what their glances and touches and voices really do to those people? Does the person ever wish for brain scans, diagnostics, something firm to back up their soft feelings?

How to best love? How to know anything, for certain, in another's heart?

Such a serious thing we are doing, and no one really knows how to do it.

PART THREE

One

I woke up with nothing. A silent apartment. I had no pain, no need. Nothing to struggle against or for. I fell asleep and when I woke again, I couldn't tell how much time had passed, how much of myself I'd given over to absence.

I had a whole bed and home to myself, days and weeks and a life to myself, and if I died, I knew I'd only be found from the smell. That's something that happened here, dying alone, your door being hacked down to find your apartment not fit for company. New Yorkers performed this anxiety as a way to bond with one another, but if you had this worry alone, if you had no one to tell, if there was no one there to tell you—*No, that won't happen to you, not you*—well. This thought can take strange shapes in an empty room. So I don't let myself worry about this anymore, but sometimes I feel as if it might be worrying about me.

A voice in another apartment disappeared into the walls between us, muffled like a song in radio static. From my bed I strained to listen to whatever was being said, and eventually I got out of bed and went to the living room to be nearer to the voice. I crouched by the wall to listen but still understood nothing. Would it have mattered to that stranger to know I had tried?

A couch was in my living room. I remembered being here when the two deliverymen unboxed it, assembled it, took away all the cardboard and plastic, but the presence of the couch still confused me. I had not yet allowed myself to sit on the couch, as I felt it did not belong to me. I had the sense that I was a stranger living as a stranger in a stranger's body in yet another stranger's home. Perhaps one of the strangers I had once been had bought it. It was pale blue, the only furniture, the only any-thing, in the living room. Sometimes when I came home from my GX shifts, it surprised me, a mute intruder.

I went to the kitchen to drink water straight from the faucet, passing the previous night's gown crumpled on the hallway floor. It reminded me a little of a snakeskin that had mesmerized me in a forest.

I wondered what the Gala had looked like beyond that sack over my head.

I thought of Clara, for some reason. I knew I should call her or find a neighbor who might check on her, something I'd been meaning to do and somehow not doing for months. I stared into a dusty corner. Eventually I felt the light shift to afternoon and I still had done nothing to prove I'd been alive today. Something potential turned suddenly kinetic in me, and I felt I had to make up for everything I had not done. I found some old newspaper and vinegar and cleaned the windows, until I began to wonder why I was doing this naked, so I went to the bedroom to put on a shirt, but I ended up just pulling the sheet off the bed and wrap-ping it around me, then realizing I hadn't yet brushed my teeth, so I went to the bathroom to do that but got distracted by the couch, which I had still been putting off sitting on for some reason so I went and sat there, saw the rotary phone I hadn't used in months and picked it up without thinking and dialed Aunt Clara's number, and as it rang, I felt aware of my legs and arms in this tangled sheet, pressing into the sofa, the sofa pushing back on me, some strange force within it.

Clara's phone rang and rang, no answer, but I was determined to reach her, if not by phone then by plane, by car, by my legs, by my face, by myself. That's what people did. People looked into the eyes of the people who had brought them here, brought them to this planet, raised them. Didn't those people have a clue about why you might be here? Didn't those people maybe have an opinion? Some ideas? I was tired of my life happening to me. I needed to make things happen.

I found the GX phone under the gown and it was, as they say, *dead*, so I plugged it in, waited for its resurrection, its messages—none—but I soon found how easy it was to find people's names and numbers and where they lived. In minutes I had the phone numbers for the homes on either side of Clara. The first call I made, a little boy picked up the phone and I asked if his mother was there (*No*) or his father (*No*) or anyone (*Not anyone*). I asked him how old he was and he said, *Four. I'm big.* I didn't know what to do so I told him bye and he said bye. Anyway, I cried for a while after that, wiping my eyes with the sheet.

The second number I called, I got this middle-aged female voice and I told her who I was, *Mrs. Parsons's niece*, and just from the way she said, *Oh, Mrs. Parsons*, I could tell and was relieved that Clara wasn't dead.

Could you go check on her? I'm just worried because I can't seem to get her on the phone.

Oh, well, I suppose I could, but I probably can't make it out there until tomorrow.

That's fine, I said, confused about why it would take so long to walk next door but not wanting to make a thing of it.

But I suppose you could just call the front desk yourself and get ahold of her a little quicker.

The front desk?

Yes, at Green Meadow?

I'm sorry?

Well, I thought you would have known. They had to move her out to a nursing home over across town a few months ago now?

I didn't—I wasn't—

Well, I can tell you what happened, you see, she hadn't been putting her trash can out for the trucks, and it had piled up in her garage, and we caught wind of it, so to speak, so I dropped in on her and it was clear she hadn't been keeping house like she used to. A little baby raccoon had even settled into the kitchen and she didn't seem to realize. I asked her if there was someone I could call for her, someone to come check on her, and she told me to call Tom, which just about broke my heart, Mary. Just about broke it. If I had known about you, I would have called, but she didn't remember having any other family. I thought she had a sister still living, so I tried looking through her papers, but I couldn't find a phone number or anything. So I didn't know who to call is what I'm saying. I'm sorry, dear, this must be a lot to take in.

I felt like that little boy, like that four-year-old. I said thank you or something, and she kept going, explained something about a social worker and Clara's pension. I hung up the phone and this time I didn't cry. I felt something sitting very still in me, something that had stopped moving altogether.

The phone screen lit up with an alert—an e-mail from Chandra, the first all week. There was no body, just an attachment: a grainy photograph of Kurt and me in the silk dress and hood. It felt so strangely foreign, like a photograph of a long-dead stranger, someone I never knew. I could have been surprised that she knew it was me or that she sent more than a dozen additional images of my anonymized body next to Kurt's extremely public one. But I wasn't shocked. I didn't have anything left in me anymore.

Two

I didn't consider buying a plane ticket, I was just suddenly leaving, arriving, renting a car, listening to a rigid voice tell me when and where to turn, how far I was from where I was going. Green Meadow was (unsurprisingly) not a meadow and not green. The squat building was surrounded on all sides by fields of sunburned straw. A nurse at the front desk was eating orange things from a foil pouch. I told her who I was and who I was here to see (*Uh-huh*, she said) and while I was alone in the waiting room full of dusty plastic plants, I fought a constant urge to go back out to that rental car, to ask that soothing plastic woman to tell me how to get somewhere, to get anywhere.

Then they wheeled this person to me, Clara or whoever Clara was now, shrunken and hunched, head nodding and nodding. The nurse yelled, *That's your niece, Mrs. Parsons. Her name is Mary. She came here to see you*, and left us to see each other. We smiled, both confused. I wanted to ask her what had happened and I wanted to say I was sorry and I wanted to say that I loved her, that I had thought of her so much more than she could ever know, but I didn't say any of that.

I said, not thinking, *Aunt Clara, I missed you.* (Not I *have* missed you, not I missed you and now you're here, but something closer to what I said to Paul that night, that I missed him to his face—because I knew the Clara I had known was now over, that I had missed her, that now this remainder of her was here, not her, but a memory of that person.)

Oh! she said. *And I missed you, too. But here we are, now.*

Her voice was bumpy and clogged, but she spoke with the rhythm of a small child, that perplexed wonder. We were quiet. I didn't know what to say. I asked her if she liked living here.

They put me out to pasture . . . on this Green Meadow. I suppose I'll stay here awhile.

Her hands were shaking as she gestured vaguely to the waiting room.

But they have all these damn fake plants! Tom had a fit. He hates these things. Hates them!

It was not at all funny but I laughed—Tom was alive and he hated fake plants.

Well, it seems we've been out here an awful long time, she said. *I'm sure you need to get going. I'm sure you've got better things to do.*

Well, no. I'm actually just here to see you.

Oh. Oh, that's right.

She nodded, staring at me with a sudden terror, and I started to reach out for her hand but she shrank away from me. We were quiet. She chewed her bottom lip, looking at different parts of my body as if trying to add me all up—my feet, my hands, my knees.

You came back.

Yes.

How?

I flew. She squinted at me. *From New York? Remember?*
Florence.

Yes, that's my mother. I'm your niece. Mary.

No. Junia.

That's— I hesitated. *Yes. That's who I am.*

Junia? Her face scrunched up as if she were going to cry, but
it seemed nothing was left in her to let out. *Did you see it happen?*

See what happen?

I just don't know how a person can be like he is. I never— She
stopped, her face slack. She was silent awhile.

Clara?

Yes, she said, not looking up, and a loudspeaker thundered
above us.

—*Good afternoon, Green Meadow! Bible study will begin shortly
in the rec room. That's Bible study, in the rec room, with Pastor Hank,
beginning shortly.*—

I reckon I've studied the Bible enough. She smiled.

I did my best to look or seem happy to be here, but I didn't
know what to say anymore, why I'd come at all. For lack of anything else to say I asked her how long she'd been here.

*They put me out to pasture. On Green Meadow. I suppose I'll stay
here awhile.*

—*For those of you who missed it, I said Bible. Study. In the rec
room. Please head to the rec room now if you want to participate in
Bible study today. Thank you!*—

I reckon I've studied the Bible enough.

I felt the phone buzzing in my pocket—I hadn't realized I
had it on me.

Well, hasn't this been nice? she asked.

—*Matheson*—

Clara—can you hold on for one second? I was already standing and heading toward the door. *I have to just answer this, just one minute.*

She waved at me.

We need you to come to the loft as soon as possible, he said.

I can't.

What?

I left town. I'm in Tennessee, with family. (The word felt strange in my mouth.)

And what on earth are you— No—it doesn't matter. You should know you're not supposed to travel without permission.

It was urgent, and I'm on a break, I thought. *My aunt—*

It's in your contract, Mary. You should know that.

I did, it was just an emergency—

And who else had an emergency recently, Mary? Have you already forgotten?

No, I understand but—

No, you don't seem to understand. That's exactly the problem. Your data from the past two weeks has been very erratic. Can you tell me what the most important requirement of your role in the experiment is?

To be Kurt's emotional . . . support?

To care. You are required to care for Kurt.

I do care.

You haven't even so much as sent him a text in three days, Mary. How is that caring?

I thought you told me—

So it's my fault? Is that it? It's my fault that you don't care?

That's not—

Listen, we need you to get here as quickly as possible. Can you do that for me?

I can fly back tomorrow.

Tomorrow. Well. I suppose that will do—and he hung up.

Clara was gone when I came back in. The same nurse at the

front desk looked up as if she'd never seen me before, as if we had to start all over.

Can I help you?

Mrs. Parsons—she was just here a minute ago.

I think you ought to come back some other day. She's not in such a good way for company.

In the car again I knew where I needed to go and I knew the rigid woman couldn't guide me there, that I would have to drive from memory.

Three

The rifle clicked before I could see him, but I knew he wouldn't shoot. He walked onto the shadow-dappled porch, holding the barrel in line with my heart. It was all for show—that one never had bullets in it, had been broken for years. It was just part of his tactic for hikers that had drifted off course, clicking the rifle, thickening his accent to tell them this was private property, though I knew he didn't even believe in property, just privacy.

I stood silent beside the car. The wind didn't move and I didn't move and I couldn't hear any birds, not even the faint cluck from the chicken coop behind the house.

When he recognized me, his face became my father's face again and I noticed how his skin hung looser, hair grayer, beard wild. He lowered the rifle slowly, as if we both had one. Here was my father at the end of all the years we'd lost.

Well, he said.

He set the gun on the porch and sat on one of the stairs. I started to say something but my jaw clicked when I opened it and my throat resisted, became achy—every greeting was too casual, asking for Mom too childish, observations all futile, his name too heavy. Why hadn't I considered this, considered how I'd have to say something?

It happened, he said. His beard had grown patchy, worn down in some places and wild in others. *I didn't think that's how it would . . .*

His voice was strangely soft and airy.

What happened?

He went to the other side of the porch, touched Mom's rocking chair.

Right here. She started praying out loud and you know she never prayed out loud, didn't like the spectacle of it. She said the Lord's Prayer, then she said it backward. He smiled in that fearful way people smile when they should not smile. *Her mind worked like that sometimes, worked backward for those last couple weeks. I went out to the sycamore and dug a hole like we said we would, picked her up and carried her there. And that was it.*

No, I thought, and I may have said it. He wasn't speaking like a man who had buried his wife and I didn't feel like a daughter who had lost her mother. This wasn't right. Something wasn't here.

This was never the plan, he said, I think, because as he spoke, I fell over, fainting with open eyes. I lay there awhile. Merle stood over me.

You're fine, he said.

My right arm was skinned up and I had dirt and little bits of bark in my mouth. I washed up in the kitchen with the same deer-tallow soap I remembered from forever ago. We said nothing for a while, then he said something about a tumor, some kind of herb she used on it, all the prayers they said and now she'd been dead almost a year. My lungs sank lower in my body, the air in them immovable.

Merle and I sat at that wooden table and I knew then that all he ever wanted was a life that made sense, a life with reasons. He wanted a reason for why he had to watch her cut that tumor from her own breast since he'd been unable to do so, had trembled too much with the scalpel, and there had to be a reason that he had cried as she just grimaced when she poured the tincture into the gaping hole in her body, then burned the wound shut.

At the end she asked for you, he said, but I didn't believe him. I didn't feel anything but the absence of what I thought I should feel. I wondered how the Research Division would have measured this moment, what it might have proved about me.

I had the urge to report this death to someone, to fill out a government form or stand in a line. I would have taken any kind of ritual, even just a document that explained what had happened. Something to say, I'm here. She's dead. It's over. I realize this.

You didn't tell anyone, I said.

Who's there to tell?

Clara.

She's as good as dead herself, he said unsoftly, looking up at the rafters. I hated his ambivalent God, his belief in a plan so infallible that it could tamp out mourning, explained all pains away as part of God's will and therefore not painful, but divine.

Clara is still alive, I said, unable to keep my anger from filling the words. *She was her sister, and you owe it to her—*

You don't know Clara as well as you think you do. She was always against me, against our marriage. And after Tom was gone she just— she was unbearable, always trying to argue with your mother . . . She had ideas about me that wouldn't change no matter what I did and once you stopped coming down here, she wouldn't even talk to us anymore. She never gave me a chance. She never did.

She was still family.

You were family, too.

I had nothing to say, nothing to tell him.

I didn't ask for this, he said. *I never asked to be alone like this. There was supposed to be a family, more children. No one was supposed to be alone—we didn't plan for that. But you were all God gave us. And you left and Florence—* But he didn't finish this sentence, covered his face, and crumpled.

Excuse me, he said a moment later, numb, *I don't know what's gotten into me.*

I knew his raging rhetoric, his silence, his contentment, even his flashes of gratefulness—but I had never seen his sorrow. I wondered if he knew about how, in the real world, sometimes two sad people cry together and the person who is crying a little less grips the person who is crying more, holds them still until their crying lessens and their body releases, lets go of something, then they bend away from each other but keep their arms around each other and they let their eyes meet and one of them will make this tiny hurt smile. Maybe, I thought, we could try to do that.

Everyone is tricking themselves. He shook his head, his eyes drying. *We try to make time easier here, in this creation, and it took my whole life for me to realize it . . . but I don't understand God. All I have is faith.*

I waited for a while, then asked, *What am I supposed to do? I mean about you, out here.*

I'm fine. I'll go to God someday. I'll go lie under that sycamore and wait for it.

I couldn't say anything to this, couldn't tell him he wouldn't, because I knew he would.

You could call me sometime, at least.

To say what?

I looked past him, above him, anywhere but his eyes, those eyes the same size and color as mine, whether I wanted it or not, just like mine.

I don't know why she went like that, why we had a daughter who lost her faith or maybe never had it. But all I have left is faith. This was the life God chose for me. I pray. I write. I wait for the end. That's all there is for me.

I left soon after that.

In my motel room I drank glasses of tap water until I was sick and sat on the bathroom floor, waiting as this slow grief reached me. Eventually I turned on the television to bring a voice into the room, to leave this room without leaving it, but the screen just showed Kurt and me with the black bag over my head. I turned the television off.

I found the motel Bible and put it on the bed, watched it as if it might do something, might move or speak, and eventually I did open it, found some verses I used to love, and as I read them, I heard the words in her voice, calm and soft, natural as birdsong. Had she believed it all? Did she ever hear these verses in my voice? Did she even remember, toward the end, what I sounded like?

I closed the Bible and as I went to put it away, I held it in front of me until my arms ached, waiting for something, it seemed, but all I felt was the weight of an object in my hands.

Four

Unlocking my apartment, I found it was already unlocked.

Kurt was sitting on the blue couch, his arm still in the sling and cast. He was drinking a green juice from his good hand.

You're back.

Yes.

A small video recorder on a tripod was aimed at me, red light above the lens.

Nice place. Very stark.

How did—

You gave me a key months ago.

We were quiet for a moment and he asked me how my flight was, sounding somehow angry, and I said something and we were quiet again. In this silence it eventually occurred to me I hadn't shut the door or taken off my backpack—with nowhere to put them I dropped my keys and bag on the floor, shut the door behind me. Finding company when I'd expected to be alone was disproportionately aggravating.

And how was your trip?

I nodded, hardly felt I'd even had one. *It was—um. I don't know if I can . . . really say.*

Interesting, he said, disinterested.

What's with the camera?

He stood and drained his juice through a straw.

Archival purposes. He walked back to the kitchen. *I'll explain.*

I heard him toss the empty bottle in the sink. He reappeared in the living room, told me to have a seat. I did, on the couch. He angled the camera to face me again and stood behind it.

Do you know the first thing I thought of when I woke up on the morning after the Gala?

I nodded no.

You.

I didn't know how to feel or react to this—the handbook protocols had gone hazy. I thought of how still and silent the forest had been as Merle explained how Florence had died. I thought about having to pull over on the drive back to my airport motel to throw up pure bile onto the passenger seat.

But I didn't hear from you at all.

I'm sorry, I said, a reflex, though the apology seemed to be for someone else. For Clara or Florence. For Chandra. It was possible I didn't care for Kurt at all unless I'd been assigned to do so and I don't know if that makes me a good employee or a bad person or both. I wanted to tell him what had happened in Tennessee, to explain myself, to not have to be the person who had done everything wrong, but I also didn't want him to ever know. These stories were mine, as personal as my spleen.

I know Matheson was probably very short with you on the phone yesterday. He's very protective of me. He understands when I am really hurting.

You look all right now.

And you actually don't look so good.

My mother died.

So did mine. He stared at me through the back of the camera. *You told Matheson it was your aunt. Now it's your mother?*

It's both. My aunt has dementia, I guess, and my mother is just . . . she's dead.

He shook his head. *We know all about you, Mary. That you're an orphan, that the woman who adopted you is named Clara Parsons, that she's been in a retirement home for a while now and you've never visited. It's not that hard to find this stuff. We knew everything the whole time. We just didn't know you were such a liar.*

I sat there, silent, unsure of what I could or should be feeling. I stared into my reflection in the camera lens.

It calls all our data into question. All of it. You've ruined so much.

I didn't care if he thought I was a liar. I didn't want him to know the truth. It was mine. I was keeping it.

One thing is clear, though—we loved each other. From a scientific perspective, at least—and maybe that's all that counts. No matter how much you've lied, you can't lie about what the research proves, and you're the one who has to face the fact that you hurt someone you loved.

To hurt someone you love—what a human activity.

What I had felt for him, I knew, hadn't been an unfettered love but instead an obligation, a sense of being owned—how sad to think that these feelings might seem like love in the brain, that from the outside the difference couldn't be seen.

Maybe I should have known better, that studying people this way was too imprecise . . . He looked down at the back of the video recorder, at the two-dimensional me. *You know, I was always very fond of you, even though you were never very good to me.*

He stared at me, waiting for a reaction. I gave him none.

What I'm really here to tell you is the project is being reorganized, and we just don't need you anymore.

The impulse came to disagree, to say he couldn't send me away. A quick panic—what would I do? What would I even do now? But I said nothing. My mouth opened but nothing came out. I wondered what the Research Division would have measured in me in that moment.

I'll miss you, he said, to the screen, and I said, *I'll miss you, too,* the incantation I'd been taught and trained in. *I love you,* he said, and I repeated this as well.

He scrutinized the camera, the little me in the camera, maybe looking for evidence of a lie. But it was too late for that. I did not love him or not-love him. There were no conclusions to make. For a long while we were silent, then he repeated both those lines—the *I'll miss you* and the *I love you*—and I repeated my repeats and he did it a third and fourth take until, on the fifth, I broke into tears that belonged somewhere else. Exhausted crying, a back stock of crying. He waited until I stopped, uncovered my face, and looked up at him. He stared at me, stared through me. I glanced at the lens. He adjusted something on the camera, then turned it off, began collapsing the tripod with his one good arm as if he had done this every day of his life.

You will still receive your full salary and benefits for a year as long as you give no interviews, anonymous or otherwise. After a year you will receive half salary and no benefits, assuming you are still able to stay away from the media and uphold the stipulations of your NDA. I should also remind you that all the contracts you've signed are still legally binding and in effect. And if you violate them in any way, I assure you we will know about it.

He moved toward the door, stopping short of it, barely turning to speak over his shoulder. *And should anything arise that you find surprising, have a look at your contracts before attempting to contact us.*

Then he was gone. I walked to the window in the kitchen and watched him from above as he left the building and got into a waiting car. And as he did, I saw Ashley dart across the street, screaming, beating on his window, trying to open the door, running after the car as it peeled away.

I wondered what could have happened between them that would make her need him this badly, but I suppose you can never tell what is happening between people. It's as private as eye contact, no room for more than two.

Five

Ed called that afternoon, wanted to know how I was doing.

Okay, I said.

He said my aura had transmitted a message to him and I didn't care if he was lying or delusional or honest or enlightened, and I didn't care if PAKing was full of shit or not—I wanted the comfort of someone in my life being calm and sure. Certain about something I couldn't see. Or maybe I just wanted the comfort of someone being in my life at all.

I asked if I could come back and he said he had room the next morning, and this is how my life went full circle, as it seems life will do, and there I was with Ed again, being stretched and pushed and pinched. I told him everything this time, and I wondered what had stopped me before, why I believed that silence could protect me from anything.

Something settled, something changed in you, he said. *You know something.*

I don't know anything.

He nodded and we were quiet for a long time.

That's something, he said eventually, but I'm not so sure.

After our session I asked if he'd heard from Chandra.

Yesterday, in fact.

I waited for him to tell me where she was, how she was, anything, everything. I felt every pound of bone within me.

She's okay. She can't talk to you, but she's okay.

Where is she?

With his head bowed he said, *It would be better for you not to know yet.*

We were quiet for a while. I didn't know where to look. I felt the same scattered feeling I'd had when Chandra played that moan-y little flute.

Chandra is the sort of person who sits very close to the light. This culture doesn't have an understanding of people like her. They're taken advantage of or diagnosed, explained away, but with her it's not so simple. She is awake to realms other people are too afraid to see, but she also . . . well, she sometimes goes into the light so deeply she can't find her way out. We must believe there are better ways of being, ways of getting better. This is the faith we have to have in healing. But no matter how much we want it, nothing is ever fixed or final.

We sat in silence a while after that until he put his hand on my shoulder and looked at me in such a way that I knew he was telling me that our work was done for good this time, that perhaps we would never see each other again, that he, too, was leaving me here, leaving me with my not-knowing. He moved his hand to my head, thumb between the eyes, and what had been our time together became a thing we had done instead of something we were doing.

I left. I knew it was time. We didn't say goodbye. I just got up and left.

I took a long, roaming route home, my direction feeling inevitable, the city somehow silent around me. Who were all these people and why did they wake up each morning? Did any of them feel what they needed to feel? Did any of them have anyone in their life that meant everything and if so, how did they know? And how did they bear it?

I realized on some narrow street somewhere that I had been shaking, that my legs could no longer carry me, so I leaned back into a wall and fell to the sidewalk, crumpled there, achy and sweating. My ending with Ed became my ending with everyone, with Paul, Chandra, Kurt, Florence and Clara and Merle. I had nothing but myself and I knew that was true for everyone, that we all had to live like this. In our bodies, in the world, a boundary always between them. I felt the shaking lessen, then end. I felt myself breathe. I felt still. I felt.

Someone walked past me, a body slumped on the sidewalk, and threw a few coins at my feet. I kept them.

As I entered my apartment, the landline was already ringing. It never did anymore, the debt collectors now satisfied and Chandra gone.

Is this Mary?

I hesitated before I said it was. I suppose I'm still not convinced.

This is Vivian. Chandra's mother? Listen, I just heard from Julian and he mentioned you had been looking for her recently? On Facebook?

She was waiting on me to say something but all I could do was wait.

Listen, I remember you being a really nice girl, very trusting, but you might not know Chandra as well as you think you do. Things have, um, not been going so well with her and you probably shouldn't try to be in touch.

But where . . . Why didn't she tell me where she—

It's just not that simple, Mary. She got wrapped up with this . . . group, but she left them, too, and it's just—it's all really too much to go into right now but I didn't want you to be worried.

I was worried, I was still worried, but I couldn't say so for some reason. Eventually I asked her if she would tell Chandra something for me, but when she said she would, no words would come. I tried to move my lips, but there were no thoughts.

I think it's just best for you to let go of this, is what I'm saying. You're a sweet girl—I remember you being sweet and I just—believe me, nothing good will come of it.

I thanked her and she thanked me, but neither of us seemed to know what for.

The next morning I opened the blinds to the grimy little window in my kitchen and saw Ashley squinting up at me from the sidewalk like an athlete letting her power build. I dropped my tea, the mug cracking into several pieces, hot liquid sloshing across my feet as I jumped back, landed on a shard, blood and chamomile mixing on the linoleum. Hobbling toward the bathroom, I could hear her shouting my name in the street. I tried to remain calm, not wanting to undo the work I'd done with Ed, but as I sat on the edge of my tub, rinsing my gashed and burned feet in cool water and applying one of Chandra's gels to the wound—there was a knock. I froze, turned off the running water to listen.

Another knock, a pounding.

I did nothing. I didn't have to answer the door just because someone was there. There was no rule about this. I did not move.

Mary?

She'd probably slipped in behind someone.

Mary, I just need to talk to you. Just—open the door. Come on.

I found a bandage for the cut, gauze left over from when I had all those lesions, reminding me how far I'd come. I tried to tally it up, all the good in my life: most of my symptoms were gone, I'd regained my appetite and put on weight, I'd gotten mostly out of debt. I had no stupid job, I had an income now for doing nothing. I could just stay inside my home, speak to no one, clean stuff, and stare. So what if a possibly dangerous woman was outside my door? So what? I could handle this, I thought, if this was all I had to handle.

I'm not going anywhere until you speak to me.

So I went nowhere and she went nowhere for some time. I sat in my living room and she pounded at the door every few minutes until I finally gave up and said, *What?*

Let me in.

I'm not letting you in.

Just tell me where he is.

Kurt?

She scoffed.

I don't know where he is, I said.

Bullshit.

I don't.

He was here. He was with you.

I don't work for him anymore.

Me either, she said with some implied irony I didn't understand.

So, I don't know where he is. Please leave me alone.

I fell asleep that night without leaving my apartment, not wanting to open the door, unsure if she might still be out there.

All week I kept my blinds down and curtains drawn, peeking out only when I needed to leave the house, and if anyone had asked me how I was doing that week (no one did), I would have told them I was terrified, though there was some odd pleasure in it, too, in feeling so hunted.

But I'd also become so tired of adventures, of travel, of debt, of people, of conflict, of noise, of working, of everything. I tried to meditate as Ed had suggested and once I attempted to go to a yoga class at one of the places that Chandra had taken me to, but when a woman with pale pink hair at the front desk smiled in such a vacant way and said, *Namaste*, I turned around and walked out and didn't even realize what I had done until I was nearly home. I ducked into a grocery store and as I considered canned sardines (another Chandra recommendation), I heard Ashley's voice behind me.

I don't hate you. You know that, right?

The other woman on the aisle didn't even look up from the label she was reading, giving us that public privacy.

I don't blame you for anything, Ashley continued. *It's just that he screwed us both over, so we have to stick together.*

I didn't know if she meant Matheson or Kurt and I mostly didn't care, except to distantly wonder if the GX was still going on, if Ashley was in on it, if I should check my contract as Kurt had last suggested, that perhaps all this time they had still been studying me, had bugged my apartment, that perhaps I had signed my whole life over to them and didn't know it. I didn't say anything to her, walked off as if she were just some insane stranger.

They must have told you something, she insisted, trailing me.

No one did. I don't know anything.

But they will—he will. You'll be the first to know. Because you were in love, weren't you? I saw the reports.

It was true I still sometimes wondered where he might be at

that moment, wondered what he was doing, saying, feeling—I didn't know if that counted as love. And if it was, I couldn't tell if it was an unseen perk of the whole thing or a terrible, embittering tax.

I don't know, I said, and kept walking. She followed me as I wandered in circles around my neighborhood. She started ranting, going on about a conspiracy, something they were doing with the surveillance tapes, something about the sensors and what they had done to all of us, that it was abuse, that they'd been controlling her mind, that she didn't even know herself anymore, that she was mush, that she had been ripped apart.

I don't know what I am, she said, *I don't know what feelings are mine anymore.*

We were standing outside my building, and though I wanted to help, I didn't have any help to give. I was out of everything.

I was afraid she would try to follow me in. She held her face in her hands and wept and I wanted to be good to her but it seemed she needed so much more than what I could give. Then she looked up and said, *Why?*

Why what?

But she didn't say what. She just asked, *Why?* again, so gently, as if she were speaking in a church.

I left her on the sidewalk, making sure the door shut behind me. I fell asleep but woke an hour later, turned on all the lights, and looked for her. Half of me knew she couldn't have gotten in, but the other half wondered if she could have slipped into the building, picked my lock, moved stealthily into my bedroom, taken a deep inhale of my hair as I slept, searching for a trace of him, searching for some sense to be made. I wondered if I'd find her waiting in the kitchen, cracking her knuckles, scalding her tongue on tea. I even went out and squinted down my building's stairwell, waited to hear a step on the lobby tile, but there was nothing—no sound, no step—just still air resting on walls and floor. I almost whispered her name into the dark silence, but all I could do was inhale and hover at the edge of the *A*.

Six

When Ed called to say we needed one last session, immediately, that afternoon—*No charge*, he said—I wasn't sure I wasn't dreaming. In the week since I'd seen him I'd been sleeping so much my waking life had become hazy and my dreams had become sharper.

I woke up facedown on Ed's table, his elbow pressed into the base of my spine as he pushed my right shoulder up.

He said, *I saw it.*

Unable to speak, I listened.

It was the strangest thing. Something told me to go for a walk last night before biking home and there was a line outside that movie theater two blocks from here and I can't think of the last time I went to a movie, but I got in the line, saw a very interesting film . . . anyway, I'm sure you know where this is going.

Though I didn't, I couldn't or just didn't want to correct him.

And then it all made sense—why we had to stop our work, all that psychic cording you didn't realize and everything you told me last week. It all made sense.

I felt unsure of what he was implying but I mostly didn't care. It felt so nice to be touched that I could have tolerated almost anything, and later when I was dressed and he was saying his final, final goodbye, I wanted to hug him or tell him something or ask him to clarify what he meant about the movie, but I felt I had to get out of there immediately. I had already mourned our work twice and there was no use in mourning it a third time. I left the building and went to that bench in that sooty little shred of a park by the street with too much traffic.

I'd been sitting there for a half hour or so when a woman, she must have been barely of drinking age, barely of any age at all, approached me with a wide smile and wild eyes.

Are you . . . ?

I looked at her, waiting on something to add up.

I just—I'm so sorry to bother you, but I'm an acting student and I've just never—I can't think of anyone who—your performance in The Walk *was the most moving thing I've ever seen. It was so authentic, so . . . charged!*

I said nothing and she kept talking.

I'd ask for your autograph but I don't have a pen or anything— do you?

No.

Can I? Can we? She held her phone up, sort of shrugging at it. I couldn't tell what she was asking but then she sat next to me and held the phone above us, our faces reflected, and just before the screen blinked I saw myself—brow bent and mouth straight.

Thank you, thank you so much. She rushed from me, as if any minute I might explode.

I went home quickly, making sure not to come close to anything like eye contact with anyone, taking the less peopled streets, weaving with intent through the crowds thronging Broadway and the avenues. When I got home, I found the GX phone, half hoping it wouldn't turn on anymore, but it did—I suppose it still counted as one of my benefits—and I immediately looked up *The Walk*, the search bar knowing me better than I knew myself, adding *Kurt Sky*. The first thing that came up was a one-minute trailer, Kurt in profile as the lead image, and though I hesitated, I played it.

A long shot of Kurt walking through a field, one I remembered from his editing room. Kurt's eyes, close-up, darting. Then there I was, sitting in his living room, then in bed, a shot of Kurt running, another shot of his eyes, then one of the more violent attacks from Ashley, me in the background, watching. More shots of Kurt in the field, running and panting, then a voice-over—*We tried to keep all these secrets*—me in the kitchen, looking up into the skylight—*but we always knew*—and cut back to Ashley, dripping in sweat, smiling—*The Walk*.

I set the phone down on the couch, went to the kitchen, and couldn't remember what I had come in there for, went to the bathroom and thought the same thing, went to the bedroom, took off my clothes, and went back to the living room. I looked at the phone without touching it. I wanted to know more and I wanted to know less. I went to the kitchen, drank a glass of tap water, refilled the glass and drank again. I went back to the living room, lay on the couch beside the phone, and pressed it on, began searching *The Walk Kurt Sky* over and over, clicking deeper and deeper in, reading reviews, reports on ticket sales, reading essays about Kurt, reading essays about why most of the actresses were uncredited, reading theories about who we were. I read the ranting ends of comment threads attacking or defending what I looked like, the sound of my voice, my *acting*. It was the year's best film according to some, or the century's worst according to others. It had only been out a few days but it seemed a whole wing of the Internet was already devoted to it, as if there were little to no distance now between every living person's opinion of something and the searchable catalog. It was groundbreaking, thrilling, boring, feminist, chauvinist, radical, predictable, avant-garde, pretentious, brilliant, tragic, highbrow, lowbrow film or movie or trash. Some said using amateur actors was a manipulative fad, that Sky was one of the greatest film artists we'd ever seen, that he was still arguably the best actor who had ever lived—by nightfall I knew everyone's opinion. I had caught up on new theories on the #baglady, and the phone grew hot in my hands, but more came up: *New Selfie of* The Walk's *Anonymous Actress with Lucky Fan!*

There I was beside a girl smiling as if in midlaugh, tilting her head at a studied angle, documenting her joy beside my whatever. Looking at it, I felt frightened in that way that large things are frightening—looking down from a great height or swimming in a part of the ocean with an unreachable floor. Being taken, having your photograph taken—I realized then that it was called this for a reason.

I nearly burned my eyes out as the battery wore down, reading and watching and listening to everything I could. Finally it died and I let it.

Seven

Days, I slept late. Nights, I wondered if I should go out somewhere, eat a meal in public, try to meet a person to put in my life, but I never did. I ate while standing over the sink. I reread my way through the bookcase. I ordered everything. Men arrived at my door with boxes and bags. Every week or so I would go out to the bank to get cash for delivery tips—my account reinflated with weekly deposits from Kurt—but I did almost everything else by telling my phone what I wanted and where I was. First it was just food and cleaning supplies—other than reading all I ever did was clean or jog dumbly up and down the short hall—but later I bought a small table and a rug and an air purifier and wads of sage. Soon everything in my home was beautiful and perfect. I cleaned so often and so deeply that no dust could settle before I had wiped it away. I didn't even have a trash can, instead I made frequent trips to the garbage chute each time an object—a napkin, an apple core, a plastic bag—lost its use. When the weather was nice, I left my windows open and blinds down, the wind rattling them like a chime without the high notes. When the weather was perfect, I tied a scarf over my head, put on large sunglasses, and sat on the metal fire escape. Sometimes tourists would point up at me— *That's what they do here, live on their escapes.*

Months went by like this, long enough for the weather to turn cold then warm again. At first I felt sure Chandra would stop by or call soon—I had these premonitions, I thought—and I didn't want to miss her. Then winter made my solitude feel noble, that being still and waiting was the correct response to snow and darkness. Faintly, I worried I was turning into Merle, wicked and away and too certain, so every day I tried to make a list of what I believed for sure, immediately crossing out each line. On the good days I wrote nothing.

After some months Mikey, the bodega's delivery guy, started showing me pictures of his baby daughter, making jokes, asking me if I heard about that explosion or the protests or something else. I'd never heard of anything since I didn't read the Internet or newspapers, but talking to Mikey reminded me that even if I wanted nothing to do with the rest of the world, there might be some good in knowing what the world was doing. So I ordered a little black radio, let its voices and music become my sole companion. In the morning I said *Good morning* to it and each night I said *Good night* before putting us both to sleep. All day it told me everything, and its tone never changed. I relied upon it. I felt more and less alone.

I started asking Mikey if he'd heard about the state senate race or refugee crisis. Often he had not. He always listened patiently as I told him what I knew.

I loved the radio's hourly news updates, especially when the same one repeated for a second or third time and I could try to recite the words with it. For a while I said the announcers' names, but eventually I inserted my own—*From NPR news in Washington I'm Mary Parsons*—until one day I said, without thinking, *I'm Junia Stone*. All afternoon I caught myself whispering, *I'm Junia Stone*, in odd corners of the house, into the couch, into the freezer, into a laundered bedsheet as I folded it.

I was listening to the radio and cleaning the tiny grooves in the hardwood with Q-tips when I heard the name Kurt Sky, something about an experiment, then his viscerally familiar voice—was I imagining this? I tried to listen but the words scattered around me, fell out of order, would not march through my mind————*extremely cutting-edge full-body virtual reality suit, not just an audiovisual experience, but one that affects the user from the inside out, internally*————*cranial electrotherapy stimulation* ————*the temporary but profound illusion that the user has become, briefly, an entirely different person*————*Identity Distance Therapy, a product from Kerensky Technologies*.

I felt confused and strange, only coming to when I heard two of the morning announcers discussing how urgently my annual contribution was needed, how they were just nothing without me, how they would just fall apart, *Please call*, so I turned the radio off and went to find the phone, found and turned on the phone, typed a *K* that immediately filled in as *Kurt Sky Technology Company*. Somehow it just knew. I lay down on the floor though I wasn't yet done cleaning it. KerenskyTechnologies.com was the first thing to appear, a sleek white-and-blue page, and soon a man in a white coat was smiling on the tiny screen, saying hello, introducing himself, thanking me for my interest in Identity Distance Therapy. The image was so clear and real I felt almost sure he was with me now, this man was here in my hand.

—*We accept that falling in love is a brief, delusional state and that despite people's best intentions, relationships usually end, almost always painfully or if they endure, they are often merely endured. Have you ever wondered what is happening in the brain that allows this to happen? Have you ever wondered if there was a way out of this terrible cycle?*

I paused the little man and leaned him (leaned the phone) against the baseboard, then sat up straight to listen, to take him as seriously as he seemed to take himself.

Our team has located a special part of the brain that shows us how the psychological motivation to find and maintain romantic love is also a desire to, in some ways, become another person—

I heard my own voice deep in memory—*Love is a compromise for only getting to be one person*—and remembered Kurt recording this, taking it and containing it in that dusk on the roof on that drug. (What was mine was not mine, was, perhaps, never mine.)

This man kept asking himself questions and immediately answering them. I got up and paced the room, felt unable to sit still, felt that someone was making me move, gripping me by the shoulders and pushing me around.

—*Identity Distance Therapy uses a system of highly advanced wearable biotechnology that changes a user's brain activity and bodily sensations to create a virtual reality experience so complete that users report a total dissolve of the self, a transcendence so profound that one believes, completely, that they are another person. And our studies have proven that a weekly ten-minute IDT session has such a profound effect on the brain that it seems to alleviate that impossible desire to be another person, that source of so much suffering that we've proven to be a primary reason for the demise of romantic love. A user's disposition is so suddenly and radically transformed that they can be in a relation-*

ship without fruitlessly trying, as so many do, to escape from the self through another person.

Unhappy couples, he explained, had become fulfilled again or for the first time ever. Single people had found sudden and real and lasting and secure love almost immediately. All their uncertainties ended. They found a better way to be.

I let the video keep playing, let the phone-contained man speak to an empty room as I went to the kitchen, as I looked out the window, washed a dish, went to the bedroom and sat on the mattress, looked at my feet, looked at my hands, wondered what, if anything, I should do with them. I heard the man talking in the other room, then a different voice, Kurt's voice, and I felt a little ache low in my chest. What was the feeling of missing someone? Was it this?

—how something makes sense that didn't make sense before, I could hear him saying, and other words, bent by the distance between us. I wondered about all the things Kurt had ever said to me that I could no longer remember. Were all those things still somehow stitched, immovably, beneath my skin?

—These are the two biggest threats to a relationship: certainty and uncertainty—

I paced my apartment again, looked at all my things, looked at my tiny plant in the kitchen window, a cactus I had ordered from somewhere in California, this living thing that barely needed me. It disturbed me, all of a sudden, and I put it out on the fire escape, shut the window behind it, went back to the living room to see a tiny Kurt on that tiny phone screen, explaining something, talking and talking—

—Some might say that romantic frustration is just part of the human condition, that it's an inescapable problem we all must deal with—but polio used to be an inescapable part of being a human and

we no longer deal with that. Life expectancies used to be half what they are now. Literacy was something reserved for royalty and clergy. We evolve emotionally just as we evolve physically and we are not done evolving. This is the next—

But the phone died while he was midsentence and I've let it be dead ever since. People think you need them but you don't.

I thought of all those billions of hearts beating out there, trying to find love or keep love going. All those people, getting in the way of each other—how do we even stand it? How do we make our way around?

I opened all the windows in my apartment. The day had been warm and bright just hours before, but had become quickly and unseasonably cold and windy. The blinds rattled and the curtains whipped and flung, as quick clouds made the sunlight flicker, darker then lighter then darker. I filled with grim thoughts, real thoughts, real questions. There are so many ways to live and die, so many ways to tell that same story, over and over, but everyone keeps trying to find a better way to tell it, a more real way to look into someone else's face to say, *I am alive like you, was born without my consent like you, will someday die and be dead in the same way you'll be dead.* What did we want from this? What did we really want from it?

I crawled onto my fire escape and felt the wet air. I closed my eyes and saw a face (perhaps yours, perhaps my own) and began to speak to it (silently or aloud, I didn't know) and I said, *You know, I've really never known what to do. I just keep making these decisions or not, making right and wrong turns that are never really right or wrong. I had a job, then a different job, then I was jobless. I was poor or I wasn't. I was ill but got better, got worse again, got better. Someone died. Someone else died. Money changed hands. People changed. I changed.*

And isn't that enough for us? And who put all this fear in us, this fear of changing when all we ever do is change? Why is it so many want to sleep through it all, sleepwalk, sleep-live, feel nothing, eyes shut? Haven't we slept enough? Can't we all wake up now, here, in this warm valley between cold mountains of sleep? Sitting on my escape, I saw that man who often sold water bottles on hot days in the street, but since the day was ending and cold and it was time to go home, he seemed to have given up and was just trying to give them away. But everyone kept rushing past him, would not accept water from a stranger.

Acknowledgments

Thank you, Emily Bell, Eric Chinski, and Anne Meadows, tireless editors and allies, and to Jin Auh, Stephanie Derbyshire, Jessica Friedman, and Alba Ziegler-Bailey for all your advocacy and advice. Thank you, Maya Binyam, Rodrigo Corral, Patrick Leger, Brian Gittis, Spenser Lee, and everyone else at Farrar, Straus and Giroux and the Wylie Agency.

Many thanks to the people at Granta Books, Actes Sud, Big Sur, Alfaguara, Das Mag, and Aufbau, especially the translators and editors, Myriam Anderson, Teressa Ciuffoletti, Martina Testa, Damià Alou, Gerda Baardman, Daniël van der Meer, Bettina Abarbanell, and Lina Muzur. You are magicians.

This work began during an autumn and was finished during a spring at the Omi International Arts Center and I'm very grateful to the people who make Omi such a beautiful place to work. I've also survived on the generosity of the Whiting Foundation, the New York Public Library Young Lions, Stony Brook

University, the Black Mountain Institute, the Late Night Library, and the morning crew at the Annex in Fort Greene—Justin, Mark, Mike, Ron, and Sasha. Thank you all.

I'm very grateful to Peter Musante for many years of solicitude, support, and helping me find a title. Also to Sean Brennan, Anu Jindal, Rebecca Novack, Sara Richardson, and especially Kendra Malone for being excellent readers and dear friends. And to Jesse Ball, for such kindness and galvanization, thank you.

Keep in touch with
Granta Books:

Visit granta.com to discover more.

GRANTA

Also by Catherine Lacey and forthcoming from Granta Books
www.granta.com

CERTAIN AMERICAN STATES

Twelve stories – each a masterful and compassionate guide to the fluctuations of the human heart – from one of *Granta* magazine's Best of Young American Novelists.

A grieving wife gives away the shirts her husband has left behind. A flirtatious widow takes a honeymooning couple to see her husband's grave. A businessman working for a shadowy organization known as 'The Company' checks in to a room in a strange and remarkable hotel.

Certain states are hard to shake, or so Catherine Lacey's characters find in these twelve tales of love, loss and longing.

NOBODY IS EVER MISSING

'Wry, surprising and blackly funny . . . a novel of uncomfortable power'
Guardian

Without telling her husband, Elyria leaves her comfortable cosmopolitan
life and boards a one-way flight to New Zealand. Once there, she embarks
on a hitchhiker's odyssey; travelling in strangers' cars, becoming entangled
in the lives of others, sleeping in fields, forests, and public parks. As she
journeys from north to south she asks herself, what is it I am missing? How
can a person be missing?

'Boundlessly brave and astute. It does what books should do – let the
reader *feel* something. A novel of uneasy, startling insight'
Samantha Harvey, author of *The Wilderness*

'Compelling and fascinating. Lacey's debut is a fable of our age'
Independent on Sunday

'[A novel] of striking intelligence and originality . . . arresting and
highly accomplished' *Daily Mail*

'Incantatory, cool . . . startlingly observant' 'Best Books of 2014',
New Yorker

'Completely – and instantly – enthralling' Geoff Dyer, author of *Zona*

'A powerful, surprising, and emotional mystery about a woman who
abandons her seemingly perfect life in New York to search for or hide
from herself' 'Best Books of 2014', *Vanity Fair*